A Day in the Life

JUST as it was supposed to do, my alarm clock rang at 6:30. By barely raising my eyelids, I could tell that the sun's rays had not yet risen to the level of the window. I closed my eyes again; my faith in my alarm clock turned into reverence for the sun.

I didn't get up until eight o'clock. If I washed and ate breakfast quickly, I'd be able to get right down to work on my writing.

After breakfast, I smoked my first cigarette of the day and arranged the things on my desk. A special delivery letter arrived: Wang, a good friend of mine, would be passing through Ji'nan, and he asked me to meet him at the train station. I stopped writing, buttoned up my shirt, put on my hat and rushed out the door. There wasn't a single ricksha to be found outside my front door. No problem; if I ran down to the end of the alley, I'd be sure to find one. I thought to myself: spending time with good friends always makes me happy. Maybe I should tell Wang to get off the train and stay with me for a few days for a few good heart-to-heart talks. When I got to the end of the alley, there was not a single ricksha to be found. Maybe I sent all the ricksha pullers away!

After running a few hundred meters, I finally found one and jumped into the seat. "Take me to the Jinpu Station." The man was moving so quickly that I was sure I'd be on time for the train. I started recalling my friend's smile and voice, and could imagine him trying to locate me on the crowded train platform.

No wonder no rickshas were available; the street we came to was full of them. Lined up as far as the eye could see, they had all stopped dead in their tracks. A silk store on the west side of the street was on fire. Seeing this, I immediately decided to go via a side street. Waiting there would have been sheer idiocy. I told the driver to make a detour. I was demonstrating how decisive and clever I could be.

Only after pulling into a side alley did the advantages of staying in the main street become evident. The alley was also jam-packed with rickshas; once you got in there, there was no backing out. I came up with another brilliant idea; giving the driver a dime, I leaped out of the ricksha with the agility of a monkey. Once I found my way out of this traffic jam, I could catch another ricksha and still make it to the station on time or at worst, ten minutes late.

The side flap of my padded cotton gown caught on the side of the ricksha, and I gave it a sharp tug. What was the loss of a single gown compared to the opportunity of seeing a good friend? I relinquished a large corner of my gown. But in tearing it free with a great burst of strength, my elbow smashed into a baby resting in its mother's arms. Without a second's hesitation, the mother let out with a crystal clear diatribe consisting of the most distasteful invectives, directed right to my face. Her voice sounded as loud and clear as if I were wearing a pair of earphones. The child was crying in a very strange manner; its mouth was as wide as the mouth of a volcano, but it didn't shed a single tear.

Offering an apology would have been fruitless. Those minor provocations which in most foreign countries are easily resolved with a polite "Excuse me" inevitably set off extended altercations in China. The entire crowd of bystanders, including five policemen, a bunch of old people, two girl students, a candy seller, two dozen street urchins and one mutt, swarmed around me so closely there was no way to escape. None of them said a word; they just stood there watching all the crying and swearing, and witnessing with big smiles on their faces every detail of my being hauled over the coals. The candy seller, bless his soul, had the makings of a saint; one glance from him and I immediately understood. I reached out and stuffed a big handful of candy into the child's arms. Instantly, the mouth of the volcano was sealed. The crowd must have been terribly disappointed. After paying the candy seller, I found an opening and thrust my way out of there.

When I got to the train station, I went directly to the China Travel Service representative. A man with tiny slit-like eyes, he was his usually polite self. And though I rarely came to the train station, he still remembered me. "Have you come to pick up your luggage, sir?"

"No, I'm here to meet someone." I didn't really have to say so much, since it was already ten o'clock. Unfortunately, my friend Wang didn't have the sort of influence required to keep the nine o'clock train waiting at the station for an hour.

The more I thought about it, the more exasperated I became. I was ready to kill myself then and there. However, when I left the station, I somehow managed to leave my suicide plans behind on the platform. Now I could go back and continue my writing.

When I got home, I discovered that my pet kitten had climbed up onto the roof. This was the first time it had behaved in this manner, and there was nothing I could do to induce it to come down. Old Tian, who is over sixty, gets dizzy every time he climbs a flight of stairs. He politely withdrew under the pretext of being too clumsy to climb up the side of the house, leaving it to me to show my stuff. I had no choice but to answer the call. I soon learned that this was no easy task, for after climbing halfway up the wall, my legs for some strange reason starting spinning around. This was no mere nervousness, but out and out trembling. Though Old Tian barely concealed his hostility behind a grin, I had to rely on him to give me a hand as I climbed.

Usually, all I had to do was call Snowball by its name and it would come over and start sniffing me and purring. But Snowball-on-the-Roof was an entirely different creature from Snowball-on-the-Ground. The more I called to it, the further it backed away. I knew that if I continued pursuing it, I'd force it over to the other side of the roof and very likely end up rolling off the roof like a snowball myself. After mouthing a lot of sweet nothings to no avail, I decided to imitate a woman's voice: "Come here, little Snowball. Come over here, sweetie pie . . . . Come and eat your liver. . . ." But again, all of this proved useless. I became impatient and started to threaten the cat, but that was equally futile.

After wasting nearly an hour at this business, my second sister arrived. She called Snowball's name once, and without the slightest regard for me, the cat leaped onto the wall — using my head as a bridge — and then into my sister's outstretched arms — using my back for a ladder.

Of all my siblings, my second sister is the closest to me. Her best quality is that she doesn't interrupt my work. If she sees me busy writing, she doesn't say a word. All I have to do is say a few polite things to her and she immediately excuses herself and goes away.

"Why don't you play with Snowball for a little while," I said to her affectionately, "I've got a little writing to do."

"If you've got a few minutes first, do you think you could write something for me?" she replied with equal affection.

Of course I had a few minutes; she was always so nice to me, how could I refuse her?

What she needed was a letter. That made it even easier. Having just climbed down from my adventure on the roof, this would be a good way for me to prepare for my other writing.

My sister's letter was to the husband of her mother-in-law's niece's godmother's cousin's niece. It took us more than half an hour to figure out how to address him. As we discussed this question, I learned many things about the personalities of, and the relationships among her mother-in-law, her mother-in-law's niece, the godmother and the cousin. Just as she was telling me how the godmother had lost a tooth in 1903, Old Tian came in and announced that lunch was ready.

After lunch, my sister told me she was going to take a short nap, and that we could continue writing after she woke up.

I'm the kind of person who can never put an unfinished task out of mind. Any attempt to ignore her mother-in-law's niece's godmother and get on with my writing was bound to result in Shakespeare ending up as somebody's niece's husband. Fortunately, my sister was only planning to take a quick nap.

But my sister's nap lasted until 3:30. She apologized profusely, telling me that the night before she had played four extra rounds of mahjong. In any case, it was now time to write the letter. But my sister suddenly decided that if she went to the Li's home near the eastern gate she could speak in person to that niece's husband's older brother, so writing the letter was no longer necessary.

After my sister left, I began to rearrange my desk and asked Old Tian to make me a pot of good strong tea. I needed something to exorcise that godmother and the rest of them from my mind.

When Old Tian brought the tea, he told me they were checking residence permits and asked me when my birthday was. I told him, "The first day of the first month in the lunar calendar."

If Old Tian heard something he suspected wasn't true, he always found someone to discuss it with. He told the policemen who were doing the checking, "It's a little hard to believe that the date he gave me is correct, since I seem to remember he was born in March. In any case I know his birthday can't be January 1." The policemen became suspicious, and seeing in this a chance to uncover a Communist Party organization, demanded to interrogate me in person. They carried out a lengthy investigation, in the course of which I explained that January in the lunar calendar was the same as March in the solar calendar, adding that I was born in the Year of the Dog. As soon as I mentioned the lunar

Preface

Hu Jieqing

IN 1956, Lao She chose thirteen of his favourite short stories from five earlier anthologies and compiled them into a book entitled *The Selected Short Stories of Lao She*. In a brief afterword, the author wrote that several of the stories in the book were about twenty-five years old, and that he could no longer remember precisely when they were written. He expressed the hope that readers would enjoy them as antiques, since antiques have their own special fascination.

The contents of the present collection of English translations differ somewhat from the volume mentioned above. Six of the original stories have been retained and six others added, leaving us a total of twelve stories. All of them were written between 1933 and 1937, the latest of them nearly fifty years ago.

It might be of interest to mention here that most of Lao She's novels have appeared in English translation, while this is so for only a relatively small percentage of his shorter fiction. The present volume represents an effort to remedy this imbalance. Actually, many of Lao She's short stories are extremely popular among readers. Lao She himself particularly liked "Crescent Moon", "A Vision", and "This Life of Mine", even though he thought he was too unsophisticated to write short stories and felt he was better suited to writing novels. We'll leave this question unresolved for the present.

On a hot summer day, though there's hardly anything more refreshing than a cold bath, a simple glass of sour plum juice provides its own special form of enjoyment; if it "hits the spot", as they say, it can leave an impression which lasts a lifetime.

This book, then, can be compared to a cup of sour plum juice. It reveals a few aspects of the crises faced by the Chinese people, the corruption of Chinese society and the tragic side of life in China, besides stimulating thoughts and associations which extend far beyond its limited perspectives.

This book is a true "thirst-quencher". Try it and see!

Beijing
May 18, 1984

calendar, they promptly forgot about the Communist Party. But it meant wasting another fifteen minutes.

Four o'clock. I just remembered that today was the last day of a painting exhibition I wanted to see. For my writing's sake, however, I decided to sacrifice the exhibition, and picked up my pen once again. With a pen in my hand, I feel like everything is going my way; no matter how much excitement I've been through, I can always sit down and get to work.

The doorbell rang. The mail had arrived, a whole pile of letters. If I didn't open them immediately, those letters would begin to play naughty tricks on me. The first was from an old-age home asking for a contribution. The second was from my uncle. Did I want to buy some imported narcissus bulbs? The third was addressed correctly but the name was wrong. I started thinking about whether I should open it or not. I stared at it for many minutes, analysing the handwriting and the postmark in great detail and applying the detective methods of Sherlock Holmes, but all in vain. I put it aside. The fourth was a new book list. I browsed through it and found nothing of interest. The fifth was from a friend asking me to help him find a job. He needed an urgent reply, and so I decided to write to him immediately. Writing letters is like curing an illness: the longer you put it off, the harder it is to cure. I finished the letter but discovered I was short a one-cent stamp. I called to Old Tian, but he had gone out. I'll run down to the post office myself, I thought, it isn't very far away anyway.

By the time I'd mailed the letter, it was already dark outside. Since it's unhealthy to write before eating, I sat down and read the newspaper.

I had two pears for desert, which I figured would aid my digestion and help me get back to my writing quicker. But just as I was finishing the pears, Old Niu and his new wife came in.

The best thing you can say about Old Niu is that he is a born ignoramus with a head full of straw. No matter how busy you are, whenever he starts to talk to you, he totally loses track of time. But since he had brought his new wife along with him today, I was certain he wouldn't stay very long.

Mrs Niu shared her husband's most salient characteristics: she was a phlegmatic blockhead. By 8:30 I figured out what was going on: they were celebrating their honeymoon in my house. I tried everything: I glanced at my writing paper; I faked several yawns; I lied and said that I had to go visit a friend; I told Old Tian to wind the clock; I asked them what time they usually went to bed; I glanced at my watch. . . . But Mr and Mrs Niu were busy competing for the prize of world's Biggest Dolt. By ten o'clock, neither of them evinced even the slightest intention of leaving.

"Let's go out for a stroll. I've got a little headache." My idea was to accompany them for a few minutes and then come back and write a few thousand words before going to bed. I write faster in the late evening when no one is around. I am also an eternal optimist.

After walking with them for a few minutes, I came home. The minute I got inside, I started sneezing. Old Tian told me that I caught a cold. He immediately poured me a cup of hot water, and ordered me to go to bed and take an aspirin. I had to obey his orders, for if I didn't go right to bed, he would call a doctor. Well, I figured, if I lie in bed and think for a while,

I can wake up early tomorrow and get right to work. "Old Tian! Set the alarm for five a.m."

Old Tian just smiled at me. It's wrong to get upset with an old man. The truth was that I wanted to punch him twice in the mouth.

I was actually feeling a little stiff all over, but I made up my mind to ignore this and try to get some sleep. I closed my eyes, but I wasn't really tired. I started counting to myself, but the more I counted the more awake I felt. By eleven o'clock or so, Old Tian's coughing finally ceased. With him asleep, I could get up now, since I couldn't sleep anyhow, and was just wasting time. But my quilt felt so warm and cuddly that I decided to stay in bed for another five minutes. There was a pleasant sensation of warmth in my stomach, probably caused by the aspirin, but extremely comfortable nonetheless. There was Old Niu back for a visit, and my sister, and Snowball. . . .

"Wake up, it's eight o'clock." It was Old Tian calling to me from outside my window.

"You didn't set the alarm? Didn't I tell you to set it for five o'clock?" I felt a great surge of anger inside me as I lay there under my quilt.

"I set it alright. It woke me up at five o'clock. You caught a cold last night, remember, and your fever must have made you a little deaf."

I sighed. Can anyone control their own destiny?

"Old Tian, did anyone from the newspaper come over asking for my article?"

The article I was supposed to write was already overdue, but I hadn't even written a single word.

"Yes, someone was here.   They said there was no rush for you to finish it.   Last night the police were there and closed down the office."

January 1933

Translated by Don J. Cohn

Filling a Prescription

THE Japanese troops were holding their regular target practice outside the Qihua Gate. As usual, the police guarding the gate were checking all the Chinese passing back and forth. Since the police were Chinese themselves, they were much more thorough and bold about guarding against Chinese spies than they were about the enemy; it was so much easier for them. Policemen were different from soldiers; they weren't responsible for foreign affairs.

Niu Ertou had unbuttoned both his short and long padded cotton jackets, and his blue cotton sash was tied loosely around his waist. Though this left a sizable portion of his bare chest exposed to the wind, he still felt hot; firstly, because he was walking very quickly; and secondly, because he was anxious and upset. His father had contracted a serious illness — the prescription cost, more than a dollar! He lived nearly ten *li* from the Qihua Gate. The gate stood directly in front of him now; if he left the city immediately and took all the shortcuts he knew, he might make it home in time to let his father take his first dose by sunset. He sped up his pace; he was carrying the medicine in one hand and a rolled-up book in the other.

This story first appeared in the magazine *Modern Times* (*Xiandai*), Vol. V, No. 1, published on May 1, 1934.

A large crowd stood in front of the gate, surrounded by the police. Ertou was in too much of a hurry to hang around and watch what was going on, and headed straight for the passageway which led through the broad gate tower.

"Where do you think you're going?" The sound of the policeman's voice echoed in the empty passageway.

Ertou was in too much of a hurry to figure out if this question was addressed to him or not, and kept on walking. Why, he wondered, was it so silent in the passageway?

"Hey, boy! I'm talking to you, you bastard. Get back here!" Someone grabbed Ertou by the arm.

"My father's waiting for me to bring him this medicine." Only then did Ertou realize that it was a policeman. "I didn't rob anybody!"

"Even if your grandfather wants to take his medicine, he also has to wait a little while." The policeman pushed Ertou towards the crowd.

Everyone there had their jackets unbuttoned. Ertou didn't have to waste his time on this, since his jackets were already unbuttoned. So he took the time to survey the scene. The people there were divided into three groups. Those dressed in silks and satins stood together in one spot; those wearing cotton gowns which weren't covered with mud made up a second group; and those dressed like Ertou formed a third. Though those in the first group had also unbuttoned their jackets, the policemen only gave them a cursory frisking and let them go. Ertou thought, "Doesn't look too bad. Fifteen minutes and I'll be on my way. I'll have to hurry when I get out of here." Things weren't going so smoothly for the men in the second group. Anyone with even the

slightest bulge in their clothing had to be frisked twice.
As the policemen worked their way through the crowd,
they came to a man in his forties with a red nose, who
refused to be searched.

"Get your supervisor over here!"

When the supervisor saw who it was, he said, "Oh
it's you, Third Master. I'm sorry, I didn't notice you
when you arrived. There's too much to do here; my
hands are tied. I'm truly sorry." Without even a smile,
the red-nosed man said, "You ought to get your eyes
fixed. What a disgrace!" Rubbing his nose, he proceed-
ed through the gate.

It seemed like hours before they got around to Ertou's
group. "Take off your coats, my good men, you won't
freeze to death," one of the policemen said with a laugh.
"While you're at it, you can pick some of the lice out
of the lining of my coat for me." This remark came from
a man who might have been a ricksha puller. "Let's
have no nonsense here; take 'em off and air 'em out."
The policeman took another man's coat and shook it a
few times. The coat's owner laughed and said, "The
only thing I've got hidden in there is dirt." Upon hearing
this wisecrack, the policeman threw the coat onto the
ground. "Have a little more dirt, then."

There were only a few people left when it came to
Ertou's turn. All those who had arrived after Ertou
were placed in a separate group.

"What's that?" The policeman pointed to the object
in his hand.

"Medicine."

"No, I mean the thing you've got rolled up there."

"It's a book I picked up in a public toilet."

"Let me see it."

The policeman glanced at the book's cover and noticed it was red. He handed it to the inspector. The inspector examined the book's cover as well and noticed it was red. Then he looked at Ertou. He flipped through the first few pages, but seemed to be unable to grasp the gist of it. Then, wetting his finger thoroughly with saliva, he flipped through another ten pages, paused for a moment, raised his head, looked at the gate tower, and glanced at Ertou again. "Take him inside," he said, and a policeman stepped forward.

Ertou instinctively took a step backwards. He knew he was in trouble now, but he didn't know why.

"My father's waiting for his medicine. I picked up this book in a public toilet."

Grabbing Ertou by the collar, the policeman said, "Listen to me, buddy. If you don't behave yourself, you're going to get your head bashed in."

"But my father's waiting for his medicine!" Though Ertou was anxious now, he didn't raise his voice. His vocal chords were immune to this sort of thing.

"Get him out of here!" The inspector's face was slightly pale; perhaps he thought Ertou was carrying a bomb on his person.

Being anxious was futile for Ertou at this point, but he couldn't stay there any longer. Suddenly tears welled up in his eyes.

The policeman took him into the station and whispered something to the sergeant on duty. The sergeant took the book and flipped through it.

The stoutly built sergeant was extremely polite. "What is your surname, huh?" He drew out the "huh" like an actor in a western-style comedy.

"Niu.* My name is Niu Ertou." His nose twitched as he answered.

"Hm, what village are you from, Ertou, huh?"

"Ten-*li* Village."

"Hm, Ten-*li* Village. That's outside the Qihua Gate." The sergeant nodded, extremely pleased with his superior knowledge of geography. "What were you doing in the city, hm?" His "hm" was even longer than his "huh".

"I was having a prescription filled, my father's sick." Tears were now rolling down his cheeks.

"Whose father, huh? Speak up! It's a good thing I'm not very suspicious. Now, I want you to tell me the truth. Who gave you this book?"

"I picked it up in a public toilet."

"If you don't tell me the truth, I'm going to make things very difficult for you." The fat sergeant appeared fatter than he had ten minutes ago; perhaps this is what happened to him every time he got angry. "Young man, don't be as stubborn as an ox with me. If you tell the truth, I'll let you go. We're looking for the man who gave you this book, understand? Huh?"

"I swear to you, I picked it up in a toilet. I don't want it anymore. Just let me go!"

"I don't think you're going anywhere right now." The sergeant took one more look at the book and decided to retain Ertou for further interrogation.

Ertou was extremely upset now. "But sir, my father is waiting for his medicine."

"You mean there aren't any pharmacies outside the gate, so you had to come into the city to buy medicine?

---

* Niu means "ox".

There must be some other reason." The sergeant was about to smile, but stopped himself. He felt extremely satisfied about his own profound wisdom.

"The doctor told me to have the prescription made up at the Huaidetang Pharmacy downtown. The medicine's better there. Sir, I beg you, let me go now. I don't want that book anymore. Is that alright?"

"No, that's not alright."

That night, they took Ertou to the Bureau of Public Security.

"Ru Yin" the writer and "Qing Yan" the literary critic were enemies, though the two of them had never met. Ru Yin earned his living by writing fiction while Qing Yan made a career out of writing criticism. When their works appeared in the magazines and newspapers, it was always Ru Yin who took the lead, with Qing Yan following close behind. No matter what Ru Yin wrote, Qing Yan always aimed the same poison arrow at him — "unsound thinking". Though this in no way affected the sale of his works, Ru Yin always felt that in the final accounting, the psychological victory belonged to Qing Yan. He didn't know whether or not the people who bought his cheap books smiled out of sympathy for him when they thought: "Who cares whether his thinking is sound or not; his stories make really entertaining reading." He hoped his readers didn't think this way and consoled himself by thinking, "Maybe there's somebody out there who really respects me." He was very much like a self-satisfied businessman. But whenever he received any fees or royalties for his writing, he imagined Qing Yan looking over his shoulder and saying, "Ahah! I see you've earned some money again! I guess that's one that got away. Just wait and see, I'm not finished with you yet!"

Once by coincidence their two photos appeared together in a magazine. This really piqued Ru Yin's imagination. In the picture, Qing Yan had a big head, long hair, protruding eyes and a pug nose like that of a Pekinese dog. The best thing you could say about him was that he looked like Socrates. It was this imaginary Socrates who very frequently haunted Ru Yin.

A number of malicious thoughts occurred to Ru Yin. Judging from his pen name alone — Qing Yan means "black swallow" — he had probably started out as an insignificant popular love story writer. But now that he had changed careers and was earning his living by condemning everything he read as "unsound thinking", it was just as well to ignore him. However, passive consolation is never quite as satisfactory as an active attack: the bullets of "unsound thinking" were still flying directly over his head.

Ru Yin wondered how he could set his thinking "straight"? The answer to this question could certainly not be found in Qing Yan's critical writings. There was one way in which Qing Yan didn't resemble Socrates: Socrates asked a lot of questions and was always full of answers; he often went around in circles, sometimes ending up lost inside his own arguments. But Qing Yan's style was to stand at the finish line of a 100 metre race, grab the slowest runner and slap him in the face. Ru Yin's only way out was to change the way he wrote. He read through a number of books which were supposed to be representative of "sound thinking" — though some of them had already been banned. He found them disappointing, since most of them were nothing more than anemic romances. He knew he could write much better than that.

He started to write in this style. He published a few pieces and waited eagerly for Qing Yan's response. But once again the response was: "Unsound thinking!"

When he made a careful comparison of his own work and that of the so-called orthodox writers, he noticed that they were written in entirely different languages: his were in Chinese, while theirs were written in some western-style Chinese. The content was also different: his stories were expressions of light and shade, sincerity and degradation, ideals and emotions; theirs were comedies laced through with "blood" and "death".

Despite this, Ru Yin's latest works ended up as "unsound thinking".

He wanted to play a joke on Qing Yan in order to shut him up once and for all. He started producing imitations of the so-called orthodox works, using foreign-style language and plots which though lively were far from realistic. He sent a number of them off to some magazines.

Strangely enough, every single story was returned to him. One in particular was accompanied by a polite letter from an editor:

> In times like these, when there is no freedom of speech, the use of such words as red, yellow, blue, white and black could get us all wiped all. Nearly all the language in your story is of this type.

Ru Yin couldn't stop laughing. So this was the way the world worked: words could really deceive people. Writers, readers, critics and censors all came from the same mould.

He now understood why Qing Yan only attacked him for his "unsound thinking" and said very little about the other aspects of his works: it was because he was scared. This was quite a fair assessment. Now more than ever, he wanted to play a trick on Qing Yan. With his own money, he printed up a short anthology of stories previously rejected by publishers. He addressed a copy to Qing Yan and sent it to him via the editorial office of a certain magazine; in this way Qing Yan would be sure to get it. Even though he had spent his own money, he felt this was a positive move. "I went out on my own and printed these stories; let's see if he has the courage to criticize them without rejecting them outright."

Qing Yan went to the editorial office of X Magazine to see if there was any "news" for him. He found three letters and a package waiting for him on his desk. He read the letters first and then opened the package. It was a book with a red cover — written by Ru Yin. Qing Yan smiled. He felt sorry for Ru Yin. All authors deserve sympathy to some degree. After breaking through the barriers erected by the editorial departments, they're inevitably subjected to the wrath of the critics. But never under any circumstances should a critic lower himself out of compassion for an author. Unfair criticism could put one in a very awkward position. This he knew very well; but truly fair criticism could have even more serious consequences. The general rule was that writing which lacked barbs couldn't be considered literary criticism.

Qing Yan was the sort of person who would never hurt a fly. But writing criticism was his way of earning a living, and most hatchet men performed their jobs in order to eat.   He knew all of this, but he still played dumb.   He also knew which publications didn't like which writers, and by keeping this in mind whenever he wrote anything, further secured his own position. You might say that he was a man without ideals; considering the overall situation, however, perhaps he could be forgiven for this.   The truth was that he never intended to be at odds with Ru Yin, since he didn't enjoy being at odds with anyone; but criticism was criticism.   If he could have come up with a more original phrase than "unsound thinking", he would have rejected those two words a long time ago, for he had no particular affection for them.   But since he had nothing more novel or convincing at hand, he had to make do with them; it was as simple at that.

He had long wanted to meet Ru Yin, to sit down for a good talk with him and even to become his friend. If they couldn't meet, at least he could write him a letter urging him to take back his red book as soon as possible, since it was a dangerous thing.   If Ru Yin wanted to carry this game any further, smoking cigarettes and fussing over pedantic stylistic changes were the least useful things he could do.   It would be better for him to think up something new.   No matter how you looked at it, writing and criticism were just two forms of pedantry.   All the flattery and hostility which were so much a part of the literary life amounted to little more than a waste of paper and ink, and no one engaged in these activities would ever contribute a single new page to human history.

The history of literature and literary criticism was little more than the history of numerous individuals flattering themselves; if these subjects never existed, libraries would certainly be a lot less empty and dull.

With his nose raised, Qing Yan let out with a snort. Rolling up the book, he left the editorial office. When he reached the southern corner of the Four Eastern Archways, he felt the urge to relieve himself. He put the book down on the mud wall surrounding the public toilet in order to facilitate tucking up his long brocade gown. As he stood in the stall, blocking the doorway, someone approached him from behind. As he was eager to allow this stranger to take his turn, he quickly straightened his gown and walked out holding his breath.

He'd gone quite a long way before he remembered the book, but he decided not to go back and look for it. Without the book in hand, he could still write his review. Fortunately, he remembered the book's title and author.

Ertou had been in jail for two days now, but he still had no idea what that book was about. All he could remember was that it was thin and had a red cover. He was totally illiterate. The more he hated that little book, the more he worried about his father's illness; that dirty rotten book was killing his father. They continued interrogating him, but he always gave the same answer: "I picked it up in a public toilet." It was hard enough for him to imagine that someone had written the book in the first place. Couldn't he find anything better to do than write a book? All Ertou'd done was pick it up. When he had nothing else to do in the winter, he'd go around collecting dung in the same way. How was that any different from picking up a book?

"Who gave it to you?" They asked him this same question over and over again.

Ertou was twenty years old, but no one had ever given him a book. How on earth could books have anything to do with him? He couldn't very well tell a lie and say that Doggy Zhang or Blackie Li had given it to him; that would mean getting innocent people in trouble. The only authentic-sounding name he could think of was Meng Zhanyuan, the head of the village martial arts society. This name, like Huang Tianba or Zhao Zilong, who were characters in popular tales, seemed like something out of a book. But he couldn't get the head of the society involved in this affair. If Meng Zhanyuan weren't there during the annual spring pilgrimage to Miaofeng Mountain, there was no guarantee that the village team wouldn't be defeated by the team from Scholartree Village in the "Five-Tiger Cudgel" contest. But when he thought about his father's illness, he could no longer worry about this sort of thing. If he could only turn into a puff of smoke and escape through a crack in the door. That damned book! That goddamned dirty book! Maybe it contained the prescription for the bogey man's magic potion!

Another day went by. Ertou was sure his father was dead.

He had no medicine to take. Ertou was nowhere to be seen. This would be enough to drive his father mad. Concluding that his father was dead, Ertou held his head in his hands. Tears began falling down his cheeks, and before long he started crying outloud despite himself.

When he stopped crying, he made up his mind to tell the policemen that Meng Zhanyuan had given him the book. This was the only name he could think of that sounded bookish enough. Neither "Doggy" nor "Blackie", not to mention "Little Seventy", seemed like appropriate names for people who gave books away.

But after giving it further consideration, he decided not to do it this way. It would be so unfair! He really and truly had picked up the book without thinking. Moreover, since he had found it in the city, Meng Zhanyuan couldn't possibly have given it to him. The facts didn't tally. His mind unresolved, Ertou's thoughts turned to his father's death. He could see all the members of his family wearing mourning dress, only he wasn't there. This was enough to drive anyone crazy!

That night, another man was put in Ertou's cell. He was young and well dressed, and had shackles around his ankles. Ertou's curiosity allowed him some respite from his worrying. Also, the sight of this cultivated man wearing shackles but displaying no sign of distress had a calming effect on him.

The new arrival was the first to speak. "What are you here for, my good man?"

"I picked up a book. Screw the ancestors of that damned book!" Ertou exploded with spite.

"What book was it?" The young man's eyes darkened slightly.

"A book with a red cover." That was all Ertou could remember. "I can't read."

"Oh!" the young man said, nodding his head.

Neither of them spoke. A few moments passed before Ertou broke the silence:

"What . . . are you here for?"

"I wrote a book!" the young man replied with a laugh.

"Oh, it was you who wrote that dirty rotten book."

Ertou had never met a person who could write books, but since this young man wrote books, he naturally assumed he was the one who had written the book with the red cover. He didn't know what to do now. He wanted to punch this writer in the nose, but there were too many policemen around. They'd already arrested him once, and he didn't want to make things any worse for himself. Having decided not to punch him, he now had no way of venting his anger. "You had nothing better to do, your hands got itchy, and so you wrote that dirty fuckin' book!" Ertou stared at the young man, gnashing his teeth.

The young man smiled mischievously. "But that book was written for your benefit."

Ertou couldn't restrain himself any longer. "I'll smack you one, you son of a bitch!" But he didn't lift a finger. Ertou was actually frightened of the young man, perhaps because his face, his manner, his youth and his clothing didn't quite match the shackles on his legs. He was very pale, but his skin was fine and smooth. His eyes were rather dull, and he was constantly smiling in a sort of an unnatural way. He was quite thin, and his narrow ankles were encumbered by those iron shackles! Ertou's fear arose from not knowing what kind of person this strange young man was.

The young man sat there smiling, and looked up at Ertou. "You can't read?"

Ertou sat there dumbly for a few moments, reluctant to answer, but he finally responded with a little grunt.

"Where did you find the book?"

"In a public toilet. Why does that matter?"

"Did they ask you about it?"

"None of your. . . !" Ertou swallowed the second half of his sentence. Besides his fear, he now felt somewhat suspicious of this young man.

"If you tell me, I'll help you get out of here." The young man's smile became more serious. He was thinking: "I wrote this dirty book for you, but you can't even read it. Isn't it my job to get you out of this mess?"

"They asked me who I got it from, but I didn't say anything."

"Let's say I tell them it was me that lost the book in the toilet. Wouldn't that solve all your problems?" By now the young man's smile looked rather silly.

"That would really be swell!" Ertou smiled. He hadn't smiled once in the last three days, so his lips remained sealed. "Shall we go talk to them now?"

"Not now. We had better wait till tomorrow when they start asking me questions."

"But my father's very sick. He may be dead by now!"

"First, tell me where you found that book."

"On the south side of the Four Eastern Archways, when I was taking a goddamned piss!" At that moment, Ertou felt something strange inside him. He could think of no way to describe this sensation properly; it was as if he were lost in the dark. He remembered one time several years ago when the locusts ate all the grain in the fields.

"Is this what you were wearing? What else did you have with you?"

"I was wearing the same outfit and I was carrying a package of medicine." Ertou began thinking of his father again.

Qing Yan returned home feeling very ill at ease. He couldn't get Ru Yin off his mind. Pacing back and forth in his room, he chuckled to himself; he still had to criticize Ru Yin's book. He could only write a short piece, since he'd lost the book. Writing literary criticism was second nature to him now, so he could easily broaden the scope of his attack and describe the binding or the cover; a literary critic was free to express his opinions on aesthetics. "If a book's red cover can symbolize the contents of a story, then this little juggling performance by Ru Yin is a cause for disappointment. For the book's cover, he has chosen thick, glossy red paper; as for the contents . . . well, the contents are full of unsound thinking." He went on from there and wrote seven or eight hundred words. In each and every sentence, he displayed his great authority. Criticism, after all, was a form of literature. He was comfortably satisfied with the precision of his writing; it had always been more severe than his thinking. It was his writing that secured him his reputation. He felt he had been unfair to Ru Yin, but this was the way it had to be. When he met Ru Yin some day, a few words of explanation would suffice to clear up any misunderstanding.

If writers obtained their pleasure at the expense of fictitious characters, then literary critics obtained theirs at the expense of the authors they criticized. After making a few minor revisions, he dropped the article in the mailbox.

Two days later, Qing Yan's article appeared in the paper. Two days after that, he learned that Ru Yin had been arrested.

Qing Yan wasn't worried about the article he had written. Critics were rarely arrested on the grounds of

sound thinking. But if that were the case, it would matter very little. Besides students who read fiction and enjoyed following the petty skirmishes fought regularly on the literary battlefield, was anyone aware that literary critics existed at all? Wasn't the whole writing business, after all, just a huge heap of rubbish? At the same time, though, Qing Yan was upset about Ru Yin. He knew there had to be something meaningful in all of this for him, though he didn't know what it was yet, and could only describe it in a negative way: this meaningful something had nothing to do with either sound or unsound thinking. Truth and nonsense are entirely different things. In other words, if an author wants to describe a soldier, it doesn't mean he has to join the army. Now he understood! The positive solution was to create a new page or two of history, not just write a few silly articles. This thought had occurred to him before, but now he was convinced it was true. Yet he still wanted to rescue Ru Yin, even though this wasn't very "meaningful" for him.

Two days later, Ertou said goodbye to Ru Yin.

When he got home, he learned that his father's burial had taken place two days before. Ertou swore that he'd never buy medicine in the city again.

Translated by Don J. Cohn

By the Temple of Great Compassion

MR Huang has been dead for more than twenty years now. Had I been living in Beiping all this time, I would have made regular visits to his grave. But it was impossible for me to remain in Beiping so long; no matter where I went, autumn winds always intensified my grief and bitterness. The proper time to visit his grave was the Double Ninth Festival — the ninth day of the ninth month in the lunar calendar — sometime around November; that was when he died. Visiting his grave was a responsibility I imposed upon myself. Of all my teachers, it was Mr Huang whom I respected and admired the most, even though he treated me no differently from my fellow students; he loved all of his students equally. Nonetheless, I tried to visit his small tomb every year. It stood under a red-leafed maple tree, not far from the Temple of Great Compassion.

It was three years since I'd been there last. During these years, I had begun to feel that my life was no longer in my own hands, and moved about from place to place without a sense of purpose. For a long time, Beiping only appeared in my dreams.

For reasons which I now forget, I went back to Beiping last year for three days. Though it was only a few days after the Mid-autumn Festival,* I made a

---

* It falls on the fifteenth day of the eighth lunar month.

special trip to the Western Hills anyway. I didn't know when I'd have another opportunity to go back there. Naturally, I went to the Western Hills especially to visit Mr Huang's grave. In order to do this, I had to put aside many other matters; the truth is that anyone who has only three days to spend in Beiping always ends up with a myriad of errands to run.

My commemorative visits were hardly spectacular; all I had to do was show up there. There was no burning of paper money or offerings of incense and wine. Mr Huang didn't believe in superstitions, nor had I ever seen him take a drink.

On the journey from the city to the Western Hills, all my memories of Mr Huang came back to me. As long as I live, he will remain immortal — I really mean that. Though he has been dead for many years, he lives on in my mind. Whenever I see a fat man wearing a long grey cotton gown, I always take a second look. Thanks to Mr Huang, a fat man wearing a grey cotton gown has become a sort of symbol for me. When I get together for a meal with my classmates, the words "And how about Mr Huang?" are frequently on the tip of my tongue, just as if he were still alive. A better way of putting it is: I thought Mr Huang would never die, and that he *should* never die, even though I know he is dead now.

How did he, as fat as he was and always wearing that long grey cotton gown, become our student supervisor? Weren't there any number of jobs he could perform a whole lot better than that of student supervisor? No matter how it came about, he finally ended up as our student supervisor. It was as if fate had decreed it; for if he hadn't been our student supervisor, how else could he have died before the age of fifty?

He was so fat that three big rolls of flesh had formed on the back of his neck. I often imagined how difficult it must have been for the barber to shave off all the short hairs that grew on those vast curved surfaces. His face resembled a big fleshy gourd, and even though I had the greatest respect for him, there was no denying that this part of his anatomy was something of a joke. And then there were his eyes!

Due to the influence of his "fat", Mr Huang's eyelids drooped rather low, causing his large eyes to resemble the ovaries of a mantis, and leaving only the narrowest slits from which shone forth unfathomable beams of black light. If you observed these two beams on their own, you could instantly drop all references to the word "fat". They were two beams of divine light which a fat man shed upon a living, joyous and responsive world. When he looked at you, this pair of tiny black orbs seemed to fix themselves upon your soul, suspending you in that kindly, generous and brilliant aura which he emitted, like a whitefish flapping about on the end of a fishing line. When he laughed in his own unique naïve fashion, you could not help falling into his embrace and totally losing yourself there. At such moments, his long grey cotton gown, which enveloped the entirety of Mr Huang's bulk, became an immortal's robe. If he were approaching in the distance, before you noticed his eyes, he appeared as some sort of unidentifiable squirming grey mass.

If a student wanted to go out and play, and could fabricate an excuse that only slightly strayed from the truth, he could ask Mr Huang for permission to leave, whereupon Mr Huang would always smile and, before hearing the excuse to the end — as if he were afraid you might give away your secret — readily fill out an Absence Permit in old-fashioned Su Dongpo calligraphy. However, you had to ask for permission; leaving school without an Absence Permit was strictly forbidden. Mr Huang handled personal matters in a personal way, but when it came to anything involving school regulations, school rules were school rules: so sayeth our big fat school supervisor!

Mr Huang was not an educated man, although he spent all his evenings reading in the students' study room. Both the books he read and the notebooks he wrote in were large in format, since it is likely that his hands would have damaged the pages of any small and fragile volume. As he read, be it winter or summer, warm beads of sweat always formed on his forehead — he was not an overly intelligent man. Whenever I happened to glance at him, I always found that his eyebrows, eyes and mouth were totally absorbed in what he was reading. It was also apparent that his teeth were clenched tightly, since his cheeks and temples trembled ever so slightly; in any case, there was tension there. Frequently, without warning, he'd grin in his own innocent way, sigh deeply, and wipe the sweat off his forehead with a white handkerchief the size of a small bedsheet.

If for no other reason, the earnestness with which he managed human relations and his naive perseverance was enough to inspire me with the deepest respect for him, a respect that was shared by most of the other students in my class. Even the most insensitive and unaware sort of people, such as adolescent students like my classmates and myself, could see that Mr

Huang's tenderness and sincerity grew out of the simplicity and frankness of his natural instincts; at the same time, his ability to carry out his responsibilities conscientiously sufficed to demonstrate that he was a kind and good person, rather than a mere coward. We also felt that he was one of "us" rather than one of the "teachers"; all the effort he expended on reading, and the tension he felt, not to mention his sweating and sighing, were all very familiar to us.

Whenever any of us encountered the sort of petty problems common among students — in our eyes, however, these were always great emergencies — Mr Huang was always the first to offer his consolation, even if he didn't provide the assistance we needed; naturally, whenever he could help he did, without being asked and before offering his consolation. Twenty years ago, a middle school student supervisor like Mr Huang would earn less than 60 dollars a month. Mr Huang earmarked one third of this sum each month for helping out us students. Whether we had financial difficulties or not, he would never keep those 20 dollars for himself. If a student got sick, in addition to providing the most kindly care, Mr Huang would buy fruit, snacks and story books and place these things on the sick student's bed while no one was watching.

However, this angel in time of distress was something of a despot in time of peace — he kept us well under control. If the dormitories were dirty, or if we did not do our exercises after class, we would all have to endure his thunderbolts, even though they were accompanied by raindrops of tears.

In this world — no, I'll be more specific: in our school, it was unfair to expect everyone to act rationally.

Quite a few of my classmates detested Mr Huang. This was not because Mr Huang's affection failed to extend to every one of us, nor because someone discovered some insincerity in him, but rather because when greatness and pettiness confront each other, it's inevitably greatness which suffers defeat; for if the opposite were true, there would be no such thing as greatness in the world. Like everyone else, this group of students enjoyed many of the benefits conferred by Mr Huang, and even acknowledged his greatness; yet they simply did not like him. Though they may have enjoyed the fruits of his generosity ten times, a single scolding from Mr Huang was enough to make him seem totally reprehensible. I didn't look down upon them because of this; I only want to mention that in this world, many people act in this manner. It's not that they don't know the difference between right and wrong, but rather that their affections extend to no one but themselves. This sort of self-love is nothing more than self-indulgence; in fact, these people are unable to tolerate even the slightest reproach. If you saved one of their lives, at the same time admonishing them with a simple remark or two, they would always remember that you had scolded them — and in fact hate you for it — while completely forgetting your kindness in saving them. Mr Huang's biggest error was to have become a student supervisor in the first place, no matter how sincere, kind or honest he was about supervising us. The world is full of irresponsible student supervisors, but there was no connection whatsoever between irresponsibility and Mr Huang.

When he first came to our school, almost everyone liked him, since he was so very different from our other teachers, who we thought of as little more than books with mouths attached to them. We felt the same respect for our teachers and our books, even though the former were somewhat more lively and interesting. In our eyes, however, they belonged to another world, and had very little to do with us. Mr Huang was a "real person"; he was completely different from every other teacher we had. He ate with us, slept with us and studied with us.

Six months after he arrived at our school, a number of students began to dislike him. Some of them had been scolded by him, others disagreed with him for no special reason. When the other students said something was good, they insisted it was bad; in this way they tried to prove that they were the only ones with minds of their own, while everyone else was stupid and did exactly as they were told.

After one minor disturbance, those who were for and against him split into two equal factions. The origin of this disturbance had nothing whatsoever to do with him. Some of students wanted to hold a meeting during class time. He tried to dissuade them, but the students accused him of interfering unreasonably. Don't forget that he was an extremely naive man — his self-confidence led him to suggest a vote to determine the suitability of holding the meeting during class time. Fortunately, those who voted along with him outnumbered the opposition by three. Though this minor conflagration was soon resolved, Mr Huang's prestige suffered a fifty-percent loss.

As a result, those students who had it in for him knew their time had come. They decided that if such a disturbance ever took place again, they'd have him fired from his job. At this time, there were three other teachers who had their eyes on taking over his position. The most determined and active of these was the arts and crafts instructor, a man who lived by his wits and his tongue. Except for the fact that he was overweight, he and Mr Huang were as distant as the North and South Poles. The arts and crafts instructor once said in class that if he were offered a monthly salary of 800 dollars, he'd be very happy to clean out chamber pots all day long. Many students liked him; anyone who slept during his class would still receive a grade of 80 or 90. With him as student supervisor, we'd all enter the Kingdom of Heaven for sure! Ever since that first little disturbance took place, he began to hold little conferences in his room every night. Before long, the seeds planted during these little meetings bore fruit. The principal's office started to receive complaints about Mr Huang, and the names "Fat Ox" and "Potato Head" frequently appeared on the blackboard.

When some of the students reported these events to Mr Huang, he surprised us by taking a day off. That evening, when we were doing our homework for the next day, the principal came in and gave us a little lecture. He told us that Mr Huang had submitted his resignation, but that he had not given him permission to leave. "If any of you are dissatisfied with our student supervisor, you are welcome to quit school. If all of you dislike him, then I'll quit too." No one could say anything. But the moment the principal left the room, a large group of students rushed into the arts and crafts instructor's room for an emergency meeting.

Two days later Mr Huang came back to work as usual, but with one less roll of fat on his neck. When afternoon classes were over, he called a meeting of the student body, but only half of the students showed up. We expected that he would have a tremendous number of things to say to us, but after stepping up onto the platform, he didn't even smile. After standing there silently for several minutes without moving, he said in a carefully modulated voice, "Let's forgive each other." That was all.

Following the summer vacation, a movement to abolish monthly examinations gained momentum rapidly, until a few days before the Double Ninth Festival, the bomb finally exploded. Our English teacher insisted on giving the examination, but the students refused to sit for it; when the teacher left the classroom, he was ushered out by the most wonderful chorus of invectives. By the time the matter reached the principal's office, the question had evolved from one of refusing to take the examination to one of hiring a new English teacher, since the principal insisted on upholding the system of monthly exams. Though some students went so far as to advocate the overthrow of the principal, most seemed willing to start by replacing the errant teacher. Since the attack was not aimed directly at the principal, the issue of refusing to sit for the examination was put aside temporarily. At this juncture, several students warned Mr Huang not to get involved.

But Mr Huang was the student supervisor, whose job it was to maintain order and discipline at school. At this time, several students came up with a way to channel this disturbance in the direction of Mr Huang.

In the end, the principal refused to replace the English teacher. And it was soon learned that during a staff meeting, Mr Huang had advocated taking severe disciplinary measures against dissenting students, that Mr Huang had urged the teachers to cooperate with him in opposing the students' demands, and that Mr Huang. . . .

The storm changed its course once again. This time Mr Huang — not the English teacher — became the principle target.

Mr Huang still spent all of his time with his students, advising us and explaining things, smiling and weeping in turn in a way which further revealed his naivete and good faith. But the die had been cast.

Those students who accepted the idea of the monthly examinations dared not open their mouths. Those who cared neither way were highly impassioned when they spoke of the exams and made big commitments, in order to win the approval of their fellow students. And those students who respected and admired Mr Huang were even too scared to caution him in private. Like an evil curse, this affair put the entire school under its spell.

I met Mr Huang in the street one day.

"Mr Huang, you must be more careful."

"Sure," he replied, smiling as usual.

"Do you realize that the storm's already changed direction?"

He nodded, and smiled again. "I'm the student supervisor."

"Tonight there's going to be a meeting of the student body. I advise you not to show up."

"But I'm the student supervisor."

"There may be violence."

"Would they attack me?" His expression suddenly changed.

I could see that he had never considered the possibility of the students using physical force with him. He had too much confidence in himself. At the same time, though, he was also aware of the potential danger. He was a "real person", not a hero made of stone. That's why I liked him so much.

"Why?" It seemed as if this question were directed at his own conscience.

"Someone's pulling strings behind the scenes."

"Huh?" He didn't understand what I meant. He added quickly, "Even if I talk to them, will they still attack me?"

He nearly made me cry. His questions were so innocent and childlike; he seemed to believe that you could never go wrong if you just treated people kindly. He couldn't imagine that the world was also full of people like the arts and crafts instructor.

"In any case, the best thing for you is not to show up at the meeting."

"But aren't I the student supervisor? If I talk to them and give them some advice, that couldn't possibly cause any trouble. Thank you very much."

I stood there not knowing what to do. With my very own eyes, I was witnessing a man sacrifice himself for the sake of his responsibilities while remaining totally unaware that he was making a sacrifice. When I mentioned the word "violence", his facial expression changed, but he didn't retreat an inch. I realized that it was impossible for him to quit his job at this time, since he would never leave the school with things in such a state of chaos. "I'm the student supervisor!" I'll never forget the way he said those words.

The meeting took place that night. Four or five of us, all close supporters of Mr Huang, took seats in the front of the room near the lectern. We'd already agreed that in the event violence broke out we'd make every possible effort to protect Mr Huang.

Five minutes into the meeting, Mr Huang opened the door and walked in. It was so quiet you could hear a pin drop. The chairman was reporting some information provided by the arts and crafts instructor — The Case Against the Student Supervisor — when the student supervisor himself walked in! I stopped breathing for nearly a minute.

It was so bright in that room that it was a few minutes before Mr Huang could open his eyes. He lowered his head and closed the door behind him; his motions were those of a blind man. When he opened his eyes finally, he directed those two big benevolent black orbs towards the assembled audience. Because of the bright lights in the room, his face appeared paler than usual. He took two steps in the direction of the lectern, placed one foot up on the platform and smiled.

"My dear students, I'm here to say a few things to you as a friend, not as your student supervisor."

"Hypocrite!"

"Traitor!"

People were shouting from behind us.

Mr Huang lowered his head. He never imagined anyone would swear at him like that. Rather than feel hate for those students who abused him in this manner, he suspected it was he himself who was insincere and dishonest. Lowering his head spelled the end for him.

When he first came in, the general silence that prevailed suggested to me that everyone still respected him; he appeared out of danger. But when he lowered his head, everyone thought that he was acknowledging these epithets and admitting his shame.

"Hit him!" It was a student closely allied with the arts and crafts instructor who shouted this first. Others immediately chimed in. "Hit him!" "Beat him!" Everyone behind us stood up. The four or five of us put our hands on each other's knees. That was our secret signal not to move. For if we so much as moved an inch, chaos would ensue for sure.

I screamed "Get out of here!" to him in as loud and nasty a voice as I could muster, though my message was full of the best intentions.

Had Mr Huang left at that moment — he was only two or three steps away from the door — there would have been no trouble at all, since the few of us would have been able to hold off the rest of the students long enough for him to escape.

But Mr Huang didn't move. Having collected his strength, he raised his head vigorously. The look in his eyes was terrifying! But a few seconds later, he lowered his head once again, and in an act of profound contrition, swallowed all of his anger. He was a "real person", attempting to use human means to raise himself to a super-human level. I understood the thinking process that went on inside him: having been cursed without having provoked anyone, he began to suspect that he had behaved improperly, though in the bottom of his heart he knew he had done nothing wrong. At this moment, someone had shouted "Hit him!" He got angry, but he felt it was wrong to express his anger. These were only young students. And so he lowered his head again.

At this point, cries of "Hit him!" and "Beat him!" fell upon him like raindrops.

If he had shown his anger, no one would have dared to touch him. Even after he lowered his head the second time, and with shouts of "Hit him!" coming from every corner of the room, no one made the slightest move. This wasn't because the students lacked courage, but rather due to the fact that the majority of them — the greater majority — had only one thing in mind: "What grounds do we have to attack this good man?" Naturally, the chairman's report convinced a number of people, but no one there could forget Mr Huang's past behaviour; in addition, many knew that the chairman's report had been fabricated by a particular faction.

I shouted "Get out of here!" to him again. I knew that "Get the hell out of here!" would have been more appropriate, but I didn't have the nerve to say such a thing.

Mr Huang still didn't budge. Once again, he raised his head. A semblance of a smile appeared on his face, and his eyes were slightly moist; he looked like a young child confronting a tiger; his expression was a mixture of admiration and fear.

Suddenly a brick smashed through the window and struck Mr Huang on the temple. The brick flew in like a comet flashing across the sky, followed by a trail of shattered glass. Mr Huang's head started to bleed and he placed his hand on the lectern to support himself. All the students behind us rushed out of the room, while we surrounded him to prevent him from falling.

"It's nothing, it's nothing at all." He was smiling as best he could, though his face was covered in blood. We went to look for the principal, the school doctor and the dean, but none of them were around, so we decided to take him to the hospital.

"Take me to my room," he said. He barely had enough strength to speak.

We had very little experience in these matters, so when

he told us to take him to his room, we simply obeyed him. When we got him there, he staggered forward a couple of steps as if he wanted to wash his hands, but fell right down on his bed. Blood was still flowing freely from his wound.

Zhang Fu, the old janitor, came in for a look and said, "Hold the teacher up. I'll get the school doctor."

When the doctor arrived, he dressed the wound, wrapped it in gauze and advised Mr Huang to go to the hospital. Mr Huang drank a glass of brandy, which seemed to restore him somewhat, and he closed his eyes and sighed. The doctor warned him that if he didn't go to the hospital, his life would be in danger. Mr Huang smiled and said softly, "I'll ... I'll die right here. I'm the student supervisor! How can I leave now? Neither the principal nor the dean is around."

Zhang Fu offered to stay with Mr Huang overnight. Though we were also eager to keep watch over him, we knew that there was a crowd of people waiting outside who looked upon our behaviour with great disdain. Young people can't stand being accused of "doing the wrong thing"; acting out of sympathy for another person or following one's own conscience was often seen as "doing the wrong thing" or "acting like a dog".* Young people are capable of acting out of great passion and cold callousness at the same time. It was better for us to leave him alone. But even though we decided not to spend the night with him, when we walked out of the school we heard people shouting, "Very pretty! Look at the ox's godsons!"

---

* A pun in Chinese.

The next morning, Zhang Fu told us that Mr Huang had become delirious during the night.

The principal came and decided to take Mr Huang to the hospital, regardless of whether he was willing to go or not.

At this moment, Mr Huang regained consciousness. We were standing outside his door listening to what was going on inside. The arts and crafts instructor was there with us, and smiled wryly when he noticed the white sign marked "Student Supervisor" on the door. But when he looked at us, he knitted his brows, as if to show us his deep concern for Mr Huang's welfare. We could hear Mr Huang saying, "Alright, I'll go to the hospital. But first I want to talk to the students."

"Where?" the principal said.

"In the auditorium. I only have a few things to say. Otherwise, I'm not going anywhere."

The bell rang. Nearly every student in the school was there.

Zhang Fu and the principal helped Mr Huang into the auditorium. His bandage was soaked through with blood; it looked as if a striped poisonous snake had coiled itself around his head. Mr Huang no longer looked like his old self. After entering the auditorium, he stood by the door without moving, making a concerted effort to open his eyes under the bandage. His eyes passed over every one of us, like a father searching for his children. He lowered his head; the effort required to hold it erect was too great for him. He spoke in a low but very clear voice. "It doesn't matter who threw the brick. I'll never . . . never make anything of it."

He left the room. No one stirred for two minutes.

Then we all got up and followed him out as he got into a car.

Three days later, he died in the hospital.

Who threw the brick at him?

It was Ding Geng.

But at that time, no one knew this. Actually, in those days, Ding Geng was known as "Miss Ding Geng"; no one could have imagined that "Miss Ding" was capable of throwing a brick.

At the time, Ding was only seventeen years old. He wore the same blue cotton robe every day; his face was covered with tiny red pimples; and his eyes were filled with "sleepy dust" that looked like eye ointment. He was an honest boy, spoke very little, but went from one person to another without becoming very close to anyone. Sometimes he would clean up his room without being told; other times he would go for days without washing his face. We called him "miss" because he was so fickle and frivolous.

After things calmed down at school, the arts and crafts instructor became our new student supervisor. And since Mr Huang had died, the principal ceased investigating the question of who had thrown the brick. The truth was that no one really knew.

However, within six months, everyone knew who had done it. Ding Geng became an entirely different person; no one could call him "miss" anymore. He became a big talker, and everything that came out of his mouth was filthy. He spent all of his time with the laziest students and started smoking cigarettes — naturally the student supervisor didn't intervene. He went out every night and often came back with the smell of alcohol on his breath. He was even chosen to act as chairman of the student association.

Actually, Ding Geng began to change the night Mr Huang died. No one had thought "Miss Ding Geng" could have thrown a brick at anyone. But now that he was no longer "Miss Ding Geng", everyone naturally assumed that he was capable of doing such a thing. The changes took place so rapidly that anything seemed possible with him now; thus, everyone concluded, it had to be "him".

Six months later, Ding Geng admitted what he had done. This was a form of self-advertisement, since he was now the school "tough guy". And the person who was most afraid of this "tough guy" was the arts and crafts instructor-*cum*-student supervisor. With the student supervisor under his thumb, any wrongdoing Ding Geng chose to admit to involved very little risk for him. Ever since the day Mr Huang ceased acting as our student supervisor, our school began to decline rapidly.

What made him throw that brick? The way Ding told it, there were at least 50 or 60 reasons, though he couldn't decide which of them was the best. Naturally, no one else could be expected to decide either.

In my own view, the real reason was that "Miss Ding Geng" was just being "Miss Ding Geng" again. That night, when everyone else was attending the meeting, he was too scared to go in and listen and stood outside watching the way the wind would blow. Suddenly inspiration struck. Perhaps Mr Huang had found fault with him once; perhaps Ding found Mr Huang's fat face amusing and wanted to see if he could hit it with a brick; or perhaps. . . . The facts were: Ding Geng was a seventeen-year-old boy who by nature was as capricious as the devil, and he had an adolescent face full of red pimples and an expression of gloominess which crossed the line between man and beast. From this, one could conclude that he was capable of perpetrating acts that might be termed accidental.

Ding Geng was just that kind of person. When Mr Huang was alive, Ding was as fickle as a chameleon, and even enjoyed it when his classmates called him Lin Daiyu.* But after Mr Huang's death, something very strange came over him. If someone said something nice to him, he'd behave himself all day by sitting at his desk and diligently practising Chinese calligraphy — in an elegant hand at that. But the very next day, he would skip class altogether.

My opportunity to observe him went beyond our student days. After graduation, we happened to get jobs in the same school and worked together for about six months. From what I was able to observe during this period, I can state with conviction that he behaved exactly like I described above. Let me cite one example: The two of us were teaching in an elementary school, I was teaching fourth grade and he was teaching third. After only two months, he made a request to switch classes with me, the sole reason being that I had three fewer students in my class. But he didn't put it this way to the principal — it would have been awkward for him to have made such a request for the sake of correcting three fewer test papers. Here's how he put it: teaching fourth grade was more prestigious than teaching third grade. He didn't want to hold a position inferior to mine.

---

* One of the leading female characters in the famous novel *A Dream of Red Mansions*.

Although this wasn't a much better excuse, it provided him with the grounds for a slightly more persuasive argument. He also told the principal that he had been the chairman of the student association when we were in high school together. Naturally, the chairman was a leader of the masses; now that we had become teachers, it was only proper for him to be teaching a higher grade.

I told the principal that it didn't matter to me either way and that I would do as he pleased. The principal thought that since we were nearly halfway through the semester, this was not a good time to make such changes, so nothing was done about it. About a month before the Chinese New Year holiday, some urgent business came up which required the principal to take two weeks off, and he asked me to take his place during his absence. Ding Geng also agreed to this. However, Ding blew up at me this time, since approaching the principal directly about this matter would have made him look bad. I forgot exactly what I said to him, but the gist of it was that I would go to the principal on Ding's behalf and tell him that I was unwilling to replace him while he was gone.

But by the time I spoke to the principal, Ding had already changed his mind; then, he suddenly quit his job, even refusing to wait till the New Year's holiday. Before the principal left, Ding had packed up and gone. It was no use saying anything to him, since nothing could stop him. That was the last time I saw him.

Visiting Mr Huang's grave brought back all the suffering and pain I had endured during the last twenty years. His gravestone seemed to have shrunk and a few wild flowers were growing in the thin soil at its base. All this natural "beauty" only intensified the melancholy of the place. I could see the sun setting through the bamboo grove next to the Temple of Great Compassion, but I had no intentions of leaving. My only wish was to talk to Mr Huang — fat old Mr Huang, dressed in his long grey cotton gown.

I noticed a man approaching. He was not wearing a hat, he had long hair, and he had on a short black jacket, though I couldn't clearly make out his features. Just someone passing by, I thought, and paid no further attention to it. But then I noticed he was no longer following the little path and was coming in my direction. Had he also come to visit someone's grave?

He didn't notice me until he was standing right next to the grave. He froze in his tracks. It wasn't easy to see me from a distance, since I was sitting in the shade of a large maple tree.

"So it's you." He spoke my name.

He surprised me, and I failed to identify him right away.

"Don't you remember me? I'm. . . ."

Before he said his name I realized it was Ding Geng. Except for the fact that he still reminded me of "Miss Ding Geng" — though I couldn't say exactly how or why — he was nothing like the Ding Geng of twenty years ago. His hair was very long and matted. His face was dark, with the same old thick layer of "sleepy dust" in his eyes. His eyes had receded into their sockets and were badly bloodshot. His teeth were blackened from smoking and I noticed that the top joints of the first two fingers of both his hands were stained a deep yellow. As he looked at me, he removed a pack of Great Wall cigarettes from his pocket.

For some strange reason, I suddenly felt a great sad-

ness. There had never been any close emotional ties between us, but we did go to high school together.... I
went over to him and shook his hand. It was trembling
violently. We looked at each other; there were tears in
our eyes. Then together we turned in the direction of
the little tombstone.

"You're here to visit his grave, I see." The words
were on the tip of my tongue but I restrained myself
and said nothing. He lit a cigarette, raised his head, exhaled a large mouthful of smoke, looked at me, looked
at the grave, and laughed.

"Yes, I'm here to visit him too. That's pretty funny,
huh?" He sat down on the ground.

I didn't know what to say, so I just laughed and sat
down with him.

He remained silent and went on smoking with his
head lowered; he seemed to be thinking about something important. After smoking half his cigarette, he
looked up and flicked off the ash in an exaggerated
manner. He laughed and said, "After twenty years, he
still hasn't forgiven me!"

"Who's that?"

"Him," he said, pointing to the grave with his cigarette.

"What?" The way he was talking made me rather
uncomfortable. I suspected he might have been somewhat insane.

"Do you remember his last words? He said, 'I won't
make anything of it.'"

I nodded my head.

"You remember when we were teaching elementary
school together, when I quit suddenly? And I asked you

to tell the principal you didn't want to take over for him? Do you remember what you said to me then?"

"No I don't."

" 'I won't make anything of it.' That's what you said. And the time I wanted to switch classes with you, you said the very same thing to me. Maybe it wasn't intentional on your part, but for me, it was a kind of . . . a kind of retaliation, or punishment. Those words were like a red strip of cloth, like a poisonous snake; they were really red. Those words turned my life into one long trembling fit. All my aspirations and my career have trembled away like autumn leaves blowing in the wind, like the leaves on this maple tree. You must know by now why I wanted to take over for the principal. For a long time, I had been trying to prevent him from taking up his position again when he came back. But then you said that. . . ."

"I didn't mean anything by it," I apologized.

"I know. After I left that school, I got a job in the Inland Waterways Bureau. It was an easy job and the pay was good. About six months later, there was an opening for a better job, and a man named Li and I both had our hearts set on it. I mobilized a number of people to help me, and he did the same. Since we both pulled about the same weight, it was a long time before the final decision came down from the top. During this time, the two of us were invited to the bureau director's home to play mahjong. While we were playing, the director hinted that the little rivalry between Mr Li and me was putting him in an awkward position. I said nothing, but Li came up with a red dragon and said, 'It's red! I give up. But I won't make anything of it.' Red! I won't make anything of it! At that moment, Mr Huang appeared before me with that blood-soaked bandage wrapped around his head. It took an enormous effort to finish that round, and by the time it was over I was covered with sweat from head to toe. I never wanted to see that Mr Li again. He was the reincarnation of Mr Huang. He put a curse on my soul that I knew would end up killing me without my shedding any blood. If there is such a thing as witchcraft in this world, this was it. So I quit. I just quit." Sweat was dripping down his forehead.

"Perhaps you were susceptible to such things because you weren't in such good physical shape." I said this partially to console him, but also because I didn't believe in ghosts.

"I swear there was nothing wrong with my health. Mr Huang is following me around, believe me. Since he's a total hypocrite, he can put hypocritical curses on people. Let me give you another example. I got married not long after I quit the job I had at the Inland Waterways Bureau." At this moment, his eyes became the eyes of a female eagle which had lost her fledglings, and he stared at a half-withered weed on the ground for several minutes. His mind seemed to have left his body. It wasn't until I cleared my throat that he was startled out of his trance. Wiping the sweat off his brow, he said, "She was beautiful, really beautiful. But — she wasn't a virgin. On our wedding night, our bedroom was like hell; only there wasn't any blood. You know what I mean? A bridal chamber without blood is just like hell. That's very old-fashioned, I know, but my wedding was old-fashioned, and naturally all my feelings then were old-fashioned too. She told me everything, she pleaded with me, she begged me to forgive her. They say that a woman's beauty can make you forgive her for anything. But my heart was hardened; I wasn't going to be a cuckold.

"The more she cried, the worse I treated her. Actually, tormenting her brought me a little relief. Finally, she stopped crying and became silent. The last thing she said was, 'Take the blood of my heart instead.' She exposed her chest and said, 'Stab me here. You have every right to do it. If I die, I won't make anything of it.' That was the end for me. Mr Huang was there in my bedroom making fun of me. I was paralysed. The next day, I ran away. I became a drifter. My home was inhabited by a bloodless woman and a bloody ghost! Suicide was out of the question. I made up my mind to fight him to the finish. He had robbed me of all my happiness. I wasn't going to let him take my life away from me as well."

"Ding, I still think it's all because you aren't well. Listen, that incident with the brick wasn't intentional on your part. Not only that, Mr Huang died because he waited too long. Had he gone to the hospital sooner, his life would never have been in danger." I tried to console him. I knew that if I said that Mr Huang was a good person who would never come back from the dead to haunt anyone, Ding Geng would get very angry with me.

"That's right, what I did was unintentional. But his way of forgiving people with false pity was a deliberate ruse; in fact, it's a curse. Otherwise, why would a dying man insist on saying what he did in the auditorium? Alright, then. I really ought to tell you what else happened since then. Since I was a man without a home, I could do whatever I pleased. I travelled through twelve or thirteen provinces.   I joined the revolutionary army in Guangdong.   By the time we'd gotten to Nanjing, I was a regiment commander.   If I'd stayed in the army, I'd at least be a army commander by now. But I quit during a purge.   This is what happened: There was a good friend of mine named Wang who was involved with the Leftists. His rank was higher than mine. If I got him out of the way, I could have taken over his position.   Framing him would have been easy; but though I had a lot of evidence against him, I didn't have the heart to turn him in.

"Even though we'd fought side by side for more than a year, and had ended up in the hospital twice together, I couldn't give up this opportunity.   Ambition has a way of making heroes ruthless.   I wasn't a 100 percent hero, though, so I came up with a rather unradical method.   I had someone tell him that the situation was very dangerous for him, and warn him that he should get away as soon as possible and turn everything over to me.   I would make plans to ensure his future safety. But he refused.   I got very angry and had no choice but to use violence.   Just as I was making my final plans, that bloody guy appeared before me, all by himself.   Some people act like that, spending their entire lives dispensing false generosity, caring nothing at all for themselves, as if death were the cheapest thing in the world. What a joke!

"Wang was the same way, he still laughed and joked with me as usual.   Before I made my final plans — since his life was in my hands anyway — I had a talk with him, with a gun in my hand.   After . . . after listening to what I had to say, he just sat there smiling at me.   'If you want to kill me,' he said, still smiling, 'go ahead. I won't make anything of it.' Was it really him that said that? Is such a coincidence possible? I knew . . . a long time ago that whenever I was on the verge of any success, 'he' would always appear with a smile on his face and seek his revenge. That hypocritical ghost could destroy people in the subtlest ways. At that moment, I couldn't even raise my arm, not to mention kill a man. Wang kept smiling and walked out of the room. With him gone, how could I get the upper hand? His position was higher than mine. It was too late for me to try to expose him with the evidence I had, since I knew he would immediately find his own way of taking care of me. My only way out was to escape. By now, some of the soldiers who were under my command are regiment commanders themselves. And look at me — I'm a married man without a home; I live in a Buddhist temple, but I'm not even a monk. I don't know what I am anymore."

While he was catching his breath, I asked him, "What temple do you live in?"

"The one right in front of you, the Temple of Great Compassion. This way I can be near him all the time." He pointed to the grave. Seeing that I had no further questions, he went on. "Since he's so close by, I can come here every day and swear at him."

I don't recall what I said then, or whether I said anything at all, but it really doesn't matter. I started down the mountain, strolling through the golden yellow light of the autumn woods, the setting sun shining on my back. I didn't dare turn around. I didn't want to take another look at that maple tree, with its leaves as red as blood.

Translated by Don J. Cohn

Mr Jodhpurs

BEFORE the train left the Beijing East Station, the gentleman occupying the upper berth in my compartment, who was wearing jodhpurs, non-prescription spectacles, a black satin sports jacket with a small Chinese writing brush stuck in its breast pocket, and a pair of low black felt boots, turned to me and said in the most pleasant manner, "Did you get on the train in Beijing too?"

I was struck dumb by this question. The train hadn't started yet, if I didn't get on at Beijing, where else could I have gotten on? I could only retaliate by asking him, in an equally pleasant manner, "And where did you get on?" I was hoping he would tell me he had gotten on at Hankou or Suiyuan, for if this were the case, Chinese trains no longer needed rails, and could travel anywhere they pleased. Wasn't that the epitome of freedom?

But he remained silent. Glancing at his berth, he mustered all the muscles in his throat — if not in his entire body — and shouted, "Steward!"

At this moment, the steward was busy helping other passengers load their baggage onto the train and locate their berths. But upon hearing this shout, which was hysterical enough to make him drop even the most pressing task, he rushed into the compartment to see what had happened.

"Bring me a blanket," Mr Jodhpurs ordered.

"If you don't mind waiting a few minutes, sir," he

replied kindly, "I'll bring you one as soon as the train starts."

Mr Jodhpurs replied by picking his nose with his index finger.

Two seconds after the steward walked out, there was another "Steward!" This time it seemed the entire train had started shaking. The steward spun around in his tracks as fast as a tornado.

"Bring me a pillow." Mr Jodhpurs had apparently decided that it was alright if the blanket arrived late, but he had to have his pillow first.

"Sir, if you don't mind waiting a few minutes until things calm down, I'll bring you your blanket and pillow together." Though he spoke rapidly, the steward was as polite as could be.

Receiving no response from Mr Jodhpurs, the steward turned to leave, but the train started trembling again. "Steward!"

This came as such a shock that he almost lost his footing, and returned to the compartment.

"Bring me some tea!"

"If you would be so kind as to wait just a few more minutes until the train starts moving, I'll bring your tea right away."

Mr Jodhpurs made not even the slightest response to this. The steward forced a smile by way of apology. Muttering to himself, he turned around slowly, as if to avoid losing his footing again. Having gotten this far, he was about to escape when a clap of thunder exploded behind him, "Steward!"

This time the steward wasn't pretending he hadn't heard anything; he had actually been deafened by Mr

Jodhpurs's voice. He sped off without even turning around.

"Steward! Steward! Steward!" Mr Jodhpurs shouted louder and louder each time. A number of people who were on the platform seeing their friends off rushed over to see whether the train was on fire or if someone was dying. But the steward didn't even turn around to look. Mr Jodhpurs picked his nose again and sat down on my berth. A moment later he cried out, "Steward!" but the steward was nowhere to be seen. Looking down at his knees, his face became so long that when he picked his nose, his face stretched out of shape and snapped back like a rubber band. Then he asked me, "Are you riding second class?" This left me very confused for a minute. I had definitely bought a second class ticket, but had I perhaps boarded the wrong train?

"How about you?" I said.

"Second class. This is second class. Second class cars have berths. We must be about to leave, right? Steward!"

I picked up my newspaper.

He stood up and started counting his luggage. The eight pieces he'd brought along with him were piled on the upper berth across from his own — he now occupied two upper berths. After finishing his count, he said to me, "Where's your luggage?"

I said nothing, but I was mistaken this time. His intentions were actually good, since he went on to say, "That damned steward. Why didn't he carry your luggage for you?"

This left me with little choice but to tell him, "I don't have any luggage."

"Oh!" That came as a real surprise to him, as if it

were a gross impropriety to travel by train without luggage. "If I'd known that earlier, I wouldn't have had my four other suitcases shipped."

It was my turn to be surprised. "Oh!" I thought. "That's a good thing. If there were four more suitcases in here there'd be no room to sleep."

The man occupying the lower berth across from mine came in. His luggage consisted of a single briefcase.

"Oh!" Mr Jodhpurs exclaimed. "If I'd known earlier that neither of you had any luggage, I could have avoided paying the shipping charge on that coffin."

I made a resolution that the next time I took a train I would bring plenty of luggage along. Can you imagine spending a night on a train with a coffin?

The steward walked past the door of our compartment.

"Steward! Bring me a face towel!"

"Wait a minute." He appeared to be gradually mounting a protest.

Mr Jodhpurs loosened his tie, removed his collar and hung them up separately on the hooks on the wall. All the hooks in the compartment were now occupied, since his hat and raincoat were hanging from the remaining two.

The train started to move. He suddenly decided to buy a newspaper. "Steward!"

But the steward didn't come. I gave him my newspaper to read; it was my eardrums that contributed this suggestion.

He climbed into the upper berth and began removing his boots right over my head, knocking the dirt off their soles. Resting his head on a small suitcase and covering his face with my newspaper, he fell asleep before the train reached the Yongdingmen Station in the south of the city.

What a relief!

When we arrived at Fengtai a few minutes later, before the train had even come to a halt, a voice called out from above, "Steward!"

But before the steward had a chance to answer, Mr Jodhpurs went back to sleep. This interruption must have been an episode in one of his dreams.

After we left Fengtai, the steward brought in two pots of tea. I started drinking and chatting with the passenger occuping the berth opposite mine. He was a man of about forty years old, and was quite average in appearance, though he had a particularly jowly face. At some point before we arrived at Langfang, there was another clap of thunder from the upper berth, "Steward!"

The steward came in, but his eyebrows were twisted in a manner that suggested his only satisfaction could come from eating a man alive.

"What do you want, mis ... ter?"

"Bring me tea!" resounded the thunder from above.

"What are these two pots of tea here?" The steward pointed to the table.

"Bring another pot for the upper berth!"

"Alright!" The steward left.

"Steward!"

The steward's eyebrows became so knotted that some of the hairs fell out.

"I don't want tea. Bring me a pot of hot water."

"Alright!"

"Steward!"

I was afraid he would lose his eyebrows entirely.

"Bring me a blanket, bring me a pillow, bring me a face towel, bring me. . . ." Actually, it seemed he didn't know *what* he wanted.

"Please be patient, sir. There'll be more passengers getting on at Tianjin. I'll take care of everything after we leave there. And I promise you that you'll be able to get to sleep in time."

Having said all of the above in a single breath, the steward turned around and left. It seemed as if he had no intention of ever coming back.

A short while later, the steward brought the water, but by this time, Mr Jodhpurs was back in dreamland. His snoring was only slightly lower in volume than his "Steward!" However, it was even and regular, and occasionally lower in terms of pitch. He made up for this deficiency by grinding his teeth.

"Your hot water, sir."

"Steward!"

"Here you are, your hot water."

"Bring me toilet paper!"

"There's some in the toilet."

"Steward! Where's the toilet?"

"There's one at each end of the car."

"Steward!"

"I'll see you later!"

"Steward! Steward! Steward!"

There was no response.

"Gragh — gragh — gragh. . . ." He'd fallen asleep again.

This man was incredible!

When we arrived in Tianjin, more passengers boarded the train. Mr Jodhpurs awoke and took a big sip of water from the spout of the teapot. Then he knocked the dust off the soles of his boots immediately above my head and put them on. As he climbed down to go out for a stroll, he picked his nose with his index finger and took a look out the window. "Steward!"

At this moment, the steward happened to be passing by the door of the compartment.

"Bring me a blanket!"

"In a minute."

Mr Jodhpurs stepped out of the compartment and stood in a daze in the middle of the passageway, as if he were trying to obstruct the movements of the passengers and porters getting on and off. He vigorously picked his nose once again and stepped down onto the platform. He inspected the pears but bought none; he glanced at the newspapers but didn't buy any; he looked at the porters' numbered uniforms but they meant nothing to him. Boarding the train, he called out to me, "Tianjin, right?" I didn't answer him. He then said to himself, "I'll ask the steward," and followed this with a clap of thunder: "Steward!" I regretted my own silence and immediately added, "You're right, this is Tianjin."

"I have to ask the steward anyway. Steward!"

I laughed out loud; I couldn't control myself any longer.

Finally the train left Tianjin.

As soon as we started moving, the steward brought Mr Jodhpurs his blanket, pillow and face towel. After spending the next fifteen minutes cleaning every accessible surface of his nostrils and ear canals with the towel, Mr Jodhpurs used it to wipe the dirt off his luggage.

I counted to myself: in the ten minutes it took to travel between the old Tianjin station and the main station, he called for the steward at least forty or fifty times. But the steward only came in once, whereupon Mr Jodhpurs asked him which direction the train was heading in. The steward replied that he didn't know, which led Mr Jodhpurs to suggest that there had to be someone aboard the train who knew, and that the steward ought to take it upon himself to find out. The steward said that the engineer didn't even know. Mr Jodhpurs's face suddenly turned very pale, "What if the train got lost?" The steward didn't answer this question, but a few more hairs fell out of his eyebrows.

Mr Jodhpurs went to sleep again, but not before shaking out his socks in my face. I was also spared a mouthful of phlegm, with which he graced the ceiling of the compartment.

Naturally I couldn't sleep. I realized soon enough that unless I had a pair of snoreproof earplugs, falling asleep would be impossible. I only felt sorry for the passengers in the adjacent compartments, few of whom had boarded the train with the intention of staying up all night. However, given his particular species of snore, with its sharp rising inflection at the end of every exhalation, it was a very minor sacrifice indeed.

My destination was Dezhou. We arrived there just before daybreak. Thank heaven!

The train stopped in Dezhou for half an hour. I found myself a ricksha, and as I headed into town, I could still hear him shouting "Steward!" as clear as ever.

It's been more than a week now, but I am still worried about that steward's eyebrows.

Translated by Don J. Cohn

A Vision

IT must have been after the Clear and Bright Festival,* for the crab-apple was coming into full bloom. Spring was late this year, of course, and butterflies still seemed fragile though the lusty bees from the very start found the whole wide world as delectable as honey. Swallows were having fun, too, pinning black letter T-s to the handful of fleecy white clouds in the sky. The willows, although there was no wind, kept their branches swaying softly to mock the hints of greenery all around. The fresh green of the fields, delicate and easily tired, crept up the hills growing fainter the higher it went, till near the top it was lost in patches of brown. The trees half-way up, even those not yet green, had a silky look about them, while the blue sky beyond the hills must have been warm, for geese were flying that way, honking, in formation. Shy epidendrums were hiding in clefts in the rock, their leaves smaller than their flowers.

The scent of the hills is best enjoyed with closed eyes to save the trouble of analysing its sources, for even last year's fallen leaves give off a good smell. The plaintive bleating of some kids in the distance just kept my pleasure within reasonable bounds. And one happened to stray my way. A little creature sprouting a beard before its horns had grown, it stood foolishly in front of a

---

* This usually falls early in April.

rock for some seconds before trotting off again shaking its comical tail.

As I basked in the sun on the hillside, my mind a blank, pearls of poetry welled up unbidden in my heart to fall noiselessly into that sea of green in my breast, while faint smiles curved my lips and faded quickly away; but not a single line did I complete. The whole universe was poetry, and I no more than one small punctuation mark in a poem.

Basking there in utter content, I knew something of the rapture in a butterfly's wings. I hugged my knees, swaying this way and that in time to the willows' motion, and saw that each small gold-green leaf on their boughs was a tiny ear pricked up to catch the voice of spring. I looked up at the sky and blessed the white cloud at whose edge a swallow, nearly melting into the blue, seemed an infinitesimal black mote in that ocean of liquid light — my heart winged towards it.

Far away a path through the hills was like a brown line on a map of green provinces. Below sloped a wheat field, sweeping down the hillside until stopped by a dark green pine wood, and I hoped against hope that beyond the pines lay the sea. I stood up and climbed higher for a better view. No, there were trees over there — hard to make out just what they were — with low cottages among them. A sudden breeze carried over the faint crow of a cock.

That note of melancholy in a distant cock-crow in spring made me wonder if the scene before my eyes was reality or illusion, or perhaps a golden thread of sound between illusion and reality? For a second I had a vision of a blood-red comb; in my mind, in that village, or in the vicinity there was a cock — and I hoped it was snowy white.

I sat down again, or rather stretched out on the turf, my eyes opened just enough to catch the blue brilliance of the sky growing deeper and higher as it let fall on my pupils blue drops of light and warmth. And presently I closed my eyes to enjoy the sunshine and laughter within my own heart.

I was not asleep but close to the land of dreams, still able to hear distinctly the twittering and warbling of birds around me. Strangely enough, in that state between sleep and waking, the same scene — just where it is I do not know — always floats before me as I start dozing off. We may as well call it the borderland of dreams.

Not large, with neither hills nor sea, it is like a garden that has no definite limits, a rough triangle whose tips reach out into shifting darkness. The tip at which I invariably look first is a mass of gold and crimson flowers, with no sunlight, nothing but darkness, behind this blaze of colour; and the dark background intensifies the crimson and gold, just as red peonies painted in a black vase flame with almost fearful beauty. That dark background, I know, helps the crimson and gold to retain their brightness instead of diffusing it; for without sunshine the brightness cannot take flight but is held and imprinted on the ground. My eyes turn here first because this part conjures up a picture of the rest in the same way that by looking at the Western Hills you know where the Temple of Azure Clouds is hidden.

From the left tip curves a long slope of wild flowers like heather, more virile than beautiful; and moonlight touching the grey tints with silver might well bring out the transcendence of poetry here; but it slips my mind whether there is a moon or not. At all events, far from disliking this heath, I delight in the frost-darkened purple which reminds me of a young mother in a dark purple gown. But the right-hand tip is the loveliest of all, for there stands a thatched cottage with a trellis before its door where pink rambler roses are a riot of pure blooms.

If I run my eyes from left to right, from the purple, the crimson and gold to the pale pink, it seems as if time has regressed from autumn to spring, as if nature's prime is not followed by decay but life ends with the two-fold glory of the scent and colour of roses.

In the middle of the triangle lies a meadow of dark green grass, soft, thick and moist, each blade thrusting up as if listening to distant rain. Not a breath of wind here, not an insect stirs. In this small world of ghostly beauty, only colours are alive.

In real life I have never seen a place like this. Yet it has a permanent existence on the threshold of my dreams. It may be descended — but who can say for certain? — from the deep green of England, the heather-clad moors of Scotland, the shadowy Black Forest of Germany. Again, take away the sunshine and there is a resemblance to the lush tropics; except that here are no snakes all colours of the rainbow, no birds of brilliant plumage. I know it, though, and that is enough for me.

I have visited it so often, it is like a picture in my heart, as real as the couplet:

> High hills and the moon dwindles;
> Low tide and rocks appear.

Yet I had never set foot inside that cottage, being either

held spellbound by those colours or hurrying from that meadow into dreams of another kind. Like men who keep meeting we knew each other's names, but because we had never had a frank, intimate talk its innermost colour remained a mystery to me, as well as its secret music. I longed to see some sign of life there.

This time I decided to investigate.

At once, without even hearing my own footsteps, I found myself by the rose trellis. Since rambler roses are linked in my mind with the Dragon Boat Festival,* I hoped to find a vermilion Judge of Hell printed on dark yellow paper between two sprays of sweet artemisia. But, no! In fancy I heard the cry "Cherry ripe!" — that was all. The place was utterly still.

The door of the cottage was shut, ivory-white matting screened both windows and door, and the sunlight was too faint for flowers to cast shadows. Not a sound could be heard inside. This was surely the very well-spring of loneliness.

Gently pushing open the door, I was welcomed in by stillness and spotlessness — yes, they welcomed me. If outside was a world of ghosts, all here belonged to man — I hardly think these epithets too far-fetched.

A curtain divided the cottage into two rooms, one large and one small. This curtain, too, was the colour of ivory and had tiny butterflies embroidered on it. The sole furniture in the outer room was a long, high table, a small oval table and a chair, all dark green and unvarnished. There was a light green cushion on the chair, a few books on the small table, and on the longer

* In early summer.

one a small pine in a pot as well as two old bronze mirrors, their patina a shade lighter than the pine.

Spread on the bed in the inner room was a green rug which hung nearly to the ground. Suspended at the head of the bed was a tiny basket of jasmine just beginning to wither. Next to an oblong rush mat on the floor lay a pair of small green slippers embroidered with white flowers.

My heart missed a beat. I had stumbled upon no intricate, splendid realm of poetry: the dominant note here was simple, everyday beauty. And this was no fantasy either, for I recognized those small green slippers embroidered with white flowers.

Most love stories are just as commonplace as spring rain or autumn frost. But ordinary people take delight in the poetry of these commonplace events, doubtless because so much else in the world is even more lacking in colour, heaven help them! I hope my tale may have some entertainment value.

We had one glorious time together, only one. Everything conspired to be perfect that day. The crab-apple tree in her courtyard was one mass of blossom like a pinky-white snow-drift, the delicate bamboo by the wall was putting out fresh shoots, the sky was a delicious blue, her parents were out and the big white cat was sound asleep under the flowers. When she heard me come, she darted out like a swallow from under the eaves, not stopping to change her shoes, and her green slippers were like soft green leaves. She was radiant as the morning sun, her cheeks much rosier than usual, as if two fountains of liquid rouge had welled up through her dimples from a sweet red spring in her heart. In those days she wore her hair in a long plait.

When her parents were at home, she could only peep through the window or seize the chance to smile at me as I arrived. Today she was like a kitten that has found a playmate: her high spirits were a revelation to me. Side by side we walked into the house. We were just seventeen. Neither of us spoke, but two pairs of eyes were exchanging rapturous signals, leaving me no time today to admire the painting, *All the Birds Pay Homage to the Phoenix* done in meticulous style, for my eyes were on her green slippers. But though she tried to tuck her feet out of sight and blushed to the tips of her ears, she went on smiling. I meant to ask about her school work, whether any of their new kittens were wholly white; but the questions remained unspoken. There was so much to ask, but something had sealed my lips; and I knew this was true of her too for her white throat moved as if swallowing back some irrelevance, while she was too shy to say what was really worth saying.

She perched on a redwood stool beside the window, and shadows of crab-apple blossom stirred on her face. From time to time she glanced outside to make sure no one was coming, and the shadows of blossom on her face glowed red with joy. With both hands in turn she fidgeted with the edge of the stool, the picture of impatience, impatient with joy. At last she threw me a searching glance and said with most palpable reluctance: "You'd better go!" By then I was so lost to the world that I saw rather than heard what she was saying. Deep down in my heart, however, I guessed its gist, for something of the sort was nagging at my mind. I hated to go but knew that go I must. I held her eyes with mine. She faltered as if tempted to lower her head, then raised it bravely to meet my gaze, fearlessly fighting down her shyness. With one accord we hung our heads, with one accord raised them again to exchange long glances. We seemed to be seeing into each other's hearts.

Slowly at last I tore myself away, and there were tears in her eyes as she saw me outside the screen. When I reached the courtyard gate and turned my head, she was standing under the crab-apple blossom. I went away walking on air.

Another chance like that never came again.

Once there was a funeral in her house — not a death that distressed them unduly. I exchanged a few words with her under the lamp while she fidgeted with the button of her white mourning. We were so close, each could almost hear the other's blood racing, as you hear the young grain growing after rain. I uttered some brief commonplaces — a movement of the lips and tongue, that was all — our thoughts were far away.

Although we were twenty-two, this was before the May Fourth Movement. Segregation of the sexes was still the rule. After graduation they made me head of a primary school and that was the proudest day of my life because she wrote me a letter of congratulation. The letter — with plum blossom printed on it — had a postscript: "Don't reply." Nor did I dare. But I was afire to do all in my power to improve that school: its success should be her answer. And in my dreams she clapped encouraging hands, hands lovely as jade.

To propose to her was out of the question. Too many senseless yet insuperable obstacles stood between us fierce and powerful as a tiger.

One consolation I had: no word of any engagement ever reached my ears thirsting for news of her. Better still, in my spare time I organized a night school and she did some teaching there. Just to see her from time to time was all I asked. But she avoided me — in her twenties she had lost the ingenuous high spirits of seventeen, acquiring in their place the dignity and mystery of a woman.

Two years later I went off to the South Seas. And the day that I called at her house to take my leave, she happened to be out.

I was abroad for several years, cut off from news of her. Unable to correspond directly and reluctant to make indirect inquiries, I had to be content with dreaming about her. Strange to say, I never dreamed of any other woman. They were unhappy as well as rapturous dreams: the fantasies of love have a flavour all their own. To me, she was still as she had been at seventeen: the same small round face, the same arch look in her clear eyes. She was not tall, but a sweet suppleness lent an indescribable grace to her walk; while to me her long black plait, seen from behind, was utterly bewitching. Though I remembered her with her hair up, I always dreamed of her with it in a long plait.

My first act, of course, on my return to China was to find out what had become of her. I could hardly credit my ears when I heard she had become a prostitute.

Not even this fearful news could damp my ardour; in fact, I longed more than ever to see and help her. I called at her house but the family had moved. Nothing could be seen but the crab-apple tree over the wall. The house had been sold.

At last I found her. Her hair was short, combed back in a large green comb. The elbow-length sleeves of her long pink gown betrayed the fact that her arms had lost their softness, nor could heavy powder hide her wrinkles and crow's-feet. Her smile was still a joy to see, not that there was any genuine gaiety in it. If not for paint and powder, she would have looked like a woman just after childbirth. Not once did she meet my eyes, although her face showed no trace of embarrassment. She talked and laughed, but her heart was not really in it— she was merely making conversation. My tentative questions as to how she was managing were brushed aside as, lighting a cigarette, she exhaled smoke like an adept, leaning back with crossed legs to watch the smoke wreaths, the picture of empty-headed brashness. The tears that sprang to my eyes can hardly have passed unnoticed but she chose to ignore them, studying her finger-nails and smoothing back her hair as if this were all she lived for. My inquiries about her family went unanswered too. I had to take my leave. I gave her my address before parting, assuring her that I was at her service. She laughed indifferently and looked away, indicating that she did not mean to see me out. When she thought I had gone, although I was still rooted in the doorway, she turned and for a second our eyes met — but instantly she looked away again.

First love, the first flower of youth, is not something to be lightly thrown away. I asked a friend to take her some money. She kept it but made no acknowledgement.

My friends saw my unhappiness — my eyes gave me away — but their wives' well-meant offers to introduce girls to me won nothing but wry smiles or a shake of the head. I had to wait for her. First love keeps its charm like childhood treasures, whether rag dolls or coloured pebbles. Later on I confided in some of my closest friends, who considerately refrained from any harsh comments, simply hinting half-jokingly that I was a fool — the woman wasn't worth loving. This only made me more stubborn. She had opened the garden of love to me, and I must stay by her till the end of time. Pity is less romantic than love but kinder. Before long I sent a friend to her with a proposal of marriage. I dared not go in person. My friend returned to report that she had laughed wildly. No other answer — simply a fit of wild laughter. Was she laughing at my folly? Fair enough, there is something of folly in all who love. That would be gratifying. Or at herself because she was too close to tears? For anguish can result in wild laughter.

Folly emboldened me to seek her out and I prepared in advance what to say, rehearsing it several times. I must succeed, I told myself: to fail was forbidden. She was out and I went twice again without finding her. The fourth time, a cheap coffin was standing inside her door — she had died after an abortion.

I sent a basket of dewy roses with my heart's blood on their petals to her grave. That was the end of my first love and the start of a futile existence. I had no desire to find out what had brought her so low. In my heart, at any rate, she would never die.

I stared blankly at the small green slippers until a rustling made me look over my shoulder. The tiny butterflies embroidered on the curtain were fluttering over her head. There she was, as she had been at seventeen, graceful as a fairy who has just alighted on the earth. I stepped back, afraid to frighten her away, and as I recoiled she changed into the woman she had been at twenty-two. She stepped back in turn, and wrinkles appeared on her face. She started laughing wildly. I sank down on the narrow bed, then sprang up and ran over to her, whereupon she changed back in a flash to the girl of seventeen. These transformations in such a brief space made her seem unfettered by time. I sat down again, holding her in my arms, conscious that my cheeks had regained the ruddiness of fifteen years before. So we sat, listening to the pulsing of our blood. Some minutes slipped by before I found my voice to whisper into her ear:

"Do you live here alone?"

"It's not here I live, but here —" she pointed to my heart.

"You never forgot me, then?" I pressed her hand.

"When other men kissed me, I had a vision of you."

"Why let them kiss you?" I felt no jealousy as I asked this.

"There was love in my heart but my lips were at a loose end. Why didn't you come and kiss me?"

"Fear of offending your parents. And then I went to the South Seas, didn't I?"

She nodded. "You lost everything through fear; and in love separation leads to despair."

She told me what had happened. The year that I went abroad her mother died, so that she had a little more freedom. A spray of blossom above the wall is bound to attract the bees and men flocked round. I was still in her thoughts, but the flesh is less patient than love — not all love is as pure as the plum blossom. A young man who resembled me became her lover. Though he adored her she could not forget me; and he possessed her body but not her heart, for a physical resemblance could not take the place of true love. When he began to suspect this, she admitted that her heart was in the South Seas. Just about the time they separated, her father went bankrupt. Marriage was her only way out and she sold herself to a rich man to be able to provide for her father.

"Couldn't you make a living by teaching?" I asked.

"I could only have taught in a primary school — the pay wouldn't have been enough for my father's opium!"

We were both at a loss. I was thinking: Supposing I'd come back then, would I have been in a position to support her father? No, I'd just have had to watch her sell herself.

"I hid my love in my heart," she said, "and kept it alive by what I earned with my flesh. I dreaded the death of the body because I thought, wrongly, that would mean the end of love. Well, never mind that now. He was insanely jealous, always trailing after me whatever I did. Wherever I went, he followed. He couldn't catch me out, but he realized I didn't love him. His resentment developed into open abuse and violence, till he forced me to admit that there was another man. Things were so unbearable by then that I couldn't even stop to consider my rice-bowl. He threw me out with nothing but the clothes I stood in. My father was still looking to me for money and I had to live myself — I'd always been used to the best of everything. So I used carnal means to satisfy carnal desires, since my body was all the capital I had. Anyone could buy my smiles. I've a lovely smile: I used to practise it in front of the mirror. In the circumstances I preferred this type of retail sale to being under the thumb of one rich husband. Although plenty of lewd remarks were made behind me in the streets, at least I was free, and I rather preened myself sometimes when I met other women dowdily dressed. I had four abortions, but once the pain was over I could smile again.

"At first I had quite a reputation. Because I'd been a rich man's plaything and had some education, men of the old school as well as the new all came to patronize me. I never stopped to think, never even tried to save. My one aim in life, all that mattered, was to be smart: tomorrow could take care of itself. Avoiding immediate unpleasantness left me too tired to worry about the future. But I couldn't keep it up. My father's opium ran away with my money and abortions were costly too. I'd never put anything by, and a bank balance doesn't mount up by itself. Soon my last shreds of foolish pride were gone and I stooped to the meanest ways of making money — plain stealing at times. If a man behind me jeered, I turned back to smile. Each abortion added two or three years to my age — the mirror doesn't lie. I had lost my looks but tried recklessly to make up for it by doing all I could to attract customers. My doors were open even when I slept: my body was on sale at any hour of the day. I sank deeper and deeper into a sea of lust, dead to sober sanity, obsessed by money. That obsession with money took the place of thinking — calculations how to make an extra fifty cents. I never cried because crying makes a woman ugly. It was money, not myself I worried about."

She stopped for breath. Her gown was wet with my tears.

"Then you came back," she went on. "You were over thirty too. I remembered you as a student of seventeen. Your eyes weren't the same as when — how long ago is it? — you stared at my green slippers. Still, you yourself were intrinsically unchanged, whereas I'd died long ago. You could go on dreaming of your first love, but not I. I'd known all along that when you came back you would want me. But I'd lost myself and what had I to give you? While you were away I'd never denied to anyone that I loved you; but when you came back all I could do was laugh wildly. It seemed a cruel trick to play — not coming back till I had sunk so low. If you'd stayed away I could have gone on dreaming of the South Seas, gone on living in your heart. But, no, you must come back, so late —"

"Late doesn't have to mean too late," I interposed.

"No, it was too late. That's why I killed myself."

"No!"

"Yes, indeed. If I could live on in your heart, live on in a poem, it was the same to me whether I lived or died. I did it when I had my last abortion. With you near, I couldn't smile any more. Without smiling I couldn't make money. The only way out was to die. You had come back too late, but I mustn't die too late. Any more delay and I had no hope of living on in your heart. I live here, here in your heart where there's no sunshine, no sound, nothing but colour. Colour lasts longer, colour paints pictures of our memories. These green slippers are a bit of colour that you and I would recognize anywhere."

"I remember your neat ankles too. Let me see them again!"

She smiled and shook her head.

I insisted, pulling down her stockings. Underneath were two white bones, no flesh on them.

"You must go now!" She shook me gently. "We can never meet again. I wanted to live in your heart, but this has finished it. I hope in your heart it will be always spring."

The sun was sinking west, a cold wind was rising, there were dark clouds in the east. All the joy had gone out of the spring while I was dreaming. I rose to my feet and stared at the dark green pines. A long, long time I stood there. In the distance a small procession was approaching, and presently a faint medley of sounds could be heard. As it drew near, the birds in the fields cried out in alarm and flew up on white wings towards my side of the hill. Raising a dust as they hurried along came a few musicians, a few mourners in white behind them, and last of all a coffin. Yes, there are dead to bury in spring too. A handful of paper money* was scattered like butterflies over the wheat field. The clouds in the east grew blacker, the green of the willows darker, tragically dark. Sick at heart, I thought of that pair of small green slippers, like the leaves on some eternal tree dreaming of spring.

Translated by Gladys Yang

---

* Offered to the dead for use in the other world.

Black Li and White Li

THOUGH love was not the central theme of the misunderstanding which arose between the two brothers, I must begin my discussion there.

Black Li was five years older than White Li. They were both schoolmates of mine, though Black Li and I graduated from middle school the same year White Li began his studies there. Black Li and I were good friends, and since I visited their home frequently, I also got to know White Li quite well. In this day and age, five years makes a big difference. The two brothers' characters were as different as their nicknames: Black Li was old-fashioned; White Li was very modern. They didn't argue about this specifically, though their points of view differed radically on every subject under the sun. Black Li wasn't really black. He was called Black Li on account of a big black birthmark over his left eyebrow. His younger brother had no such marks, so he became White Li. Their classmates in middle school, who had given them these names, thought this was quite logical. Actually, both brothers' complexions were rather pale, and they looked very much alike.

They were both chasing the same woman — pardon me for not mentioning her name. She herself couldn't decide which of the brothers she loved more, though at the same time she wouldn't admit that she didn't love either of them. We were all very worried about them on account of this. Though we knew that neither of them was looking for a fight, we also knew that the game of love wasn't always played according to the rules of friendship.

Finally, Black Li surrendered.

I recall what happened very clearly. On a drizzly night in early summer, I went to have a chat with him in his home. He was sitting alone in his room with four fine porcelain tea bowls decorated with red fish standing on the table before him. We were very informal whenever we got together. I sat down and lit a cigarette while he played with his tea bowls. He turned them around, one by one, until the fish designs painted on them were all facing him. Once they were arranged in this manner he leaned back, examining them like a painter who had just completed a section of a new painting. Next he rearranged them so that the fish on the other side of the bowls were all lined up neatly in front of him. Once again, he leaned back to get a better look, and then turned and smiled at me. His smile was as innocent as a child's.

He was fond of playing this sort of game. He had no great talents, yet he dabbled in many areas. He never pretended to be an expert in any field, but he believed that everything he did contributed to moulding his temperament. There was no question about his being good natured. If he had a hobby to persue, such as repairing an old scroll painting, he could very easily while away an entire day at it.

Calling my name, he smiled and said, "I let Number Four have her." In terms of seniority in their family, White Li was number four, since an uncle on their father's side had two sons. "Brothers shouldn't become estranged on account of a woman."

"That's why they call you old-fashioned," I said with a chuckle.

"You're wrong, you can't teach an old bear new tricks. I couldn't handle a *menage a trois* anyway. So I said to her, no matter who she loves, I couldn't see her any more. You can't imagine how much better I felt after that."

"First time I've ever heard of a love affair like that."

"The first time? Then perhaps I shouldn't say any more. She can do as she pleases, but at least Number Four and I won't have any more arguments. If this sort of thing happened between us, I certainly hope one of us would give in the same way."

"Then there'd be peace on earth, right?"

We both laughed.

About ten days later, Black Li came to see me. I knew by now that whenever a grey shadow hovered over his forehead, there was something important on his mind. On occasions such as these, we'd always drink half a catty of Lotus brandy. I got the drinks ready quickly, since his forehead was looking unusually dim.

When he was drinking the second cup, his hands began trembling. It was hard for Black Li to conceal his feelings. If something was upsetting him, no matter how hard he tried to remain calm, it always showed on his face. He was such a kind and outgoing person.

"I went and had a talk with her," he said, smiling in a rather silly manner. But this was a genuine smile, since he was getting ready to pour out all his troubles to a close friend. If Black Li had no close friends, he wouldn't have survived for long.

I didn't press him, and there was no need for us to hurry anyway. Our feelings could very easily fill in the little silences which occurred in our conversations. We glanced at each other and grinned. Our facial expressions and intuitive understanding of each other were more important than anything we might say. For this reason White Li always called us "two bumps on a log".

"Number Four got nice and upset with me," he said. I knew exactly what he meant by "nice": First, he didn't want to admit that they had an argument; and second, he didn't want to put all the blame on his younger brother, even though it was White Li who was in the wrong. The word "nice" was a complex expression of his unwillingness to say what was really on his mind. "It was all because of her. It's my fault, I don't know anything about feminine psychology. Remember the other day I told you that I had surrendered? I had no qualms about that whatsoever, but she took it very differently. She thought I was trying to humiliate her. You're right when you say I'm old-fashioned. For me, love is a matter of doing what's right. Little did I know that our lady friend's out to get the whole world chasing after her. Now she hates me. So what does she do to get her revenge? I rejected her, so she stops seeing Number Four. Number Four blew up in front of me. So today I went to apologize to her. If she had just cursed me and let off some steam, maybe she and Number Four could get back together again. Anyway, that's what I was hoping. But you know what? She didn't curse me at all. She said she wanted Num-

ber Four and I to be her friends.   Of course that's impossible for me, though I didn't tell that to her directly.
I came over here to talk to you about it.   Problem is,
if I don't do as she says, she'll ignore Number Four, and
he'll start up with me all over again."

"A very difficult situation."   I tacked this on for
his benefit.   A few moments passed.   Then I said,
"Why don't I go explain everything to Number Four?"

"That would be fine," he said, holding up his wine-
cup, "but it might not do any good. Anyway, I'm finished with her.   If Number Four wants to make an issue
of it with me, I just won't say anything, that's all there
is to it."

We shifted the topic of our conversation onto some
other subjects.   He told me he'd been reading about
religion the last few days.   I knew that his studying
religion was purely a whim; Black Li wasn't the type
to take up religion out of pessimism, or because he was
undergoing some spiritual crisis.

Shortly after Black Li left, White Li came in.   He
rarely came to visit me, so I guessed that something
important had happened.   Though still a college student, White Li looked much more astute than his older
brother.   He gave you the immediate impression that
he was capable of being a great leader.   The things he
said would either lead you down the very path he
wanted you to follow or strap you to the guillotine. His
manner was extremely direct, the very opposite of his
brother.   I was also quite direct with him, lest he call
me a "bump on a log".

"Number Two came to see you of course." Black Li
was the second oldest in their extended family. "And of

course he's been telling you all about what's going on."
Naturally, there was no need for me to reply in a hurry,
since he said "of course" twice. But before I even had
a chance to open my mouth, he went on, "You know, I
just did it to make a point."

I told him I didn't know that.

"You think I'm really after that woman?" He smiled
at me with Black Li's smile, except that Black Li's smiles
were never so disdainful. "The only reason I got involved with her at all was to cause trouble for Number
Two; otherwise, why would I want to waste my time
with her? Aren't all relations between men and women
based purely on animal desire? What do I need her
for then? Number Two believes that animal desire is
sacred, so he went out of his way to kowtow to her.
Now that she's rejected him, he thinks it's my turn to
kowtow to her. I'm sorry, that's not my style." He
laughed loudly.

I didn't smile, nor did I dare interrupt him. I listened
carefully to what he had to say and paid even closer attention to his facial expression. Black Li and White
Li's faces were similar in every respect, except for the
fact that Black Li had none of his younger brother's
arrogance. For this reason, one moment I felt I was talking to a very close friend, and the next as if I were sitting across from a complete stranger. This was quite
discomfiting; the face before me was familiar, but the
expression was very strange.

"You see, I didn't even kowtow to her once. At the
proper moment, I kissed her. She really liked that, a
whole lot more than all that kowtowing. But that's not
the main point. What I mean is, do you think Number
Two and I ought to go on living together?"

I couldn't answer this question immediately.

He smiled — probably he was thinking to himself how I was just a "bump on a log". "I've got my own life to live, my own plans; the same is true for him. The best thing would be for both of us to go our own ways, don't you think?"

"Yes. What are your plans then?" It was no easy task coming up with this question; I already felt extremely awkward.

"This is no time to talk about my plans. Once we divide our family property and start living apart, you'll find out what my plans are."

"You started an argument with Number Two just because you want to move out? Is that the point you're getting to?" Now I was being clever.

He nodded with a smile but said nothing, knowing I probably had more to say. I continued, "Why didn't you discuss it with him peacefully instead of having an argument?"

"Do you think he's capable of understanding me? You may be able to hold a reasonable dialogue with him, but not me. As soon as I mention living apart to him, he starts crying. Then it's the same old thing — 'What did Mother say before she died? Didn't she tell us we should always be good to each other?' He brings that up every time, as if the dead were supposed to run the lives of the living. Not only that, if I mention dividing up the estate, he'll disagree, I swear to you, and tell me how he wants to sign everything over to me. But I don't want to take advantage of him like that. He always treats me like a little brother. He thinks he can control other people's behaviour. He pretends to understand me, but actually he's just a big anachronism.

The present belongs to me; why do I need him to tell me what to do?" His expression suddenly became very serious.

Looking at his face, I gradually began to see things in a different light. White Li was a proud young man who looked down on us two "bumps on a log". All he really wanted was to stand on his own two feet. I also realized that if the two of them tried to talk over their differences, they'd get carried away for hours discussing the whole range of fraternal obligations. If White Li didn't bring this up, Black Li certainly would. A quick argument was preferable to all of this, lest their conflict drag out indefinitely. White Li wanted a clean break, after which each of them could go their own way. Furthermore, if they held a proper discussion on the matter, Black Li would never respond in a straightforward manner. If White Li kicked up a storm first and Black Li offered a lot of resistance, Black Li would appear to be trying to appropriate White Li's share of the estate. At this point I suddenly felt enlightened.

"So you want me to go and talk to Number Two about it, right?"

"That's right. This way we can avoid a big argument." He smiled again. "Of course you shouldn't put him on the spot. We're still brothers." It seemed he felt very uncomfortable with the word "brothers".

I agreed to do as he said.

"The more insistent you are the better. I propose that he and I have nothing to do with each other for the next twenty years." He paused for a moment, forcing a grin. "You can tell him that if he wants to forget about me, he should get married and have a nice fat baby as soon as possible. In twenty years, I'll be old-fashioned myself. If I'm still alive then, I'll come home and play uncle. Make sure you tell him that when he's courting his future wife, he should kiss more and kowtow less; he should spend his energy chasing her rather than kneeling down before her." He stood up, paused for a moment, and then said, "Thank you." It was evident that these last two words were intended for me, but also that he really didn't want to bear the responsibility for having said them.

I discussed this matter nearly every day with Black Li. Every time I went to visit him he had the Lotus wine ready. We'd eat, drink and talk a lot together, but never came up with any conclusions. This went on for at least two weeks. He understood and appreciated everything I said and even expressed the hope that his younger brother would go out in the world and make a name for himself. But his last words always were: "How can I get along without him?"

"What could Number Four's plans possibly be?" He asked himself this question pacing back and forth in his room. His black birthmark sunk into the creases on his forehead and seemed to have shrunk somewhat. "What are his plans? Why don't you ask him. If you could find out, I could stop worrying so much."

"He won't tell me." I must have told him that at least fifty times.

"That's dangerous though. He's my only brother. Let him come and argue it out with me; there's nothing wrong with two brothers having an argument. He was never this way with me before. We only started disagreeing with each other very recently. It must be on account of that woman. He wants me to get married?

I didn't get married, and looked what happened. I'll get married then! What could his plans possibly be? Really! He wants to divide up the family property? Let him take whatever he wants. I probably offended him in some way. Though I never wanted to start a fight with him, I know I have my own opinions on things. So what are his plans then? He can do as he pleases. Why do we have to divide up the estate?"

Once he started on this topic, you could be sure he would drone on for more than an hour. His hobbies increased in number day by day: divination by tossing coins or using the Eight Trigrams, analysing Chinese charaters, reading about religion. . . . But none of these hobbies helped him to figure out what Number Four's plans were; on the contrary, they only increased his anxiety. This is not to say that he appeared any more nervous than usual. Actually, he was his usual maudlin self. It seemed as if his actions could never keep up with his emotions. No matter how agitated he was inside, he always moved slowly; he seemed to be playing with his life as if it were a toy.

I told him that Number Four's plans involved his future career and had nothing to do with the present. But he only shook his head.

In this manner, more than a month went by.

"You know," I said, appealing to reason, "Number Four isn't pressing me, so it must be that he has some long range plans. He's not about to run off and do anything big right now."

He just shook his head again.

As time passed, the number of stories about him increased. One Sunday morning I happened to see him entering a church, where I assumed he was looking for a friend. I waited for him outside, but he didn't come out. I had to go somewhere, and as I walked away I thought about how the recent events in his life must have been upsetting for him — his broken love affair; his falling out with his brother; and perhaps there were more things I didn't know about. But two things alone seemed to be too much for him to bear. His actions revealed that life was just a game for him, but this was because he was so preoccupied with the most trivial matters. It made him uncomfortable if the patterns on tea bowls were out of line. Similarly, he arranged things neatly in his mind to soothe his conscience. Perhaps by going to church and praying he could put his mind at rest. While his conscience had been provided to him by the wise sages of yore, at the same time he didn't reject all modern things and modern thinking. As a result, his own "way of thinking" was never quite as coherent as "the way things really were", making it difficult for him to know how to act properly. He was probably in love with her, but he had to reject her for his brother's sake; he certainly never mentioned falling out of love with her to me. He often said, "Let's take a ride in an airplane." Then he'd laugh, but it wasn't really him laughing, it was "the flesh and bones he'd inherited from his parents" that were laughing.

One afternoon I went to see him. It was our custom to begin talking about Number Four immediately — at least this had been the pattern over the last month or so. But that day he looked like an entirely different person. His eyes were bright and he had an expression of great contentment on his face. It was as if he'd just purchased a fine edition of a rare book.

I began the conversation. "What's the good news?"

He nodded, smiling. "Very interesting!" He always said this after experiencing something for the first time. If someone told him an old ghost story, you could be sure he would respond with "Very interesting!" He wouldn't argue with you about whether ghosts existed or not since he believed in the supernatural. "Who knows, there must be stranger things in the world than that," he would say. In his mind, anything was possible. Thus he accepted new things quite readily, but without understanding them very thoroughly. It wasn't that he lacked the desire to understand things. However, on those occasions when he should have used his brain, he used his emotions.

"The principle is the same," he said, "people should make sacrifices for others."

"Didn't you sacrifice your girlfriend for him already?" I was trying to remain rational.

"That doesn't count. That was a passive separation; I wasn't giving up anything that belonged to me. I've spent the last two weeks reading the Four Gospels, and I've made up my mind. I ought to support Number Four; it's wrong for me to try to stop him from moving out. Think about it for a moment. If it's only a matter of dividing up our estate, why can't he just come and talk to me about it?"

"He's afraid you'll disagree with him," I said.

"No. The last few days, I've been thinking about it. He must have something specific in mind, probably something very dangerous, but he wants to make a clean break with me so that I won't get implicated if he gets in trouble. You think he's just young and impulsive? He acts that way just to fool us. He's actually going out of his way for my benefit, since he doesn't want me to suffer unjustly on account of anything he does. He wants to make sure I'm safe first, so he can do whatever he wants on his own with a clear conscience. I'm sure that's it. But I can't let him go now; I've got to make sacrifices for him too. Right before Mother died, she...." He stopped there, knowing I'd heard it all before.

I never thought he would take it so far, and I still didn't believe everything he said. Perhaps under the influence of religion he was giving vent to some previously hidden emotions.

I decided to speak to White Li about it on the very slim chance that Black Li was right. Though I didn't believe that what he said was true, I couldn't afford to take any chances.

I looked everywhere for White Li, but he was nowhere to be found. There was no trace of him on the campus, in the dormitories, in the library, on the tennis courts or in any of the little restaurants he frequented. No one I asked had seen him for days. White Li was like that. If Black Li went away for a few days, he would have notified all of his friends. But White Li would disappear like a puff of smoke. I came up with a possible solution: I asked "her" if she knew anything about his whereabouts.

Since I spent so much time with Black Li, she already knew who I was. But she hadn't seen White Li for a long time either. She seemed to be quite disappointed in both of them, especially Black Li. When I asked her specifically about White Li, she directed the conversation back to Black Li. I could see that she cared a lot about —or perhaps even loved — Black Li. She seemed to want to capture Black Li and preserve him like a specimen. If she could find someone better than him, she would let Black Li go; in the event she failed, she'd probably marry him after all. Since I was only guessing, I chose not to play matchmaker for the two of them. On principle I should have done that, but I was much too fond of Black Li and believed that he deserved to marry nothing less than an angel.

By the time I left her place, my heart was pounding. Where was White Li? I couldn't tell Black Li about it, since as soon as he found out he'd put a notice in the newspaper and stay up all night divining with his coins and poring over his characters. But if I didn't tell him, I wouldn't be able to think about anything else. Why couldn't I just forget about the whole thing? No, that wouldn't work either.

From outside his study, I could hear Black Li humming. He only hummed when he was very happy about something. He hummed on a more or less regular basis when he recited poetry or sang those famous lines, "deep in the boudoir, there lies a piece of flawless jade," though this was not what he was humming now. Listening carefully, I discovered he was reciting the Psalms over and over. He didn't have a very musical ear, so all music sounded the same to him. Likewise, everything he sang came out sounding the same. In any case, I could tell that he was extremely happy now. What brought this about?

The moment I walked in, he put down his book of Psalms. He looked ecstatic. "You're here at just the right time. I was just about to go and see you. Number Four just left. He asked me to give him a thousand dollars. He didn't mention dividing the estate, not even once."

It was evident that he hadn't asked his brother why he needed the money, otherwise he wouldn't have been in such a good mood. He probably had begged his brother to keep living with him, and promised him not to meddle in his affairs. It seemed now that even if White Li had a dangerous mission to accomplish, as long as they didn't split up the family estate, Black Li would have nothing to be afraid about. I could see this quite clearly.

"Praying really works," he said quite seriously. "I've been praying for the last few days, and it turned out that Number Four didn't bring up that old business. Even if he throws away the money I gave him, at least I still have a brother."

I suggested we drink our customary pot of Lotus wine, but he smiled and shook his head. "Go ahead, I'll have something to eat instead. I'm giving up drinking."

I didn't drink either, nor did I tell him how I'd searched everywhere for White Li. Now that White Li was back, why bring it up again? I mentioned "her" to him, but he didn't say a word, and only smiled.

We had very little to say about White Li's relationship with "her", so he told me some Bible stories. While listening to him, I thought there was something a little strange about the way Black Li behaved towards his brother and his girlfriend, though I couldn't put my finger on it. I felt very uneasy about this and continued to feel this way when I got home.

Four or five days passed, but this matter remained on my mind. One evening, Wang Five came to see me.

Wang, the Li's ricksha puller, had been working for them for four years.

Wang Five was as straightforward and reliable as they come. A man in his early thirties, he had a prominent scar on his head. It was said that this was the result of a donkey bite when he was a child. Wang's only weakness was that he enjoyed a drink once in a while.

He'd drunk a bit too much on the night he visited me, which made the scar on his head appear somewhat redder than usual.

"Wang Five, what brings you here this evening?" I was on good terms with him; whenever I left the Li's home late at night, they always got him to take me home, and I always gave him a little money to buy drinks with.

"I've come to see you," he said, taking a seat.

I knew he'd come to tell me something. "I just made a pot of tea. Would you like some?"

"That would be very nice. I'll pour it myself. I'm really thirsty."

I offered him a cigarette and started off the conversation by asking him, "What's on your mind?"

"Ah. . . . I just finished off two pots of wine, but there's something I can't get off my mind. It's something I really shouldn't be talking about at all." He took a long drag on his cigarette.

"If it's anything to do with the Li's, it's perfectly alright for you to tell me."

"That's what I was thinking too." He paused for a moment, but due to the effects of the wine could not remain silent for long. "I've been working for the Li's for a total of four years and thirty-five days. I'm in a very difficult position now. Second Master treats me very kindly and all, but Fourth Master, well, he's my friend. So it's hard for me to know what to do. I can't tell Second Master what Fourth Master's been up to, but Second Master's such a nice guy. If I told Second Master, I would be unworthy of Fourth Master's trust — he's my friend. But when I try not to think about it I get all confused inside. In principle, you know, I ought to be on Fourth Master's side. Second Master's a nice guy, there's no doubt about it. But in the end he's my boss. No matter how nice he is, he's still my boss. There's no way we can treat each other as brothers. He's good to me. For instance, on really hot days, when I'm pulling Second Master around, he'll always find some place along the way to stop for a little while to buy a box of matches or take a look at a book stall. Why does he do that? So I can rest and catch my breath. That's what I mean when I say he's a good boss. And since he's good to me, I've got to treat him with respect too. Like they say, one good turn deserves another. You learn that when you pull a ricksha for a few years."

I offered him another bowl of tea as a way of demonstrating I wasn't ignorant of the proper etiquette. When he finished his tea, he pointed to his chest with his cigarette. "Here, it's right here where I feel for Fourth Master. Why is that? Because Fourth Master is young and doesn't treat me like a ricksha puller. Those two guys — I mean their personalities — are very different. On hot days, Second Master always gives me time to rest, but that would never occur to Fourth Master. No matter how hot it is he's always telling me to run like the wind. But when Fourth Master and I sit around talking, he'll say, 'Who says that some people have to be ricksha pullers?' He's talking about how unfair things are for us — I mean all the ricksha pullers in the world.

Second Master treats me well, but he doesn't give a damn about the rest of us ricksha men. You see what I mean? Second Master is narrow-minded while Fourth Master looks at the bigger picture. Fourth Master doesn't give a damn about my legs, but he cares about my heart. Second Master cares about the little things, he takes pity on my legs — but he doesn't give a damn about this here." He pointed to his heart again.

I knew he had more to say, but I was really afraid that tongue-loosening effects of the wine he drank would be diluted by the strong tea, so I encouraged him a little, "Go on, Wang. Tell me everything. I'm not an old lady who's going to give all your secrets away."

He rubbed his scar and lowered his head for a few moments of contemplation. Then he pulled his chair up close to mine and lowered his voice. "Have you heard they've almost finished installing the new streetcar line? When that starts operating, we ricksha pullers are done for. I'm not worried about myself; I'm talking about everybody." He looked up at me.

I nodded to him.

"Fourth Master knows all about it; we're close friends, right? He said to me, 'Wang, you've got to find a way out.' I said, 'Fourth Master, I've got an idea. We'll destroy them!' He said, 'Wang, that's the right idea, we'll destroy them!' So we worked it all out then and there. I can't tell you the details. This is what I came here to tell you." He lowered his voice again. "There's someone following Fourth Master around. It doesn't necessarily have anything to do with the streetcar business, but it's bad having someone tailing you all the time. The worst thing is, if I tell Second Master, how can I face Fourth Master? But if I don't tell him, he might get dragged in for no reason at all. I don't know what to do."

After seeing Wang Five out, I thought it all over carefully.

Black Li surmised correctly that White Li was involved in something dangerous. In addition to wrecking trolley cars, he probably had something more formidable in mind. Thus his desire to move away from his brother was for the purpose of avoiding implicating him. He was not afraid of sacrificing his own life, or the lives of others, but he was unwilling to sacrifice his brother unless there were a good reason for it — such an act would come to no avail. And with the action against the streetcar company about to take place, he had no time to worry about Black Li anyway.

Where was I to turn? Warning Black Li would only stir up a wave of warm feelings in him for his brother. Speaking to White Li was not only useless; it would incriminate Wang Five as well.

The situation grew tenser day by day. The streetcar company announced the opening of the new line. I couldn't wait any longer. I had to go and tell Black Li.

He wasn't home, but Wang Five was still there.

"Where's Number Two?"

"He went out."

"You didn't take him?"

"He hasn't taken the ricksha for a long time."

From the expression on his face, I knew the answer to my question: "Wang, did you tell him?"

Wang Five's scar turned a bright purple. "I drank too much. I couldn't help it."

"What did he say?"

"He started crying."

"What did he say?"

"He asked me one question: 'Wang, what are you going to do?' I said, 'I'll do whatever Fourth Master says.' All he said was, 'OK'. He goes out every day now, but he never rides in the ricksha."

I waited there for three hours. After sunset, he finally came back.

"What's up?" These two words summed up everything I wanted to know.

He smiled. "Not much." I never expected him to answer me this way. There was no need for me to ask him any more questions, since I knew his mind was already made up. I felt I needed a drink, but it's no fun drinking alone. I decided to go. Before leaving, I said to him, "Why don't the two of us go away for a couple of days."

"Let's discuss that in a few days, shall we?" That was all he said.

Passionate men are capable of acting with great indifference. I never imagined him treating me this way.

The night before the opening of the trolley line, I went to his house again, but he wasn't in. I waited until midnight, but he didn't come back. He was probably trying to avoid me.

Wang Five came in and smiled at me. "Tomorrow's the big day!"

"Where's Number Two?"

"I haven't seen him. After you left the other day, he used some strange chemical and burned off the black birthmark over his eyebrow. Then he just sat there staring at himself in the mirror."

It was all over now. Without his black birthmark,

there was no more Black Li. I didn't have to wait for him any longer. When I walked out, Wang Five called to me, "If anything happens to me tomorrow," he said, scratching his scar, "take care of my mother for me."

About five o'clock the next afternoon Wang Five rushed into my room. His pants were soaked through with sweat. "We smashed all the trolley cars to bits." After that he said nothing and just sat there panting for several minutes. When he recovered his breath, he picked up the teapot and took a long drink directly from the spout.

"We destroyed everything! No one left till they brought in the cavalry troops. They took Little Ma Six away, I saw it with my own eyes. If only we had guns! But all we had was bricks. Little Ma Six is done for."

"What about Number Four?"

"I didn't see him at all." He bit his lower lip and thought for a moment. "There was a hell of a lot of excitement there. If they caught anyone else, I guess Fourth Master would have to be among them. He was one of the people in charge. Don't forget though, Fourth Master's no fool, even though he's very young. Little Ma Six is done for, but I'm not so sure about Fourth Master."

"You didn't see Number Two?"

"He didn't come home last night." He thought for a moment. "I'm going to lay low here for a couple of days."

"That's fine."

The next day, the papers carried the following news:

The ringleader of a bunch of violent hooligans who destroyed the trolley cars, a Mr Li, was arrested on the spot. A student and five ricksha pullers were taken into custody as well.

Wang Five could only recognize one word in the head-line: the surname Li. "Fourth Master is done for! Fourth Master is done for!" He lowered his head and pretended to be scratching his scar, while his tears dropped onto the newspaper.

The news spread quickly through the city — Li and Little Ma Six were going to be paraded through the streets and shot.

The cruel sun beat down on the cobblestone streets, heating them to the point where you could feel the heat through your shoes, yet the streets were lined with huge crowds of spectators. The two men were seated in a large open wagon with their hands tied behind their backs. They were guarded on either side by policemen in khaki uniforms and soldiers dressed in grey. As the wagon drew near, the two blades of their bayonets reflected the sunlight with a chilling brilliance. The wooden placards announcing their crimes could be seen swaying back and forth above their heads. The man seated in front had his eyes closed; his forehead was dotted with beads of sweat and his lips were moving as if he were mouthing a prayer. The wagon was very close, and I watched him sway past me. I broke down and cried, stopping only after he had gone past. I followed the wagon all the way to the execution ground. Not once did he raise his head.

His eyebrows were knitted; his mouth hung open. The blood spurted forth from his chest, as if he were praying the moment he died. I took his body away.

Two months later, I ran into White Li in Shanghai. If I hadn't called to him, he probably would have walked right past me. "Number Four!" I called out to him.

"Huhh?" He appeared startled. "Hey, is that you? Sounded just like Number Two."

Maybe the way I called to him reminded him of Black Li's voice, but this was totally unintentional on my part. Or maybe it was Black Li himself, alive somewhere inside me, who called out on my behalf.

White Li seemed to have aged, and looked more like his older brother than ever. We said very little to each other. He didn't have much to say to me anyway.

I remember two things he did say though:

"Number Two must have gone to heaven; that's a perfect place for him. But I'm still here smashing the gates of hell."

Translated by Don J. Cohn

The Eyeglasses

ALTHOUGH Song Xiushen was studying science, there was nothing scientific about the way he conducted his life. He firmly believed that all restaurant flies had been disinfected; thus when he ordered cold noodles with sesame sauce he made no effort to shoo them away. He had a pair of near-sighted eyes, and a pair of near-sighted glasses to match them, though he only used the latter for reading. According to conventional wisdom, wearing glasses made one's sight worse; he was sure of this. Thus he wore his glasses as infrequently as possible. For instance, whenever he went for a stroll downtown or attended an athletic event, he held his glasses in his hands. If this prevented him from seeing what was going on, or caused him chronic dizziness, well, he deserved it!

One day he was on his way to school. He kept very close to the city wall to avoid running into people, though he would occasionally collide with a dog. Today, he'd wrapped his glasses in the folds of two thick scientific magazines. He knew this was somewhat risky, and therefore stopped every few steps to make sure his glasses were still there. If he lost them, he'd be totally helpless in class. And since he wasn't rich, purchasing a new pair might drive him into bankruptcy. He usually put his glasses case in one of his pockets, but today his pockets were occupied by notebooks, handkerchiefs, pencils, erasers, two small bottles and the remains of a half-eaten bun. Carrying his glasses in this way required only a little extra care; and in any case, if he dropped them, he'd be sure to hear them when they hit the ground.

Turning a corner, he ran into one of his classmates. Since it was his classmate who had called to him, it would have been difficult for him not to respond. They stood there talking for a few minutes. A car approached, and he instinctively drew his hands out of the way. Actually, this movement was unnecessary, but his poor eyesight made him extra cautious, and he pressed his nose to the wall. After the car and the friend left, he started running, since he was afraid of being late. But when he got to school, he discovered that his glasses case was missing. Beads of sweat formed on his forehead. He rushed back to look for it, but it was nowhere to be found. A few ricksha pullers had parked their vehicles by the corner of the wall where he'd stopped to talk. He asked them about his glasses, but none of them had seen them — perhaps they were all near-sighted too. He headed back to school, but all he had to show was two hands covered with dirt. He had never been so frustrated in his entire life! He removed the uneaten portion of his bun from his pocket and threw it angrily against the school entrance. If only he had fewer things in his pockets! If only he hadn't run into his friend! If only he hadn't flinched to avoid that car which was being driven so recklessly! Was all of this coincidental? If so, it was enough to drive anyone batty. One of the ricksha men must have lied to his face. What a world this was! He walked by here every day. When he lost something, shouldn't they at least tell him about it, rather than pick it up and put it in their pocket? What use was a pair of near-sighted glasses to them anyway?

Song Xiushen's glasses fell when he had pressed his nose against the wall. Wang Four, one of the ricksha pullers, had noticed this.

Wang Four was about to say something, but when he realized who it was — that strange boy who walked along the wall everyday and never took a ricksha — he held back the words that were on the tip of his tongue. After the car turned the corner, he picked up the case and stuck it in his pocket.

He didn't dare take it out and examine it in front of the other ricksha pullers. Rather, he sat contentedly in the seat of his ricksha with a broad smile across his lips.

When he saw Song Xiushen come back all sweaty and nervous, his heart went out to him, and he was about to return the glasses case to him. But since none of the other ricksha pullers admitted to having seen it, this would have been embarrassing to him — like spitting something up after having swallowed it. There was probably nothing in it for him anyhow, since he doubted the boy would offer him a reward. If he gave it back for nothing, he'd be the laughing stock of the ricksha pullers: "You took it and didn't say anything; you thought we were going to steal it from you?" "You think you're so generous, don't you, handing it back to him for nothing?" It was easier to deny having seen it in the first place. It was his now, that's all that mattered. Students are richer than ricksha pullers anyway.

After Song Xiushen went back to school, Wang Four prepared to leave and said rather self-consciously, "No need to hang around here any longer; I'll head east for a while." At the same time, he said to himself, "Even if I don't get a single customer today, I ought to be able to sell these glasses along with the case for about two dollars." He found a quiet place, parked his ricksha and sat down to examine his find.

The case was in such bad condition that the match seller would probably trade him only one box of matches for it. The cloth cover had been rubbed off entirely, leaving a greasy surface impregnated with something sticky like persimmon juice. The glasses' thick black frames were in better condition, though. Wang Four had never liked glasses with thin wire frames. Whenever he saw someone wearing them, he would avoid asking them if they wanted a ricksha. He flicked the earpieces with his finger. They didn't look like iron, nor did they appear to be made of wood; maybe they were tortoise-shell! His heart skipped a beat!

The lenses were filthy, and bulged out in their centers. They were ground in a series of concentric circles, each of which was outlined in a ring of greasy dust. This accumulation was thicker on the outer circles than on the inner. A broken matchstick lay in the bottom of the case. Wang Four struck it and tossed it on the ground. He then removed a shaggy cloth duster from his ricksha. Breathing on the lenses, he began to polish them with the cloth strips of his duster. After repeating this operation four times, the lenses began to take on the appearance of real lenses; he then applied a coating of saliva and completed the cleaning. He tried them on, but they didn't fit; the frames were far too small for his head. Song Xiushen was small in stature and had a small head. "Nobody wants to buy them, and I can't even wear them as a joke!" Wang Four was disappointed, though he rationalized as follows: "It doesn't look right for a ricksha puller to wear glasses anyway. Why don't I just try to sell them?"

He picked up the shafts of his ricksha and went around until he found a junk seller. "Hey! You want to buy these?"

"No!" The junk seller, a man with a red nose and yellow eyes, didn't even look at them, even though his stock of goods included many pairs of glasses, and even some old-fashioned embroidered glasses cases.

Not wanting to pick a fight with this man, Wang Four went away without even saying, "Aren't you a polite son of a bitch!"

He soon came upon another junk dealer who was carrying his wares in two baskets suspended at the end of a pole. "Hey, you want to buy these? They've got real tortoise-shell frames."

"First time I've seen tortoise-shell like that," the junk dealer said, glancing at the frames. "How much you want for them?"

"What'll you give me?" Wang Four handed him the glasses.

"Twenty cents."

"What?" Wang Four grabbed them back.

"That's a darned good price! Plain lenses and far-sighted glasses go pretty quickly. But those are near-sighted lenses. Those frames are made out of celluloid. They'll probably break just sitting in my baskets. Then I'd be out twenty cents."

Wang Four was discouraged, but he couldn't sell at such a low price. Twenty cents? If he'd known that, he would have given the glasses back to the boy.

He decided then to return them to their rightful owner the next day. That way, he at least had a chance of earning a few dimes' reward.

The next morning, Wang Four parked his ricksha at the corner of the wall. The school bell rang, but the near-sighted boy didn't appear. By ten o'clock there was still no sign of him. He picked up a passenger and made it back by noon. The students were going home for lunch, but the near-sighted boy was nowhere to be seen.

Song Xiushen didn't go to school that day.

The day before, when he had lost his glasses, he went to class as usual. Though he sat in the front of the classroom, he couldn't even make out what the teacher wrote on the blackboard. The fuzzier the words became, the more he strained his eyes, and by the end of the class he had a splitting headache. The second class that day was mathematics. Pressing his nose to the paper, he worked through several problems, but he was all itchy inside and his head was burning. He felt lost. Mathematics had always been his favorite subject, but today the sight of all those numbers only made him nervous. The formulas he knew so well were now accompanied by something new in his mind; his glasses, an automobile and a ricksha puller. This new combination of elements transformed his favorite subject into the most intolerable grind. He felt very confined in the classroom and longed to escape to some wide open space where he could shout at the top of his lungs. Today, things he had been loath to think about before — such as the meaning of life — totally occupied his mind. No matter how useless an old pair of near-sighted glasses was, the ricksha puller had taken them. If someone is poor, even a single stick of firewood is a good thing; in the end, then, he couldn't very well blame the ricksha puller for what he did. He rationalized it this way, but he was still very upset. He wouldn't be able to finish today's homework assignment, and tomorrow there would be more headaches. He certainly couldn't afford a new pair of glasses. At the beginning of the semester, his family had given him about seventy dollars, but there were still two more months of meals to pay for. The wheat harvest at home had been a good one, but they couldn't sell what they grew. He thought about how his father and brother slaved away day in and day out; yet they were still unable to sell what they reaped.

He never had the time — nor the need — to think about such things before, but today they settled down in his mind next to those mathematical formulas. He could think of no way out. This was the first time he had ever experienced such despair. It was as if all those aspects of his life which had been stable up to now had vanished along with his glasses. Everything appeared hazy and unresolved before him. He was reluctant to quit school, but continuing his studies seemed totally meaningless.

The next hour passed like an eternity. When the bell rang, there was something peculiar about it. It sounded as if it were ordering everyone to go out into the wild and shout at the top of their lungs. He walked out of the classroom; a strong sense of resentment led him out of the school courtyard. He failed to attend the third class that morning, nor did he ask to be excused. He was no longer aware that there was such a thing as a third class, or that he should have asked for permission to be excused.

As he walked along the wall, his mind was in a fog.

When he got to the corner, he suddenly recalled his glasses. Several ricksha pullers were there chatting, but just as he was about to ask them about his glasses again, he changed his mind; lowering his head, he walked right by them.

The next day, he didn't go to school.

Wang Four didn't wait any longer for the near-sighted boy. For the rest of the day, he couldn't take his mind off the glove compartment of his ricksha, where he'd put the old glasses case for safe keeping. For some strange reason, he just couldn't stop thinking about it.

Just as he was about to put his ricksha away for the day, Little Zhao turned up. Little Zhao's family ran a small grocery shop, but he himself took no part in it. His father was eager for him to work in the shop, but he knew that if he did he would only end up stealing from the till; hired clerks were much more reliable. Whenever Little Zhao's father went out on a social call or to a temple to burn incense, he always wore a pair of non-prescription glasses with plain lenses, which he had picked up at a little stand in the street for about eighty cents. Big shop owners and cashiers always wore glasses with plain lenses when attending the theatre or temple fairs as a means of displaying their position on the social ladder. Similarly, owners of small shops felt it necessary to keep up with their wealthier counterparts.

Little Zhao was in no particular hurry for his father to pass away, nor would his death matter very much to him. If his father did die, however, the only way he could show the world that he was the new proprietor of the shop was to wear a pair of glasses with plain lenses. Though the glasses cost only eighty cents, their true value was inestimable. Shopkeepers who had established businesses wore them as a sign that their pockets were always full of money.

He spent a lot of time with Wang Four and the other ricksha pullers. Whenever he succeeded in extricating some spare change from the shop, he'd gamble with the ricksha men or entertain himself in a low class brothel. The ricksha men called him "Little Zhao", though he became "Young Manager" whenever his face turned red in the excitement of a good game. Actually, it was only at such climactic moments that he became conscious of his elevated position in society. At all other times, he was free of all pretensions, and treated Wang Four and the other ricksha pullers like best friends.

"Let's play a round. I'll be banker." Little Zhao held up a fistful of dirty red ten-cent notes for all to see, took out a cigarette and lit it.

Wang Four removed a half-smoked cigarette from behind his ear and lit it from Little Zhao's match.

They were all squatting down behind the parked rickshas.

Before very long, all of Wang Four's coppers found a new owner. The muscles in his forehead were visibly tense. He was eager to recoup his losses. "Hey, Redeyes, lend me a few coppers, will you?"

Redeyes bet all the coppers in his hand on five numbers. Since he was cleaned out himself, naturally he felt no need to respond, so he squinted with his red eyes in the direction of the dice.

Wang Four was in a quandary. He stood up angrily and looked around to see if there were any policemen nearby. Though he had lost all his money, if a policeman grabbed him, he still wouldn't be able to get away.

Little Zhao was ahead quite a bit now, and asked if anyone wanted to continue playing. They all responded in the affirmative, though Little Zhao was going to have to lend them each some capital to gamble with. With his filthy hands, Little Zhao picked up the coins and ten-cent notes he'd won and stuffed it all into his pocket. "Don't be sissies. You all want to play, don't you? Put your money where your mouths are!"

They were all getting ready to call Little Zhao "Young Manager", when Li Six, who sold baked sweet potatoes, arrived. "Everyone take one, courtesy of Manager Zhao!" Little Zhao treated them all to sweet potatoes. "You're a good man, Little Zhao!" They all crowded around the sweet potato seller's portable oven. Wang Four chose one for himself, and gulped it down in big bites accompanied by deep breaths.

When he finished eating, Wang Four said, "Little Zhao, I have something for you." He removed the glasses from the back of his ricksha. "The case is in pretty bad shape, but wait till you see what's inside."

The moment Little Zhao set eyes on the glasses, the word "Manager" lit up inside his head. He tossed the remainder of his potato on the ground, adding a stray dog to his list of guests. What a fine pair of glasses, even better looking than his father's! He tried them on. "Hey, these are near-sighted glasses; they make me dizzy."

"You'll get used to them," Wang Four said with a chuckle.

"Get used to them? I'll have to get near-sighted first!" Little Zhao thought that was too high a price to pay, but he really liked glasses. He put them back on and started to walk around. When he took them off and looked at his friends, they all approved of the way they looked on him.

Wang Four said, "Very stylish!"

"But they make me dizzy," Little Zhao said, but he was still reluctant to part with them.

"You'll get used to them." Wang Four thought this was the best thing he could say in this situation.

Little Zhao tried them on again and looked up at the sky. "It's no good, they still make me dizzy."

"Take them anyway, just take them." Wang Four was being as ingratiating as he possibly could. "They're a gift for you; I can't use them. You take them; in two years, if your eyes start going bad, they'll be just right for you."

"You're giving these to me?" Little Zhao asked. "Really? Shit, it'll cost me half a dollar to buy a new case for them."

"Yes, they're for you. I can't do anything with them. I'd only get about two dollars if I sold them." Wang Four was acting even more ingratiating.

"Let me see what I have here." Little Zhao took out all of his ten-cent notes and paid Li Six for the sweet potatoes. "I've only got 60 cents left. Goddammit, I'm only up twenty cents."

"You still have a pocketful of coppers," someone reminded him.

"Couldn't be more than a dime's worth." Though he didn't take them out and count them, no one believed him. Little Zhao wasn't upset because he had won so little money; he was actually quite satisfied with himself since he usually lost when he gambled. Losing a few dimes meant less to him than the embarrassment of being called a "turkey". But today he had won his reputation back, even though he only won about thirty cents, including the coppers — maybe more, since those coppers were quite heavy. "Wang Four, I can't accept these as a gift. Here, I've got sixty cents altogether. You take half and I take half, that's only fair."

Wang Four hadn't expected to get so much, but since Little Zhao was being so generous, he pressed him for a little more: "How about throwing in a few coppers as well. That was easy money for you anyway."

"Whoa! That's my lucky money. I better keep that, since we're going to play tomorrow, right?" Little Zhao believed that if he showed up the next day, he'd be sure to win again. The last few days, the dice had been rolling in his favor.

"Alright, thirty cents it is. Thirty cents for such a fine pair of glasses." Wang Four took the money and put it in one of his inner pockets.

"Didn't you say you wanted to give them to me as a gift? Son of a bitch!"

"Alright, alright! Good friends shouldn't argue over such small amounts."

Little Zhao put the glasses back in their case and made ready to leave. "See you all tomorrow!" He took a few steps and opened the case to take another look. When he turned around to look, he saw that none of the ricksha men were watching him, so he put the glasses on. Though everything went blurry in front of him, he didn't want to take them off now; he'd get used to them sooner or later. Wang Four was right. There was nothing more frustrating than owning a pair of glasses and not being able to wear them, especially since all shop managers had to wear glasses. With a pair of glasses, a watch and a gold inlay in one of his front teeth, he'd have no trouble winning the heart of Little Pheonix, who lived in Nangangzi.

As Little Zhao turned the corner, a loud horn sounded in his ears. Since he couldn't see where the car was coming from, he quickly removed his glasses. . . .

After that, neither the near-sighted boy who walked along the city wall, Little Zhao nor Wang Four were seen in the vicinity of the school. Li Six announced, "Wang Four's been hanging around the southern part of the city recently."

Translated by Don J. Cohn

Brother You Takes Office

BROTHER You set out to take office.

When he came in sight of the building where he would be working, he slowed down. It wasn't very large. He knew the place. He had visited nearly all the offices, gambling houses and opium dens in the city. He remembered this place — when the door was open you could see the Mountain of the Thousand Buddhas. Naturally at the moment he had no interest in the Mountain of the Thousand Buddhas; his duties would be heavy! But he showed no agitation. He'd knocked about for years, he knew how to make his feelings. You walked slower still.

Fat, fortyish, heavy brows, a sallow clean-shaven face. A grey serge gown, wide sleeves, black satin shoes. He moved sedately, with never a glance at the Mountain of the Thousand Buddhas. Maybe I should have come in a car, he thought. No, what for? His men were all his own kind. Everyone knew each other. Why put on a show? Besides, his was an important job. Why throw his weight around? It wasn't as if he had anything to worry about. Black satin shoes, grey serge gown — just right for a man of his position. You strolled slowly, calm and composed. No need to wear a military uniform. A "hard guy" was stuck in his belt beneath his gown. You smiled to himself.

No signboard hung outside the two-room office but, like You's clothing, there were hard guys inside. The door was open. His four men were seated on stools, smoking, their heads down. No one was looking at the Mountain of the Thousand Buddhas. On a large table by the wall were several teacups. On the floor, a new iron kettle was surrounded by cigarette butts. One was still burning. As the men rose to greet him, You again thought about the car. Assuming office this way really was a little cheap. But his old friends stood very ceremoniously. Although everyone was smiling warmly, there was respect in their manner. They didn't look down on him because he hadn't arrived in a car. When you came to think of it, the inspector and his office operated secretly. The less attention they attracted, the better. Of course, his men knew this. You felt somewhat easier.

After pausing before the large table and smiling at the men, he went into the inner room. Its furnishings consisted of a desk and two chairs. On the wall was a calendar, decorated with the blood of a departed bedbug. The office is a bit too bare, You mused. But he couldn't think of what to add.

Zhao brought in a cup of tea with a piece of twig floating in it. You didn't speak to him. Rubbing his forehead, You got an idea. Ah, that's right, he needed a wash basin. But he didn't tell Zhao to buy one. He had to think this over carefully. The money for the office expenses was in his hands. Should he use it, or keep it all for himself? His salary was a hundred and twenty dollars. The expense account gave him eighty more. On a job where you risked your life, another eighty wasn't too much. But weren't his men also risking their lives? And they were old friends. You had eaten and drunk with them for years. When they lived in the earthen cave dwelling, hadn't they all slept on the same platform bed? No, he couldn't keep the whole expense account for himself.

Zhao went out. When Zhao was leader of his own band, had he ever privately pocketed money? You blushed. From the next room, Liu glanced at him through the open door. Although over fifty, Liu had come to work as one of his men. But three years ago, Liu had fifty rapid fire rifles under his command. No, he could't keep all the expense money. But in that case, what was the use of being boss? Share the eighty with the others? Of course they too had been leaders, but only of bandit gangs in the mountains. Although You kept in constant touch with them, he had never formally become a bandit. There was a difference. They, to put it bluntly, were crooks who had given up crime to join the forces of law and order. He was an official. An official had his own way of doing things. Very well, then, he'd run his office in an official manner — the eighty dollars would be reserved for his personal use. But he still needed that wash basin, and a couple of towels, too.

There were also certain things he ought to do. For instance, an inspector ought to read the newspaper, or lecture his men. The newspaper he had to have. Whether he read it or not didn't matter. Just spreading it on his desk would make an impression. As for lecturing people, he was no novice at that. He had been a corporal in the army, and a member of the tax commission. Yes, he'd have to lecture his men, otherwise it wouldn't seem like a real office-taking. Anyhow, these fellows had all been up in the hills, and at various times they'd been in the army. If he didn't give them a couple of stingers, they wouldn't respect him.

Zhao had left the room. Liu kept coughing. He definitely had to lecture them. He'd teach them how to behave. You cleared his throat and stood up. He wanted to wash his face. But he still had no basin and towel. He sat down again. He'd lecture them. What should he say? Hadn't he made everything clear when he asked them to help? Hadn't he said exactly the same thing to Zhao and Liu and Wang and Chu? "Give me a hand, old friend. When there's food on You's table, nobody goes hungry. We're brothers!" And he'd said it more than once. Why repeat it?

As for their duties, they were all quite clear. It was simply a case of set a thief to catch a thief. Every one of them knew it, though it wasn't a good idea to put it into words.

The main thing was to look out for himself, to protect his own neck. If he really tried to make good on this job and arrested a few of his underworld friends, Liu and the others might let their pistols off in his direction. It was best for him to keep one eye closed. He couldn't start off with a big flourish. They'd all be meeting again some day. But could You say this? How could he lecture them? Get a load of the eyes of that Liu — those lids wouldn't close even when he was dead. The help the men were giving You was a form of bandit loyalty. He couldn't get rid of the code of the hills in one sweep. True, the police commissioner had put him on this job to nab bandits. But they were all his friends. Intimate friends. A tough problem!

You took off his grey serge gown, then went out and smiled at his men.

"Inspector," Liu hailed him. Contempt was plain in his eyes. "How about assigning us some work?" he said.

You nodded. He'd show them. "I'm going to write a list. I have to make a report to Commissioner Li. As I told you brothers the other day, our job is to help Commissioner Li nab bandits. The commissioner called me in and said, "You, you've got to help me, I don't know the layout here. How could I refuse? He's an old friend too. I can do it, I thought. Why? Because I thought of you fellows. I know the setup pretty well, and you know it right down to the ground. Working together, we can put it over. Commissioner, I said, leave it to me. Since he did me the honour of offering me the job, I couldn't be ungrateful enough to refuse. Brothers, whatever Commissioner Li gets, there's a share for me. Whatever I get, you're in it too. I've got it all figured out. Now I'm going to write this list — who does what. After we've talked it over, I'll hand it in, then we'll get started. We'll do it all official and proper. Right?" You asked with a laugh.

No one replied. Chu blinked. Although there wasn't any awkward silence, You couldn't very well say any more. He'd have to prepare his list, write it out with a pomp that would crush Liu and his pals. After all, You recalled, wasn't he the one who wrote the ransom note the year Chu kidnapped that rich young Wang? Yes, he'd certainly wriggle that writing brush. But where was his brush and ink slab? These men couldn't get anything done!

"Say, Zhao. . . ." You thought he'd send Zhao to buy the writing brush. But then he checked himself. Why Zhao? You had to be discriminating where money was involved. This wasn't up in the hills where they did things any old way. This was official business. Who should do the buying, who should deliver letters

— these jobs had to be assigned right. It wasn't easy. The man who bought things got a rake-off from the store. You didn't earn anything delivering letters. Who should be stuck with the messenger job?

"Ah ... nothing ... nothing," he told Zhao. He wouldn't buy the writing brush just yet. He'd have to give the matter more thought. You was rather disturbed. He never imagined being an inspector was so troublesome. It wasn't such a wonderful job. Yet it might not be too bad, particularly if he could keep the eighty dollars expense money. But he couldn't do that. His men had all been bandits. If he held on to the money too tightly, their pistols might pump him full of "black dates". That wouldn't be so funny.

It was a tricky situation. An official with bandits for his assistants. What kind of an official was that? Yet he couldn't operate without them. Could he nab crooks by himself? A fat chance! He patted the pistol in his belt.

"Brothers, have you got your hardware?"

Everyone nodded.

Are the bastards mute! What was the idea? Was it scorn, or fear? Just nodding, that was no way for a friend to behave. If they had anything to say, they ought to say it. Look at that Liu, his face all grim and solemn. You laughed again. He wasn't being quite officious enough. But he couldn't be too officious with this crowd. Maybe they'd like it better if he swore at them. But he didn't dare. He wasn't a real bandit. You felt as if he were standing with his feet in two different boats. He hated himself for not being a genuine bandit. At the same time, he felt he was high-class. If he weren't, would he have been made an official? Lighting a cigarette, he pondered. He'd have to feed this bunch. He could hang on to the office expense money, but he'd have to spend a bit on food.

"Let's go, brothers, to the Wufu Restaurant!" You went to put on his grey serge gown.

Zhou's face cracked into wrinkles, like an overripe pumpkin. Two smile lines appeared in Liu's fifty-year-old stony cheeks. Wang and Chu also revived. Moisture had evidently returned to everyone's throat. Those who couldn't find anything to say, licked their lips.

At the restaurant, they were all great friends again. They didn't stand on ceremony. For their joint feast this one proposed a jellied fresh ham, that one wanted a mixed roast with sea-slugs. Liu suggested grilled whole chicken — two of them. When they were half full, they started to talk business. Liu, of course, spoke first, since he was by far the eldest. His stony cheeks were red with feasting. He took another drink of liquor, another bite of the ham, another drag on his cigarette.

"Inspector," he began. His eyes swept the other. "Opium pedlars, pimps — we can take them easy. But with bandits, we've got to be careful. Are we going to sell our brothers for a small heap of silver dollars?"

Drink had given You courage. "That's no way to talk, Brother Liu. Commissioner Li appointed us to catch bandits. There are too many of them around. If we don't nab some, fast, Commissioner Li may lose his job. If he goes, where will that leave us?"

"Suppose we do nab some, knock a couple off?" A strong liquor breath accompanied the smoke Zhao exhaled. "Sure, we've got guns, but so have they. Anyhow we're not going to keep these jobs for ever. It's not that I'm scared."

"Whoever's scared is a son of a bitch," was the analysis Chu drew.

"A stinking son of a bitch," Zhao confirmed. And he added, "Nobody's scared, and everybody's willing to give Commissioner Li a hand. Fraternity — that's the problem. It's true you've helped us, Brother You, and you've been around more than we, but you've never been up in the hills."

"Don't I know what the code is?" You gazed off into space and laughed coldly.

"Who says you don't?" countered gourd-mouthed Wang.

"It's this way, brothers." You decided to needle them. "If we're friends, you'll stick with me. If you don't want to stick with me," again he laughed off into space, "that's all right too."

"Inspector." Once more it was Liu. His eyes were piercing. "If you really want us to go at it, we will. But don't forget this. We're just your assistants, you're the head man. Any comebacks will go direct to you. You're a friend, so I'm talking straight. If you want us to nab guys, that's a cinch. Nothing to it."

The lovely sea-slugs You had consumed turned to ice in his stomach. This was just what he was afraid of. His men would do the work and he would report the victories. But when the bandits started dishing out black dates, he would be first on the list!

He mustn't worry in advance. He'd take things as they came. Eating black dates was uncomfortable, but reporting success and being rewarded was very sweet. He had been around for years. He knew no matter what you did, you had to strike first. When you played, you played for keeps! You was over forty. If he didn't get much out of this himself, at least he could leave a little something for his son. He wasn't going to be like Liu and the others. Always guarding their heads but leaving their backsides sticking out. Doing dirty work all their lives but ending up without even a burial plot to lie in when they died. He was shrewd, he could plan. He wouldn't listen to Liu. You decided to go ahead. He'd play along with Commissioner Li. If he cracked a couple of cases, he might even be transferred to headquarters. Who could tell? With a car to ride around in wherever he went. He couldn't always walk to take office!

The concluding soup expanded spirits and stomachs together. Everyone grew much more cordial. Although You was still quite firm, his tone mellowed:

"You've got to help me, brothers. Pick someone with no connections and bring him in. It'll serve him right. We've got to put on some kind of a show. We're all carrying hardware. How will it look if we just nab a few pimps? All right, then. This is how we'll do it. First find some small fry. Nab the kind that can't cause any trouble, then we'll see. When we finish that, We'll come back here for another feed, what do you say? That cold ham wasn't bad."

"It's autumn, it's getting cool. We ought to have hot roast pork from now on." Wang didn't talk much, but when he said something it was to the point.

You decided to keep Wang with him in the office and send the other three out to investigate. No need to write a list. When they came back he'd make a report. Yes, he'd have to buy a writing brush and an ink slab, and also a wash basin. He'd buy it himself so there'd be no question of favouritism. What he needed was a secretary, but he had forgotten to mention this to Commissioner Li. For the time being, he'd do his own writing. He'd ask for a secretary after they'd cracked their first case. There was no rush. You was a man who kept both feet on the ground. People said Erdie's son could write. You would give him a start in the world. He'd make Erdie's son his secretary. Good. For his first day in office he wasn't doing badly.

Chatting with Wang on the way back, he forgot all about the brush and the ink slab. The office wasn't a bit like a real office. Still, it was just as well. All that business about writing with a great flourish was only something in his mind. When it came to actually writing, he didn't know many words. They always seemed to escape him whenever he wanted to put them down on paper. It was just as well that he had no brush and ink slab.

But what should he do with his time? He ought to have a newspaper, even if it was only to look at the pictures. He couldn't just keep gabbing with Wang. Although they were old friends, he was an official and Wang was an underling. You had to think of his dignity. He had already stood in the doorway. He couldn't drink any more tea. He had looked twice through the pages of the calendar. There was nothing else for him to do. You thought over his family finances. Their condition was hopeful. Salary a hundred and twenty, plus eighty dollars expense money — even if he didn't take it all. He could count on at least a hundred and fifty a month. Gradually, he could save up for a little house.

Mother's — ! Dog Shang did just one job with warlord Zhang Zongchang and they raked in a hundred thousand! There was never anything like it. Never. They were the kind of bandits Commissioner Li was after. Who could be as careful with his money as Dog Shang? With money in your hands, you went dizzy. Take himself for instance. You had picked up twenty or thirty thousand when he was working in the tax office. And now where was it? No wonder men went crooked. He was used to eating and drinking and playing around. Live on bran muffins again? He couldn't stand it. Nobody could stand it.

Yes, to tell the truth, they all — including You — were waiting for Marshal Zhang's return. Naturally. Mother's —! Ding the Third alone was storing two trunks full of military notes* which Zhang had printed. If Zhang came back, Ding would be a rich man with those trunks!

How could You talk about arresting bandits? They were all old friends. But on a salary of a hundred and twenty, plus eighty in expense money, what else could he do? He had to! Mother's! Get on with it. Who could worry about so much? Every man for himself. Whose fault was it that Marshal Zhang couldn't come back? Nab them! Shoot a couple! You had never been up in the hills. He wouldn't be betraying any of his own gang.

It was after four, and still no sign of Liu and the other two. Had they really gone to pry into nests, or were they just fooling around? He'd have to set office hours. Everyone must be back by four-thirty to re-

---

* At that time China was ruled by various big warlords, who issued notes which they used as money in the areas under their control.

port. What kind of an office would it be like, if they never showed up? Without them he couldn't operate. With them, they were a headache. Mother's — !

He wouldn't wait for them any longer than five. He started work at eight, at five he quit. His men could go out whenever they liked. It wasn't unusual for arrests to be made in the middle of the night. But the inspector couldn't always be waiting around for his assistants. He ought to tell them, but it was rather hard to say. What was so hard about it? Wasn't he the boss? He immediately notified Wang. Wang grunted. What did that mean?

"It's five o'clock!" You glanced at the Mountain of the Thousand Buddhas. The sun was gilding its summit. In the sunlight the autumn grass still had a bit of green. "Look after things, Wang. See you tomorrow at eight."

Wang's gourd-shaped mouth was closed in a tight line.

The next morning You deliberately came a half hour late. He had to hold back. Suppose he arrived before his men? How embarrassing.

But the men were all there, seated on stools, smoking, their heads down. You felt like punching them. What clods! When he entered, they rose as they had the day before, but very slowly, as if they all had athlete's foot. You smiled at them, though he felt more like swearing. It would be awkward if he did. He had to act big. Who told him to become a leader of men? He had to act shrewd. You gave a grandiose laugh. Casual, unconcerned.

"Ah, Liu, do any business?" Natural, pleasant, humorous. You mentally praised himself.

"There was business," Liu, grim-visaged, bored into You with his eyes. "But we didn't do any."

"Why not?" You laughed.

"We didn't have to. They'll be coming in themselves soon."

"Oh!" You tried to laugh again, but no sound emerged. "What about you?" he asked Zhao and Chu.

The two just shook their heads.

"Shall we go out again today?" queried Liu.

"Ah, wait a while," You walked towards his room. "Let me think." He turned his head back and looked. The men were again seated, their eyes on the cigarette butts. They weren't saying a word. Clods.

You sat down in his office. He was puzzled. They'll be coming in themselves? He couldn't ask Liu what that meant. He couldn't admit they had him stumped. They'd lose respect. But what did it mean — they'll be coming in themselves? He'd just have to wait and see.

Should he send Liu and the others out on their rounds today? That had to be decided immediately. "Hey, Chu, get going. Keep your eyes open, do you hear?" You waited for them all to laugh. That would show they appreciated his carefree humour. No one laughed.

"Liu, you'd better wait. Didn't you say they were coming to see me? You and I will keep them company. We're all old friends." He didn't send Wang and Zhao out either. The more men he had around the more secure he'd feel. But suppose they wanted to go out themselves? He couldn't stop them. You had to act reserved on a job like this. If they asked him, then he'd speak. But Wang and Zhao didn't say anything, so that was all right.

It was on the tip of his tongue to ask, "How many

of them are coming?" but he swallowed back the words. Didn't he have three assistants with him, all packing guns? If they came in a big gang, well, he'd just have to close his eyes. He'd act according to the situation. Mother's — !

He still had no newspaper. What kind of an office was this anyhow! The official had to sit around waiting for bandits. It was really too much. Why not telephone Commissioner Li to send down a company of soldiers, nab the bandits as they came in, then shoot the whole lot! No, better not be too hasty. Better wait and see. Nine thirty.

"Hey, Liu, when are they coming?"

"Soon, inspector." Was there a mocking note in Liu's voice?

"Go out and get me a paper." You simply had to have his newspaper.

When it was brought, he turned to the local news section. He pretended to chuckle at something he saw. He'd read it learnedly aloud. But there were too many words he didn't recognize. Like the name of that café hostess there. What the devil was it?

"They're here, inspector." Liu was quite formal.

You was calm. Setting aside the irritating café hostess, he said softly, "Come in." He felt for the pistol in his belt.

A whole crowd entered, headed by Big Yang. Following him was Fancy Brow, another hulking brute. Walking between them, Monkey Four looked particularly small. Sixth Horse, Big-mouth Cao and White Zhang Fei also walked into the room.

"Brother You," they hailed him cordially.

He had to admit he knew them.   You stood up and smiled.

Everybody talked at the same time.   There was such a clamour no one could hear himself think.

"Big Yang, you tell him."   Gradually everyone's interest focussed on one point.   They urged one another: "Listen to Big Yang!"

Frowning, Big Yang leaned forward and rested his hands on the desk.   His mouth virtually against You's nose, he said: "We've come to congratulate you, Brother You."

"Listen!" White Zhang Fei gave Monkey Four a poke in the back.

"Congratulations are congratulations, but you ought to give us a treat.   Actually, we should be treating you, but the last few days we're a little short of this."   Big Yang's index finger and thumb pinched together in a circle like a silver dollar.   "So you'll have to treat us."

"Anything I can do, brothers — " You began.

Big Yang rolled right on.   "You don't have to invite us to a restaurant.   That's not necessary.   We want this."   Again his thumb and index finger formed a circle.   "We want money for train tickets."

"Train tickets?" said You.

"That's right."   Big Yang nodded thoughtfully.   "You see, brother, you're now in charge of this district.   How can we keep on operating here?   We're all friends.   You come, we go.   There can't be any squabbles between us.   You do your official job.   We'll go back to the hills.   You pay the fare.   No hard words.   We part friends.   We'll be meeting again some day."   Big Yang turned to his cronies.   "Isn't that the idea?"

"Right. It's just that," cried Monkey Four. "Now let's hear from Brother You."

This was something You had never expected. He hadn't thought that it would be so easy. But he certainly hadn't expected it would be so hard either. These six wanted train fares. Suppose another sixty, or another six hundred, came in, all wanting him to pay their fares? Besides, Commissioner Li had appointed him to arrest them. If You gave them all fares, spoke to them gently, and sent them off one by one, how would it look? And where would the money come from? He could hardly ask Li for it. Should he spend his hundred and twenty dollars salary, plus eighty dollars expense money?

The trouble was these birds were giving him a lot of face. Not a hard word out of them. "You come, we go." Short and sweet. Spoken like a real friend. It was easy enough, if a man was willing to lay out the money. With a smiling face, You invited them to have some tea. He couldn't make up his mind. He didn't dare offend them. They might talk nicely, but they also could be very rough. If they said they'd go, they'd definitely go. But they wouldn't leave unless You gave them the fares. It would make an awful dent in his expense money. And he'd have to pretend to be happy about it, too. They wouldn't stand for any tough talk.

"How much, friends?" he asked casually.

"Ten dollars apiece," said Big Yang, speaking for all.

"It's just the train fare. Once we're up in the hills, we'll manage fine," Monkey Four added.

"We'll leave this afternoon, friend. When we say a thing we mean it," said Big-mouth Cao.

You couldn't be so decisive. Ten dollars apiece meant sixty dollars! Three-fourths of his eighty dollars expense money!

White Zhang Fei got a bit impatient. "Fork over the sixty dollars and we'll be moving along. It's either you or us. With you here, we've got to leave. Isn't that the answer? If you give us the money, we'll go. If you don't — but why talk about that? We understand each other. Real men don't beat about the bush. Brother You, I'm holding out my hand for that train fare."

"Right, we're all holding out our hands. We'll pay it back later. Our friendship hasn't been just for a day," said Big Yang. The others also chimed in. Although their words were different, the meaning was the same.

You could no longer delay. He took out the wallet next to the pistol in his belt and counted out sixty dollars. "Here you are, brothers." He didn't smile.

"Thanks, brother," chorused Big Yang and his gang. Monkey Four rolled up the bills and stuffed them into his waist-band. "We'll be seeing you, brother," he said. The bandits left. In the outer room they nodded at Liu and the others. "Come up and see us in the hills." You's men smiled and escorted them to the door.

You was miserable. If he had known this was going to happen he would have sent for soldiers and had those six birds arrested. But maybe this way of handling it was better. He'd be running into them in the future. Sixty dollars gone. A few more visits like this and his hundred and twenty dollars of salary would also vanish. What kind of an inspector was he? An inspector who gets squeezed by bandits. He was like a mute who's eaten wormwood — it was more bitter than he could say. Had Liu been trying to be helpful, or was he just kidding around? He ought to ask him! Not only hadn't Liu captured any bandits — he had invited them to the office. Was that any way to do things?

Still, maybe he shouldn't be too strict with Liu. He might go back to the hills. You had to have him. He couldn't afford to offend anyone. What a life. If he had brought a couple of green hands along when he took office, when those bandits came he'd have had to eat black dates. Those sixty dollars bought him his life. If you looked at it that way, it was worth it.

You had no choice. What's done was done. He was only afraid that another gang might show up tomorrow asking for railway fares. He couldn't tell this to his men. He had to smile, show that You was big-hearted to his friends, as if sixty dollars or a hundred were nothing at all. But if he kept handing money out at this rate what would the inspector have to eat? The northwest wind? A fine thing!

Again he picked up the newspaper, but he'd lost interest. He had no interest in anything. Like a fool he'd given away sixty dollars. It was really sickening. He ought to be ashamed — being afraid for his life. It was as if his life didn't belong to him — he had to buy it. Mother's —! He had to admire Monkey Four and the others. They dared come to the inspector's office and demand train fares. Weren't they afraid of being nabbed? No, the devils. But he, You had lost face. Not only hadn't he arrested them, he hadn't even dared to speak a harsh word. What a disgrace. Next time would be different. He wouldn't act so soft again. It wasn't worth going soft just to remain an inspector. An inspector had to arrest people. There were no two ways about it. Blast that café hostess. What *was* her name?

Chu had returned. At least he ought to come in and report. The inspector couldn't very well run out and question him. In the next room Chu and Liu talked and talked. He would wait. He'd see whether Chu came in or not. Who could reason with bandits?

Finally Chu entered. "Brother . . . er . . . inspector. There's a gang holed up north of the city. Want to go see them?"

"Where are they?" You couldn't be afraid again. Sixty dollars gone already. If he had to die, then he'd die. He'd go even if they were gods.

"On the lake shore."

"Take your gun. Let's go." You didn't hesitate. He'd clean out that nest. No one would get any more railway fare out of him.

"Just us two?" Chu certainly could be infuriating.

"What kind of talk is that? Tell me the address and I'll go myself." If he didn't act bold, his assistants wouldn't know what sort of man the inspector was. Just handing out train fares, not cracking a single case. How could he face the commissioner? What was he being paid a salary of a hundred and twenty a month for?

Silently, Chu poured himself a bowl of tea. He seemed to be getting ready to go along. Ignoring him, You stalked out. Chu followed. That was more like it. You felt a little braver. Of course two on this job were much better than one. If they ran into trouble they could talk it over.

By the lakeside was a lane about the size of a nostril. In it was a small inn. You was very familiar with this area. Of course he recognized the inn. You needed only one look to see that it was a nest of thieves. He should have brought more men along. You, he said to himself, you've wasted your years of experience. When you lost your temper, your brains went with it. Why didn't you bring more men? Who told you to get mad at them?

Since he'd come, he'd have to see it through. He'd show his men — although he'd never been up in the hills, he had plenty of guts. If he could haul a couple of crooks out of this place, the next time he spoke his words would carry a lot more weight. He'd try his luck. Maybe he was a goner. Who could tell?

"Chu, will you guard the door or shall I?"

"There they are," said Chu, pointing inside. "No need to guard the door. None of them want to run."

Another farce. Yes, they would talk about fraternity. Mother's —! You looked in. Several toughs were sitting in a small hallway: Coloured Butterfly, Nose Six, Burly Song, Young Desheng, and two others he hadn't seen before. Finished. Again old friends.

"Come in, Brother You. We haven't even dared go to congratulate you. Come in and meet the gang. Dog Zhang, Jewels Xu, this is Brother You. Old friends. Our own brother." Greetings exchanged, the gangsters chatted animatedly.

"Have a seat, brother." Young Desheng — his pa, Old Desheng, had just been executed in Henan Province — was particularly courteous.

You hated himself. Why couldn't he think of what to say? In the end it was Chu who found just the right words.

"Brothers, the inspector has come personally. Speak up if you have anything on your mind."

The inspector smiled and nodded.

"Then we'll talk frankly," said Nose Six. "Brother Song, take Brother You and show him."

"This way, Brother You." Burly Song jerked his thumb towards the rear and went into a small room.

You followed. There was no danger. He was sure of that. He couldn't risk his life even if he wanted to. How irritating. The little room was pitch dark. Its earthen floor stank of mildew. Against the wall was a small wooden bed strewn with straw. Burly Song pulled the bed away from the wall and squatted in the corner. Removing two or three moist bricks, he extracted several pistols and threw them on the bed.

"That's the lot." Burly Song smiled and wiped his hands on his tunic. "Things are too hot around here. If we carry those, we can't even get on a train. That's our problem. We didn't know you were in charge till Brother Chu dropped in. Now we have a way out. We'll turn this pile over to you. You give us a little railway fare and have Chu put us on the train. That's how it's got to be. We're asking you this favour."

You wanted to vomit. The stench of the mildew was seeping into his brain. Holding his nose, he said: "Why give them to me?" As they went back to the hallway, he added: "I can't keep that stuff for you."

"But if we take them with us, we can't leave. The heat's on," Burly Song explained earnestly.

"If I take them, I can hand them over to the authorities. I'm not turning in any men. At least if I've got some weapons to show, that will be something. You've got to think of it from my angle. Right?" You was enraged to hear himself speak like this. Much too soft.

"That's up to you, Brother You."

He had been hoping they would refuse.

"Whatever you say, brother. Of course you know we need guns in our line of work. Would we give them up if we had any other way out? Do whatever you like with them. All we want is to hit the road right now. Without your help we can't get away. Have Brother Chu put us on the train."

The bandits were giving orders to the inspector. Their own brother. You had nothing to say. He had no ideas, no energy. He had ideas, but they didn't work. He had a position, but he couldn't use it. The truth was out. He scratched his head. He couldn't turn in those weapons. But could he refuse to take them? He'd have to give the gang railway fares and look after their guns to boot. What kind of official business was that? The only alternative was to refuse the weapons and not give them any money either. Let them do as they pleased. But did he dare? Arresting them was even more unthinkable. A dead body could be pushed off the lake bank at any time. You didn't want to end up in a watery grave.

"Brother You," Burly Song was extremely sincere, "it's hard for you. Anyone who says different is a son of a bitch. But we can't help it. Take the hardware, give us a couple of dollars, and we'll say no more. The words are in our hearts."

"How much?" You gave a sickly smile.

"Six sixes are thirty-six. The man's a bastard who asks for a dollar more. Thirty-six dollars."

"But I don't want those guns."

"That's up to you. Anyhow, we can't take them along. If we're nabbed, at most we'll get six months. But if they catch us with that hardware on us, it's black dates or something very much like it. That's the truth. We're not scared — we brothers don't have to boast — but when you ought to be careful, you'd better be careful. Well then brother, thirty-six dollars, and we'll be seeing you again." Burly Song turned up his palm.

Thirty-six dollars changed hands. The inspector had no choice. "What are we going to do with these guns, Chu?"

"Brother Chu," called the gangsters, "take us to the train."

"Brother You," they were very polite, "thanks a lot."

"Thanks" was all You got. So many guns in one bundle would be too heavy to carry. He divided them with Chu, and each tucked several in his belt. How awesome. A belt full of pistols. But You couldn't fire a single one. These fellows all trusted him. That's why they gave him their guns. It never occurred to them that he might turn them down. How could he even think of arresting them. They had guts. He had to admire them. By now, he had spent sixteen dollars more than his eighty dollars office expense money. What else could he do? He'd probably lose his hundred and twenty dollars salary too.

You's lunch was tasteless to him that day, though he drank two big tumblers of liquor. What was the use of talking? He was a dud. He had let Commissioner Li down. You was not without a sense of dignity. He thought it over. One more fiasco and the only course left would be to resign. But what a disgrace — to resign. And where else could he find a job paying a hundred and twenty a month these days? Commissioner Li certainly wouldn't give him another appointment. Not only hadn't he captured any bandits — on the contrary, the bandits had taken him in. What a joke. When they got back to the hills, they'd surely laugh at him. He was just one big joke. The more he thought about it, the worse You felt.

The best thing to do was capture some opium. Could opium be considered illegal? Yes. But what a dull pastime for an inspector of a special bureau. Anyhow, he couldn't resign. First he'd collect some opium; it wasn't a bad idea. You determined his policy. He'd confiscate opium for a while, then he'd see. At least here he knew his ground.

A week passed. Several stores of opium were brought in. Commissioner Li wanted bandits, but You couldn't push his men. His expense money was already sixteen dollars overdrawn.

It was a Monday, and his men were all out looking for opium, (opium!) when a big swarthy fellow swaggered into You's office.

"Brother You," he called smilingly.

"You, Money Five? You've got your nerve."

"With Brother You in office, what have I to fear?" Money Five sat down. "Give me a smoke."

"What have you come for?" You reached for his money pouch. More railway fare.

"First to congratulate you, second to thank you. When the brothers got back to the hills, they all praised you. That's the truth."

Oh? They didn't laugh at me? You thought to himself.

"Brother," Money Five pulled out a roll of bills. "We can't let you lose anything. The brothers in the hills will never forget your kindness."

"Really —" You tried to make a show of courteous refusal.

"Not a word, brother. Take it. Now where is Brother Song's hardware?"

Am I a weapons keeper, or something? You didn't dare say it aloud. "Chu's got them," he replied.

"Good, I'll ask him for them."

"Just down from the hills?" You felt he ought to make conversation.

"Just down from the hills. I've come to advise you to chuck this job." Money Five was very sincere.

"You want me to resign?"

"That's right. Maybe you're one of us, maybe you're not. Anyhow, with you in office, we stay out of the way. You couldn't operate if we were here. You're good to us, and we're good to you. Leave this job. That's all I've got to say. I have over three hundred men up in the hills, but I've come down to say this to you personally. We're friends. When I tell you to quit, you'd better quit. A smart fellow catches on fast. I'm going, brother. Tell Chu I'll be waiting for him in the inn by the lakeshore."

"Tell me one thing, brother." You stood up. "If I quit, what will our friends think?"

"No one will laugh. Don't worry about that, brother. Well, goodbye."

Two or three days later, there was a new man in the post of inspector. You, fat and stately, often strolled down the street. At times, he glanced serenely at the Mountain of the Thousand Buddhas.

Translated by Sidney Shapiro

The Soul-Slaying Spear

Everything in life is a game; this thought
often occurred to me in the past; only now
do I understand the truth of it.

THE headquarters of the escort agency where Dragon
Sha used to work had long been converted into an inn.

The time had come for Asia to wake up from its
dream. The sound of rifle fire overpowered the roaring of tigers in the jungles of the Malay Peninsula and
India. Half awake, the peoples of Asia rubbed their
sleepy eyes and offered prayers to their ancestors and
gods; but before long, they lost all of their land, their
freedom and their rights. Men with different-colored
faces stood outside their doors, the barrels of their guns
still warm. Of what use were their long spears, powerful bows and poisonous arrows, and thick shields
covered in gorgeous snakeskin? Their ancestors and the
divinities worshipped by their ancestors were totally im-
potent. China, with its dragon banners, was no longer
the great mystery it had been in the past. Now China
had railroads running through its graveyards, destroying
all auspicious geomantic influences. The fringed ma-
roon banner of the escort agency, the steel sword in a
green sharkskin sheath, the horse hung with a string of
bells, the accumulated wisdom and argot of the escort
trade as well as the code of justice and pride of repu-

tation — for Dragon Sha, all of these things, including his mastery of the martial arts and his career as a swordman — had vanished like a dream. This was the age of the iron horse, of automatic rifles, of treaty ports and of terrorism. There were even rumors about that people were out to chop off the emperor's head!

At the point in history when our story takes place, acting as an armed escort was no longer a viable profession, though this was before either the Revolutionary Party or the educationalists had begun to promote the traditional martial arts as a national pastime.

In the past, Dragon Sha was known far and wide for his short and lean figure, his agility, his powerful physique and his piercing eyes which shone like stars on a frosty winter night. By now, however, he'd put on some weight. When the escort agency was converted into an inn, he moved into the northernmost rooms in the small rear courtyard. His long spear stood in one corner of his room, and he raised pigeons in the courtyard as well. In the evenings, he would close the gate leading into his courtyard and run through the routine which had made him famous: the "Five Tigers Soul-slaying Spear". His spear, and the series of exercises he performed with it, represented twenty years of experience in the Northeast, and had earned him the name "Magic Spear Sha". In those days, he had never suffered a single defeat. Now, however, his spear no longer could confer glory upon him or win him any victories; only when he passed his hand over the spear's cool, smooth, quivering staff could he lessen his despair somewhat. And only at night, when he practiced by himself in the privacy of his courtyard, did "Magic Spear Sha" come back to life. During the daytime, he rarely talked about the martial arts or the past; his world had been blown away by a storm.

Some of the young men he had trained as boys came to see him frequently. Most of them were unemployed. They had mastered some of the martial arts, but had no real opportunity to use them. Some of them gave performances at temple fairs. First flexing their legs, they would go through a series of exercises which would conclude with a few fancy somersaults; after such a display, they'd try to peddle some tonic pills. In this way they could earn themselves a few strings of cash. Those who couldn't afford to live in this manner hauled big baskets of fruit or beans into town in the early morning and hawked them in the streets. In those days, rice and pork were relatively inexpensive, and a man willing to do a little hard physical labor could easily earn enough to fill his belly. But this kind of life couldn't satisfy Dragon Sha's disciples. Not only did they have huge appetites; they also had to eat well — no hard buns or hot pepper pancakes for them. Moreover, they frequently took part in pilgrimages into the mountains, which included contests of "Five-Tiger Cudgels", wielding a sword at the head of the procession, and donning huge masks to participate in the lion dances. Although these pilgrimages never brought in much money — in comparison with working as an armed escort — they at least gave these young men an opportunity to get out in public and flex their muscles. These affairs were also a way of advertising one's skills. The participants had to dress up in their finest costumes: a typical outfit would include a pair of trousers made of European-style black crepe, a short jacket of fine white bleached cotton and a pair of fancy cotton shoes, though black satin fighting boots were generally considered more impressive. They were the disciples of "Magic Spear Sha" — though Dragon Sha himself would never have acknowledged this. Public performances often meant incurring some expenses, not to mention risking the possibility of getting into a brawl. When they ran out of money, these "disciples" often came to Dragon Sha for a loan. Dragon Sha was not one to beat around the bush in such matters, and would help them out as best he could; in any case, they never went away empty-handed. On the other hand, if they wanted to learn a new fighting trick or a fancy display piece, or asked their master to show them some countermoves, such as "snatching a sword empty-handed" or "spear vs. tiger-head hooks", Dragon Sha would usually brush them off with a quip, "What countermoves can I show you? I'd sooner shoo you!" And sometimes he would simply kick them out of his house. They had no idea why Master Sha acted this way, and often left rather reluctantly.

These disciples, however, sung Dragon Sha's praises wherever they went. On the one hand, they wanted people to know that they were the inheritors of an authentic martial arts tradition and had studied under a real master; and on the other, they all wanted to stir up Master Sha's pride: if someday a particularly stubborn adversary insisted on meeting Dragon Sha in person, they wanted to be sure he would show them his stuff. Thus they boasted that Master Sha could knock a bull off its feet with a single blow, and could easily send a man flying over the roof with a single kick. Though no one had ever seen him perform these miracles, the more they spoke about them, the more sincerely they believed they were true. They even went so far as to specify the time and place these miracles had taken place, and swore to the ends of the earth that they weren't exaggerating.

One day, Wang Sansheng — "Three Victories Wang" — one of Dragon Sha's more mature disciples, marked off a circle in the courtyard of the Temple of the Earth God and laid out his weapons. After taking a big pinch of snuff the color of tea leaves he began to swing his long segmented iron whip around his head to enlarge the circle. He put his whip down on the ground and without performing the customary bow to the assembled crowd, placed his hands on his hips and recited the following couplet: "I'm a man who's fought his way through this world; my fists have made me a hero throughout the length and breadth of the empire." He surveyed the crowd with a sweeping glance, and continued: "My good friends and neighbors, my name is Wang Sansheng. I'm no sideshow performer, but a true expert of the martial arts. When I worked as a escort in the Northeast, I met some of the best men in the business. I'm out of work now and have a bit of time to spare, so I thought I'd set up here and offer you gentlemen a chance to step into the ring with me. Anyone here who loves the martial arts is welcome; but remember, it's friendship first with me. If one of you would be so kind as to step up here, I'll be glad to entertain you. My master is Dragon Sha with a magic spear; that means my fighting is the real McCoy. Gentlemen, is there anyone here willing to join me?" He surveyed the crowd once again, but he knew that no one would have the nerve to step forward. His speech was impressive, but his iron whip was more so, weighing some nine kilograms.

Wang Sansheng was tall and had a tough muscular face. He opened his big black eyes wide and glanced through the crowd a third time. No one made a single sound. He removed his short jacket and tightened his wide pale blue fighting belt, which aided him in contracting his stomach. Spitting into the palms of his hands, he picked up his long-handled broadsword.

"Gentlemen, first I'll give you all a little sword demonstration. I'm not doing this for nothing, mind you, so when I'm finished, if you've got a few spare coins, toss 'em this way; but if you don't, then just shout a little something encouraging. Just remember, I'm not in it for the money. Alright then, here we go."

He held the sword against his body and opened his eyes wide, stretching all the muscles in his face. His chest muscles stuck out like two twisted birch roots. He stamped his foot and raised his sword before him, its long red tassels swinging back and forth in front of his shoulders. He brandished the sword in a series of fancy movements, squatted down, and spun around. The sword revolved like a tornado with a loud whirring. Finally, he bent down and set the sword spinning on the palm of his right hand. Not a single sound arose from the crowd; all that could be heard was the tinkling of the bells attached to the tassels of his sword. With an elegant gesture, he placed his sword on the ground in front of him and stamped his foot again. Straightening up until he was a head taller than anyone in the crowd, he stood there like a black pagoda, and then resumed his normal posture. "Ladies and gentlemen!" Holding the sword in one hand and placing his other hand on his waist, he surveyed the crowd once again. A few people tossed a few coins at his feet; he nodded in approval. "Ladies and gentlemen!" He waited a few more minutes, but the scattered bright and well-worn coins on the ground failed to grow in number, and people on the periphery of the circle began to leave. He took a deep breath. "No one appreciates me." Though he said this under his breath, everyone heard him clearly.

"Well done!" an old man with a scraggly beard shouted from the northwest corner of the circle.

"Eh?" Wang Sansheng made as if he hadn't heard the man.

"I said: You ... performed ... very ... well!" The man's tone of voice was slightly abrasive.

Putting his sword down on the ground, Wang Sansheng looked in the direction the voice was coming from. No one in the crowd had noticed this old man before, but now they all turned to look at him. He was short and wiry and had a coarse blue cotton long gown slung over his shoulder. His face was wizened and his eyes were set deeply in their sockets; his beard was composed of little more than a few sparse brownish hairs. The queue resting on his shoulder seemed to be made of straw. It was about as thick as a chopstick, but much less straight. Despite the old man's unformidable appearance, Wang Sansheng could tell he possessed real fighting skills. His forehead shone with a mysterious radiance, and his pupils were like two tiny wells shimmering with a black lustre. But Wang Sansheng had nothing to fear. His ability to identify a real fighter boosted his confidence in his own fighting: he was Dragon Sha's righthand man.

"How about joining me for a few rounds, Uncle?" Wang Sansheng addressed him with due deference.

Nodding his head, the old man entered the ring. At this moment, the crowd broke out laughing at the way he walked. His arms hardly moved at all; and each time he took a step with his left foot, he had to slide his right foot along the ground to catch up with it. In this fashion, he dragged himself forward, bending over and straightening up at each step. He looked as if he had suffered from paralysis at some time in the past. Making his way to the center of the circle, he threw his gown on the ground, oblivious to the ridicule being directed at him from all sides.

"So, you're a disciple of Dragon Sha with his magic spear, eh? Well then, you fight with a spear, but what about me?" The old man came right to the point; he seemed to be itching for a fight.

All those who had started to stray from the circle came back to watch. And no matter how loudly the man with the trained bear banged on his gong, no one paid any attention to him.

"How about me fighting with a spear and you using a set of triple-sticks?" Wang Sansheng wanted to give the old man a chance to prove himself. The triple-sticks — three heavy wooden rods connected in a line with two short chains — was not the sort of weapon an amateur could fight with.

The old man nodded and picked the sticks up from the ground.

Wang Sansheng glared at his opponent and started rattling his spear. He had a very unpleasant expression on his face.

The pupils of the old man's eyes darkened and receded into their sockets; they resembled the burning tips of two incense sticks, and followed the tip of Wang Sansheng's spear as he swung it in circles through the air. Wang Sansheng had a strange feeling that the old man was about to swallow the tip of his spear with those eyes of his. The spectators surged forward to the edge of the circle until there was hardly any breathing space between them. They were all aware that the old man possessed extraordinary powers. In order to divert the old man's eyes, Wang Sansheng executed an elaborate flourish with his spear.

The old man's scraggly beard fluttered once. He said, "After you." Wang Sansheng held his spear out in front of him and lunged forward, bending one knee. The sharp point of his spear was aimed directly at the old man's throat, and the red tassels surrounding the shaft swung around with the thrust. All at once the old man came alive; leaning slightly to one side to avoid the tip of the spear, he struck the spear with a downward stroke of one section of his triple-sticks while forcing Wang Sansheng's hands upwards with the other. There were two loud cracks and Wang Sansheng's spear fell to the ground. The crowd shouted their approval. Wang Sansheng blushed deep purple from his face down to his chest and picked up his spear. With a fancy flourish, he charged forward again, this time directing the tip of his spear towards the old man's belly. The old man's jet black eyes glowed in anger. Nimbly bending one leg, he parried the spearhead with one section of his triple-sticks and with another struck the spear's handle just as Wang was about to pull it away. With a bang, Wang Sansheng's spear fell to the ground once again.

More applause and cheers arose from the crowd. Wang Sansheng was now sweating all over. But this time he didn't pick up his spear; he simply remained standing there fixed to the spot, staring straight ahead. The old man threw down the sticks, picked up his gown and, dragging his right leg behind him, started walking at a somewhat faster pace than before. With his robe over his shoulder, he went up to Wang Sansheng and patted him on the arm. "You need a little more practice, boy."

"Where do you think you're going?" Wang Sansheng wiped the sweat from his brow. "Stay here a minute. I lost this one, but there's something I want to ask you. Do you dare take on Master Sha?"

"That's what I came here for in the first place." The old man twisted up his wizened face in a semblance of a smile. "Let's go. Get your things together. I'm taking you to dinner."

Wang Sansheng gathered up his weapons and left them with the magician Second Pockmarks. As they walked out of the temple, a large crowd was following them. Wang Sansheng shouted a few obscenities in their direction and they scattered.

"What is your family name?" Wang Sansheng asked.

"Sun's the name." The old man's speech was as coarse as the rest of him. "I love the martial arts, and I've always wanted to meet Dragon Sha."

"Dragon Sha's going to beat you into a pulp," Wang Sansheng thought to himself. He quickened his pace, but Mr Sun had no problem keeping up with him. Wang Sansheng knew that the old man's way of walking with consecutive leaps was characteristic of Zha Family Boxing — there was no doubt in his mind that he could kick up a storm in a fight. But no matter how agile his legs were, he was certainly no match for Dragon Sha. Convinced of this, Wang Sansheng felt a little better inside, and slowed his pace.

"Uncle Sun, where is your hometown?"

"Hejian County.* Just a small town." Sun seemed to be warming up a little. "You can master the cudgel in a month. You can master the sword in a year. But it takes a lifetime to master the spear. To tell you the truth, you've got a really fine pair of hands there."

Beads of sweat broke out on Wang Sansheng's forehead, but he said nothing.

When they arrived at the inn, Wang Sansheng's heart was beating wildly. His worst fear was that Master Sha would not be at home; he was very eager to get his revenge. He knew Master Sha generally avoided becoming involved in conflicts of this sort, and that many of his fellow disciples had been spurned by Master Sha in similar situations. But Wang Sansheng believed Master Sha would agree this time; first, since he was Master Sha's eldest disciple, in a different class from the rest of those youngsters who hung around him; and second, because Dragon Sha's name had come up in front of the crowd at the temple fair; he could hardly afford to lose "face" in such a situation.

"Sansheng, what brings you here?" Dragon Sha was lying in bed reading the classical novel *Canonization of the Gods*.

Sansheng blushed a deep crimson. His lips trembled but no sound came out.

---

* In Hebei Province.

Dragon Sha sat up. "What's the matter, Sansheng?"
"I got whipped."

Master Sha yawned but said nothing to him.

Wang Sansheng was very upset, but didn't want to show it; it was much more important to rouse Master Sha to action.

"There's an old man named Sun waiting outside to see you. My spear ... he knocked my spear out of my hands twice!" Wang Sansheng knew the effect the word "spear" would have on Dragon Sha. Before Dragon Sha could say a word, Sansheng rushed out the door.

When the visitor entered, Dragon Sha was waiting for him in the main room of his flat. They greeted each other politely in the traditional manner and sat down. Dragon Sha told Wang Sansheng to make tea. Sansheng hoped they would get right down to business and start fighting, but resigned himself for the moment to making tea. Mr Sun remained silent and sized up Dragon Sha with his deepset eyes.

Master Sha was extremely deferential. "If Sansheng offended you in any way, forget about it. He's just a youngster."

Mr Sun was disappointed in this response, but knew Dragon Sha was very astute. Unsure of how to react, Mr Sun knew that a man's astuteness was not necessarily an indication of his attainments in the martial arts. "I've come to learn spear fighting from you," he spurted out.

Dragon Sha said nothing. Wang Sansheng came in holding a teapot — he was so eager for them to come to grips that he had poured the water into the pot before it had boiled.

Raising his tea bowl, Dragon Sha said, "Sansheng, go round up Little Shun and the rest of them and tell them to meet us at the Tianhui Restaurant. We're taking Mr Sun out to dinner."

"What?" Wang Sansheng's eyes nearly fell out of their sockets. He glanced at Dragon Sha. Though his heart was filled with inexpressable anger, he responded with a simple "Yes, sir!" and walked out, pouting his big lips.

Mr Sun said, "It's hard work teaching disciples."

"I've never had any disciples. Let's go now, this water isn't boiled. We'll go to a teahouse and drink tea till we get hungry." Dragon Sha picked up his waistpouch from the table, put his snuff-bottle in one pocket and some money in the other, and hung it over his belt.

"I'm not hungry. Let's not go out yet." Mr Sun's two "nots" were insistent enough to knock his little queue off his shoulder.

"We'll chat for a while longer then."

"I've come especially to observe the way you fight with a spear."

"Five Tigers Soul-slaying Spear?" Dragon Sha said, pointing to his belly. "Look how much weight I've put on."

"Here's my idea." Mr Sun looked intensely at Dragon Sha. "We don't have to fight. Just teach me your 'Five Tigers Soul-slaying Spear' routine."

"Five Tigers Soul-slaying Spear?" Dragon Sha laughed. "I haven't done that for years. I couldn't do it now if I tried. I've got a better idea. Why don't you stay here with me for a few days. I'll show you around town, and when you're ready to go, I'll give you a little something to help you out on the way home."

"I don't want to go anywhere and I don't need any money from you. All I want is to learn the martial arts." Mr Sun stood up. "I'll go through one of my routines for you so you can decide if I'm qualified or not." He stood up and literally leaped into the courtyard in a single bound, scaring the pigeons away. Spreading his legs in the proper starting posture, he performed an entire routine of Zha Family Boxing. His footwork was nimble, his hands full of grace; leaping and landing on one leg, his little queue remained suspended in the air and descended slowly like a kite on a windless day. Though his movements were rapid, all his postures were well balanced and a delight to watch. He circled the courtyard six times, covering every inch of space in it; all of his movements were fluent and finely coordinated. His body remained in one place while his spirit permeated every corner of the courtyard. He finished by bringing his hands together in front of his chest, shrinking back to his normal posture. It was as if a flock of swallows flying madly about the courtyard had all returned to their nests.

"Excellent! Excellent!" Dragon Sha nodded his approval from his front steps. Still holding his hands together in front of him, Mr Sun said, "Teach me your spear routine!"

Dragon Sha came down the steps and returned the salutation. "My dear Mr Sun, to tell you the truth, that spear and that spear routine are going to be buried with me when I die."

"Then you won't teach me?"

"No."

Mr Sun's mouth and beard quivered nervously for a few moments, but there was very little he could say. He went back inside, picked up his blue cotton gown and limped out. "Sorry to bother you then. Goodbye."

"Why don't you stay for dinner?"

Mr Sun said nothing.

After escorting his guest to the gate of the courtyard, Dragon Sha returned to his room and stood nodding in the direction of the corner where his spear stood.

He went alone to the Tianhui Restaurant, since he was afraid Wang Sansheng and the others were waiting for him there. But when he got there, he found out that they had not come at all.

Wang Sansheng, Little Shun and the others stopped giving performances at the Temple of the God of Earth, and no longer boasted about Dragon Sha's feats. On the contrary, they began spreading the word that Dragon Sha had thrown in the towel and was even too scared to fight with an old man. In fact, they now began telling people that Mr Sun could kill a bull with a single kick. It meant very little to anyone that Wang Sansheng had lost to him; but Dragon Sha hadn't even tried. In any case, Wang Sansheng had had a chance to test himself in the ring with the old man, while Dragon Sha was too much of a coward even to stick up for himself. Before long, everyone seemed to have forgotten about "Magic Spear Sha".

One quiet evening when no one was about, Dragon Sha bolted the outside gate and ran through the sixty-four thrusts of his entire routine. Leaning on his spear in the middle of the courtyard, he gazed up at the stars and thought back on the good old days, when he enjoyed a fine reputation in the country inns and all through the wilderness. Sighing, he rubbed his hands over the cool, smooth handle of his spear and smiled. "No, I won't teach this to anyone. I won't teach this to anyone."

Translated by Don J. Cohn

"The Fire Chariot*"

IT was New Year's Eve, according to the lunar calendar. Nobody paid any attention to the western calendar in those days.

As the train started moving, one could hear the wailing of the train whistle and the soft sighing of the passengers. Some passengers were counting hours to themselves: seven, eight, nine, ten; if the train arrived at the station by ten o'clock, they could be home by midnight. That wasn't too late, though the children would probably be asleep by then. The overhead racks were piled high with canned food, fresh and dried fruit and toys. Glancing at these gifts, the travellers could hear their children calling out to them: "Daddy!" But before long, they would return to their daydreams. Others, knowing they would not reach home until the following morning, sought out a familiar face among the other passengers, but none were to be found. By the time they got home, it would be next year already! Others. . . . How slowly the train was moving! Though they'd already arrived home a hundred times in their minds, their bodies were very much on the train. They smoked, drank tea, yawned, daydreamed about going home, hoped, made wishes and looked out the window at the black and endless night; when they turned away

---

* Literally, "The train".

from the windows, their faces were entirely devoid of expression; they would lower their heads, on the verge of tears, and yawn.

There were very few people in the second class car. Big fat Mr Zhang and scrawny little Mr Qiao sat across from each other. When they first boarded the train, they had each laid out their blankets across an entire seat as a way of reserving them for their exclusive use. When the train left and they discovered that there were very few other passengers on board, the bitterness they felt about having to travel on New Year's Eve became intensified, while at the same time they regretted having occupied only a single seat each; this gave them something to commiserate with each other about. Both gentlemen were holding borrowed railroad passes, but the passes' owners had been unwilling to part with them even a day earlier. The two of them agreed on the following point: if people with railroad passes chose to make you wait until the last day of the year, then you just had to wait. The passes' owners seemed to enjoy watching their friends get nervous and impatient, even to the point of blowing up in anger! They sighed together: friends today — can you really call them friends? It's not like what it used to be. Nowadays, no one gives their passes away until New Years' Eve, and even then you would owe the passes' owners numerous favors. They nodded in agreement: it was entirely their friends' fault that they wouldn't make it home for New Year's Eve. At any other time of the year, borrowing a railroad pass was never a problem; but come new year's time, people got stubborn and starting making things difficult. The two travellers were perhaps too embarrassed to say what was really on their minds: Goddamn them all!

Fat Mr Zhang removed his fox fur riding jacket and attempted to sit cross-legged on his seat; but he was so fat it was nearly impossible for him to remain upright that way. It was also terribly hot in the train car and his broad forehead was covered with beads of sweat. "Steward! Bring me a hot towel!" He turned to skinny Mr Qiao and said, "Why do they always overheat these trains? It must be much cooler travelling by airplane."

Mr Qiao had taken off his overcoat, and although he was wearing a fur-lined robe with a satin padded vest on top of it, he wasn't feeling hot at all. "There're a lot of airplane passes floating around, actually," he said, smiling wryly.

"Better not take any risks!" Mr Zhang made another concerted effort to cross his stocky legs, but was again unsuccessful. "Steward! Bring me a towel!"

The steward came into the car supporting a tall stack of hot towels on the palm of his hand. He was about forty years old, extremely tall and thin, and gave one the impression that he could very comfortably disconnect his head from his shoulders and replace it whenever he pleased. Normally disposed to providing the finest service, he was nursing a particular grievance today. The moment he entered the car, he addressed Little Cui, "You know what happened, don't you? I worked two days in a row on the 27th and 28th, so I should have a day off on the 30th. Alright then, I was already to take off when Mr Liu comes in and tells me, 'Old Five, I'm afraid you've got to work on the 30th.' Ai! You know what I mean? More than sixty people working on this train and he still can't do without me? I don't care about celebrating New Year's. That's not the point. It's having to work today that pisses me off." He glanced down the aisle at fat Mr Zhang and shifted the hot towels from one hand to the other. He removed one from the pile and offered it to Little Cui. "Have a towel. Here's what I should have said to Mr Liu: 'I don't care about celebrating New Year's. But I ought to get off on the 30th. After working a solid year on this train, why should I have such bad luck? There're more than sixty people working on this train. What's the big difference if I . . . ?' " His resentment flowed, bubbling forth falteringly like water from an inverted bottle. It was nearly impossible for him to contain himself.

When Little Cui handed the towel back to him, Old Five continued, "What a pain in the ass! Who needs all this? I tell you, screw this whole crazy business! You kill yourself the whole goddamned year, and then. . . ."

A touch of animation which one might interpret as a smile transfused Little Cui's sickly complexion. He nodded his head, and was about to bend it even further as a way of expressing his sympathy for Old Five, but stopped there in order not to compromise his principles in such a casual manner. All the people who worked on the train — from the chief conductor to Old Five and even the couplers at every station — were Little Cui's friends. His sickly face was a veritable second class ticket; if he ever got into trouble with the Ministry of Railroads, there were very few people who would deny this ticket's validity. Similarly, no one who knew he always carried a few hundred ounces of opium with him at all times dared to deny him the right to do this. Little Cui offended no one; if a friend of his got into trouble, he could ill afford to show too much sympathy, lest his other friends become jealous. And since he never offended anyone, he was never afraid of anyone either. Little Cui's train ticket — his sickly face — was stamped all over with wisdom and intelligence.

"Shit, you work a whole goddamned year without a break!" By venting some of his own bitterness, Little Cui provided Old Five with an opportunity to relieve himself of some of the anger stored up in his heart. Evidently, he was aware of what Aristotle wrote about the effect of tragedy. "I'm in the same trap. It's the 30th, and here I am riding the same old train. But that's not all. Tomorrow, the first day of the New Year, I've got to go see that bitch Pinky. Everyone else's going after the God of Wealth, but I've got to go see that slut. Shit!" He parted his sickly lips, revealing several blackened teeth. Then he closed his mouth, cleared his throat and landed a huge gob of phlegm on the floor.

As expected, Old Five instantly ceased worrying about his own problems, and was moved by Little Cui's plight. When he extended his neck in Little Cui's direction, Old Five looked a lot like a camel — with a kind and tender face. The face towels had cooled, so he went to the next car and poured some hot water over them. When he returned and passed by Little Cui, he didn't say anything, though he winked once to indicate that his resentment hadn't died away altogether. The train shook, and he nearly lost his balance. Righting himself, he went up to Mr Gou. "Have a hot towel.

Couldn't get away till the 30th, eh?" His real purpose in asking Mr Gou this question was to revive his own grumbling. Though Old Five knew Mr Gou quite well, he knew Little Cui better, so with Mr Gou it was necessary to approach his favorite subject by a slightly circuitous route.

Mr Gou was very well dressed. He apparently felt on need to take off his black woolen overcoat with its otter collar, nor his brand new black satin skullcap. Splendidly attired, he sat there quite formally; he could easily pass for the chairman of a large corporation preparing to address an audience from the rostrum. In order to take the towel proffered by Old Five, he had to stretch his arms forward, thus shortening somewhat the very long sleeves of his overcoat. Then, with the towel in his hands, instead of simply bending his arms, he made a wide semi-circular motion, and when his hands finally reached his face, he began to scrub in the most gentlemanly manner. His sparkling face set off his square head and large ears to good advantage. He nodded slightly to Old Five, but didn't explain why he was travelling on New Year's Eve.

"Do you know what we have to go through to make a living?" Old Five couldn't bear wasting an opportunity to vent his spleen in front of Mr Gou, but he wanted to avoid repeating the same old rigmarole to him. Thus by carefully measuring his words, he injected just the right dose of respect and intimacy into the conversation. "I ought to have a day off on the 30th, but here I am still working. There's no way out." Taking the towel back from Mr Gou, Old Five added, "How about another one?"

Mr Gou shook his head, both as a way of refusing

a second towel as well as to show a little sympathy for Old Five. But he said nothing. Everyone on the line knew Mr Gou was related to Mr Song, head of this section of the railroad, which gave him every right to ride in the second class car for free. It was therefore quite beneath his dignity to enter into a casual conversation with a steward.

Old Five felt that Mr Gou's shaking his head was rather brusque, but when a relative of Mr Song, the section chief, deigned to shake his head, one ought to be grateful. A moment later, the train shook violently, and he walked down the aisle as if he were on a swing-boat. With a flourish, he unfurled a towel that had been twisted up like a cruller, holding it by its corners in a manner both dainty and professional. "Wipe your face, sir?" Mr Zhang placed the hottest part of the towel over the palm of his hand, slapped himself in the face with it, and began rubbing as if he were polishing a mirror. "And you, sir?" Old Five offered a towel to Mr Qiao. Mr Qiao was not particularly keen on rubbing his face, and only left on his towel whatever finely ground fertile filth he could produce from inside his nostrils and under his fingernails.

"They'll be inspecting tickets shortly." Old Five thought it was wrong to start complaining to strangers, so he began with a short detour. "After we check your tickets, you two gentlemen can take a nice rest; if you need any pillows, just let me know. There're only a few passengers on the train, so you should be able to get some sleep. It's New Year's Eve, so it looks like you two gentlemen are going to have to celebrate on board this year. When you work on the railroad . . . you don't even have a choice." He didn't want to say everything at once; better he should observe their reactions first. He offered Mr Zhang another towel. Mr Zhang was reluctant to exert so much effort a second time, but he had not yet wiped his hair after his haircut earlier that morning. For this, a few passes of the towel would suffice, though his scalp required a little vigorous rubbing as well. After going through all the motions, he breathed a sigh of relief. At this point, Mr Qiao couldn't possibly accept a second towel, since it looked like Mr Zhang had used up all the energy available for rubbing. Instead, he started picking his teeth with his freshly-cleaned fingernails.

"Why do you have to make it so hot in this car?" Mr Zhang said when he tossed the towel back to Old Five.

"I wouldn't open that window if I were you unless you want to freeze. Believe me, no one gives a damn about anything that happens on this train." In a single leap, Old Five arrived at his favorite subject. "What do you think, shouldn't a guy who works the whole year have a day off on New Year's Eve? Ah, forget it, what's the use of talking about it?"

One good reason was because the train had stopped at a small station.

A number of people got off from the third class cars. They were all carrying sacks over their shoulders or baskets in their hands. As they headed out of the station, some hesitated for a moment, perhaps wondering whether they had left anything on the train. Those who remained on board stared out of the windows, envious of those who were nearly home, and anxious for the train to move a little faster. No one in the second class car got off, but seven or eight men in military uniforms boarded, their leather shoes pounding noisily through the carriage and their polished leather belts shining in the light. They carried on four bundles of extra-large fireworks wrapped in red paper stamped with gold characters. These fireworks were so large there was hardly any place to put them. The soldiers marched up and down the aisles, shouting and cursing at each other. The more heated their arguments, the more difficult it became for them to reach any conclusions, until the assistant battalion commander ordered, "Lay 'em flat on the floor!" "Put 'em on the floor!" echoed the platoon lieutenant.

In perfect unison, the soldiers bent down, straightened up, patted the dust off their uniforms, stood at attention and saluted.

The assistant battalion commander returned the salute. "Alright then, dismissed!" The platoon lieutenant echoed, "Dismissed!" Accompanied by the sound of loud footsteps, all the grey caps, grey puttees and leather belts moved in the direction of the train door. "On the double!" The whistle sounded; the engine huffed and puffed. Electric lights, human shadows and the sound of turning wheels all blended into one as the train moved out of the station.

Old Five wandered up and down the aisle — whether this could be considered work it was hard to tell — and glanced at the assistant battalion commander, the platoon lieutenant and the fireworks piled on the floor. Feeling too timid to say anything to them, he sat down with Little Cui and started in on his favorite topic, this time with an even more detailed report about what it meant not to be able to take the day off. Little Cui responded by saying that both Pinky and Big Trumpet, another friend of his, were both stinking bitches.

Old Five was becoming slightly anxious about the fireworks, so he ambled back to where the two officers were sitting. The assistant battalion commander was lying down and appeared thoroughly exhausted. He had placed his gun on the little table next to his seat. The platoon lieutenant felt it would have been improper for him to lie down so soon, but in the meantime had removed his cap and was actively engaged in scratching his scalp. Old Five didn't want to disturb the battalion commander, so he smiled at the platoon lieutenant from a distance and said, "How about letting me put these firecrackers on the overhead rack for you?"

"Why?" The lieutenant took a deep breath and scratched his scalp with such force that his mouth was pulled out of shape.

"Someone might knock them over," Old Five said, retracting his neck.

"Who's going to knock them over? Why would anyone want to do that?" The lieutenant opened his single-fold eyelids, but the effect was lost on Old Five.

"Well, it doesn't matter then." Old Five smiled, but it was as if a boulder were pressing down on his head, giving his face a very squashed look. "It doesn't matter. Where are you getting off?"

"You looking for trouble?" The lieutenant felt a great vacuum inside himself, and thought it appropriate to vent a bit of spleen.

Old Five knew there was no use in picking a fight, so he withdrew tactfully to where Mr Zhang was sitting. "We're going to begin checking tickets now, sir."

Fatty Zhang and Scrawny Qiao were right in the midst of the liveliest conversation. It turned out that both gentlemen knew a man named Ziqing, and that Ziqing was actually a distant relative of Mr Qiao. From Ziqing their conversation shifted to Ganchen; both Mr Zhang and Mr Qiao knew Ganchen too. He could play twenty rounds of mahjong at a single sitting; even if he lost every penny he had, Ganchen always discarded his tiles in the most gracious manner, a broad smile perpetually spread across his lips. Ganchen was a man of the world, and extremely clever. Was it last year, or the year before, that Ganchen had found himself a lovely and gifted concubine? Ganchen was quite a guy, and a good friend as well.

The ticket inspectors began their rounds: The first two, wearing caps decorated with golden braids, came in frowning. In the second class car, however, one would smile while the other frowned. In the first class car, naturally, they both smiled. The third ticket collector, a tall husky Tianjin type, was sporting a pistol in a leather holster and a beltful of bullets. The fourth was a tall Shandong type, and in addition to pistol and bullets had a large knife in his kit. The fifth, Old Five, just stood there not knowing what to do with his long slender neck, so he simply tilted his head slightly to the right. They entered the car together and passed by where Little Cui was sitting.

By now, Little Cui's sickly complexion and stained teeth were familiar sights to them all. As usual, when they saw him this time and Little Cui smiled, it only made them all feel uncomfortable. The head ticket inspector with the golden braid on his cap stared off into the distance as if there were something on his mind and clicked his little silver ticket punch against his leg, while the second in command, wearing the same sort of cap, actually nodded to Little Cui. The Tianjin type smiled for an instant but immediately resumed his frown; he could turn his smile on and off like a light. The man from Shandong fidgeted with the peak of his cap, and though he had many things to say to Little Cui, decided to wait until later; there was a rather elusive look in his eyes. Old Five was feeling somewhat embarrassed for Little Cui, and apologized to him on behalf of all the ticket men. "Don't get up, there're hardly any passengers today. When we're done we'll come back for a chat." Little Cui felt left out, and a dark cloud passed over his sickly face as he sat down.

Old Five went up to Mr Gou and addressed him, "Mr Gou!" But the head ticket inspector thought this was rather presumptuous and immediately interrupted him by shaking Mr Gou's hand. "How's our section cheif Mr Song these days? How is it you're travelling today?" Mr Gou smiled and, looking more dignified than ever, quickly withdrew his shaking hand and clasped his two hands together in front of his chest in the traditional gesture of greeting. He mumbled something incomprehensible, but it was instantly understood by all present that he was just trying his best to be polite. The two men from Tianjin and Shandong stood there not knowing what to say or do, while feeling somewhat inferior to their colleagues. Nonetheless, they maintained their dignity by straightening their backs as stiff as boards.

At the apposite moment, Old Five walked briskly up to Mr Zhang and Mr Qiao and announced that it was time to inspect their tickets. When he saw that they were both carrying free passes, his respect for them rose to great heights. Old Five returned Mr Zhang's pass to him first and lingered for a few moments over Mr Qiao's since the latter's pass had been issued to a woman, and Mr Qiao, without a doubt, was a man. The number two ticket inspector poked his head in for a glance but withdrew immediately, nodding his head in forgiveness: on New Year's Eve, a woman could easily turn into a man. Holding Mr Qiao's pass in his two hands, Old Five returned it to him in the most apologetic manner.

The assistant battalion commander was snoring. Sensing the imminent arrival of the ticket inspectors, the platoon lieutenant quickly put his feet up on the seat in order to appear asleep and discourage them from disturbing him. As all eyes turned towards the fireworks on the floor, the man from Shandong nodded in admiration — they were so long and fat. The Tianjin type turned to the second in command and said, "These must be for Brigadier-General Cao!" And since nobody raised any objections, they continued on their way. As they were going out the door, the chief ticket inspector issued a brief order to Old Five: "Tell them to put those fireworks up on the rack." In an effort to lessen the difficulty of such a task, the second in command added, "You can do it for them." Old Five nodded several times, and his whole body nodded as well. He said nothing to them, but he had it all worked out in his mind: "Since you don't have the nerve to tell them yourselves, all I have to do is nod. Nodding my head and whether I put the firework on the rack are entirely different questions." The Tianjin type was the most conservative of them all: "Don't forget they're for Brigadier-General Cao." Hearing this, Old Five came to the enlightened conclusion that there was no way the fireworks could be moved.

When Old Five returned to where Little Cui was sitting, he could tell from the shadow on his face that he needed a glass of water, and went to fetch it for him without saying a word. Little Cui couldn't afford the time to thank him at this moment, and took a tiny piece of something out of his pocket — not even Old Five could see what it was. He placed the tip of his right thumb on his left palm and cured up the fingers of his left hand so that it resembled the sort of shoe worn by a woman with bound feet; at the same time he grinned, but his face was sickly pale and he was sweating; he looked like an onion which had sprouted after being stored in a warm place. He placed the little shoe over his mouth, tossed back his head and closed his eyes. Bringing the glass to his lips, he drew in his hollow cheeks as if he were gargling, and took a deep breath which produced a sound in his throat. When he opened his eyes, a broad smile appeared on his sickly face.

Old Five cocked his head and nodded in approval. "It's so important to eat well."

"Yes, eating well's very important", Little Cui replied, his spirits restored.

Mr Gou could no longer stand the heat with his overcoat on. As he began to remove it, he glanced around him and stopped. On the one hand, he wanted to put his coat in the safest possible position; on the other, he was concerned about maintaining his dignity. The coat hooks were placed too low. If he hung it there, the coat's lower half would rest on the seat, resulting in a few unattractive creases. Laying it flat on an empty seat would place it at a disadvantageous distance from himself, and estrange him from the otter-fur collar. Nor was it proper for him to hold it on his lap for very long, just as it was unacceptable to have one's concubine sitting on one's lap in public. Unable to make up his mind, he looked up at the overhead luggage rack where his eighteen pieces of luggage were arranged in a row: four bundles, five large baskets, two small baskets, two suitcases, one handbag, two bottles, a parcel wrapped in newspaper and another wrapped in glossy paper. He counted them. They occupied some six meters of space on the rack. To his great satisfaction, they were laid out without the slightest crowding. He was still clinging to his overcoat, and since he couldn't figure out what to do with it, he sat up even straighter.

"New Year's Eve, not home yet. New Year's Eve, not home yet." The rhythmic clicking of the wheels urged the train forward, but it moved as slowly as ever. The starry sky rose and fell; clusters of mountains, trees, villages and cemeteries receded into the darkness. After breaking out of one spell of blackness, the train would rush into the next. Smoke and sparks belched forth from the engine, while clouds of white steam and spray gushed out from the wheels and remained suspended in space after the train had gone; rushing ahead, rushing ahead, not missing a single breath, the train flew through the night. One moment of darkness, richly textured, faded away; another moment of darkness, perfectly empty, faded into the distance. Here there were snow banks, there a small range of hills; the snow was glistening white, the hills were dark and murky; all these things quickly disappeared. However, the train moved slowly, relentlessly slowly. "New Year's Eve, not home yet." The carriages were brightly lit and comfortably heated, but the passengers were anxious and impatient. Who could go to sleep at a time like this? "New Year's Eve, not home yet." Out with the old, in with the new; sacrifice to the Gods; bow down to the ancestors; paste New Year couplets up on door panels; set off firecrackers; make dumplings; eat mixed sweets. Fine wines and sumptuous cuisine were all there in their minds, in their mouths, by their ears, before their noses; but their laughter quickly faded into melancholy. Here they were on the train, but the only sounds they could hear were "New Year's Eve, not home yet." Outside, one dark shadow followed upon another; the starry sky rose and fell; out among the snow drifts, no human voices could be heard, nor a single horse-drawn cart; there was simply nothing to be seen. This unending, unfathomable darkness embraced the well-lit and comfortably heated train cars, dragging them along as if it would never let go. "New Year's Eve, not home yet."

Mr Zhang took two bottles of strong liquor down from the rack and rinsed out two tea bowls. "We're old friends now. Let's drink to it. We can celebrate again when we get home, but there's no reason we shouldn't enjoy ourselves here on the train. Enjoy today, forget tomorrow. Bottoms up, bottoms up! This is vintage wine from Yingkou — twenty years old. You can't buy this anywhere. I got it from a Manchurian bigwig who had a few bottles to spare. Drink up, this is fine stuff!"

Mr Qiao was hard put to refuse, but at the same time didn't feel like drinking right away. He stared at the little bowl in front of him, not knowing whether to take it or not. He sat for a moment trying to figure out what to do. From the overhead rack, he took down a large package wrapped in paper and opened it gently. Inside were a large number of small paper packages, each of which he felt with his fingers, the same way clerks in Chinese medicine shops check the contents of medicine bags against the doctor's prescription. He identified three bags accurately: dried lichees, dates, and five-spice-flavored dried beancurd. He only smiled in the direction of the wine after opening these packages. "Just like old friends. Let's not stand on ceremony!"

Mr Zhang cracked open a lichee with his fat fingers. The shell split with a festive "pop", a proper reminder of New Year's firecrackers. He watched while Mr Qiao took a drink and when he'd finished swallowing asked him, "How do you like it?"

"Excellent! Excellent!" Mr Qiao rolled back his tongue to prevent the heady fragrance from escaping from his mouth. "This is wine money can't buy!"

After exchanging several polite toasts, their faces turned bright red. They chatted about their families, their jobs, their friends, the difficulty of making a living, railroad passes.... When they clinked their bowls together, their hearts touched as well; their eyes were moist with tears, and their hearts burned so passionately that they couldn't help but open up to each other: Mr Qiao took out a package of candied kumquats. Mr Zhang thought he ought to open up a few packages of his own, but since he had already opened *two* bottles of wine, why not capitalize on that and prove to Mr Qiao that he wasn't a stingy person? "We're going to empty both of these bottles, one for you and one for me; down to the last drop! We're going to celebrate New Year's right! Anyway, it's not wine that makes you drunk. When good friends get together, it doesn't matter if we drink our fill. Drink up! Drink up!"

"But I'm not much of a drinker."

"What are you talking about? This is vintage stuff, twenty years old. You'll be perfectly all right. It's destiny that brings good people together for the first time on New Year's Eve."

Mr Qiao was moved by his candor. "Alright, then, I'll drink with you, to hell with the consequences!"

Little Cui seemed to have something on his mind, but Old Five felt the urge to go to the dining car for a nip or two and leave Little Cui behind to take a nap. "What do you say, shall we head for the dining car?" Old Five stood up and surveyed the interior of the car.

Little Cui made no response. Old Five noticed that Mr Gou was lying down across his seat, his feet resting on the armrest. He also noticed that Mr Gou's new light brown cotton and wool blend socks still had fresh creases in them. Mr Zhang and Mr Qiao, the two free pass holders, were drinking merrily. The battalion commander and the lieutenant were soundly asleep. The fireworks were resting quietly on the floor of the car, their red wrappers glistening like fresh blood. Old Five sneaked off to the dining car.

Little Cui curled up on his seat and closed his eyes, a half-smoked cigarette dangling from his lips.

Mr Zhang had nearly finished his bottle. He loosened his clothing, and sweat dripped down from his temples to his cheeks. His eyes were bloodshot and his tongue was numb, but he never stopped babbling. Because he'd lost partial control of his tongue, some of the things he said were somewhat on the coarse side, though he was still thinking straight. He was about to use abusive language with Mr Qiao, but he managed to curb his tongue, transforming his denunciations into bursts of strong emotion. But he didn't become impolite on account of having too much to drink. Mr Qiao had only drunk half a bottle, but his face was a ghostly pale. He fished out a pack of cigarettes and threw one to Mr Zhang. They both lit up. With smoke streaming from his mouth, Mr Zhang lay down on his back, his legs dangling over the edge of his seat. He had no cares in the world. He would have started singing "I've fallen into a drunken stupor. . . ." but his throat was hot and dry, in no condition for singing. He snorted through his nose like an angry bull. Mr Qiao lay down as well, cigarette in hand, with his eyes fixed diagonally across the aisle upon the lieutenant's feet. His heart was beating rapidly, he burped, and his pallid face felt itchy.

"New Year's Eve, not home yet." The sound of the train wheels clicked rapidly in Mr Zhang's ears. The faster they went, the more rapidly his heart beat, and soon all he could hear was a loud buzzing. His head started to spin like a rope swinging in the breeze. Everything around him — including his mind and his body — turned bright red, and a series of red circles appeared before his eyes. But a minute later, the buzzing stopped, the spinning diminished to a gentle sensation inside his body, and he opened his eyes cautiously. He recovered somewhat and, as if nothing at all had happened, groped for a match with his pudgy fingers. He relit his half-smoked cigarette and tossed the match away. Instantly, a large thick puff of smoke rose up from the table; the bowls, bottles and table top began to glow with a faint green light which shuddered as it rose gradually and began to spread. Mr Qiao woke up startled to discover that his cigarette was on fire. He tossed it onto the floor and groped in the direction of the table, knocking over the bottles and bowls and spilling the liquor, while the little paper packages started to burn in a rainbow of colors. A ring of flames revolved around Mr Zhang's face like a torch dance. Mr Qiao thought about getting up and running away, but the flames from the burning packages on the table spread to all the paper parcels on the luggage rack, which seemed to stretch out their arms to embrace them. Mr Qiao was on fire head to toe; his eyebrows were singed off; his hair smoldered with a crackle; and when the flames reached his lips, still dripping with liquor, they too started to burn. Mr Qiao looked like the statue of the celestial judge who spits forth flames from his mouth.

Suddenly there was a loud series of explosions. The platoon lieutenant had just awoken from his nap when a "double charger" blew up by the side of his nose, spattering blood and sparks all over him; he stood up in a panic; there were more explosions all around him, as if he had walked into the center of a minefield. Before the battalion commander could stand up, his entire body was covered in flames, and his right eye had been blown to bits.

Mr Gou awoke with a start. He glanced up at the luggage rack, and noticed that some of his paper packages were burning. The flames bore down upon him like a fiery dragon with its pointed scales made of flames. He made up his mind to break a window and jump out, and removed one of his shoes to accomplish this. The window shattered; the wind rushed in, feeding the flames. His otter-fur collar, his four bundles and five baskets, and all his clothing were perfect fuel for the flames. The train sped on through the night, the wind whistling and the fireworks exploding one after another. Mr Gou panicked.

Little Cui was so inured to train travel that nothing could wake him up. The fire began at his feet, searing his entire body, fusing all the opium he was carrying on his person into a single sticky mass. He sat up quickly, and was nearly blinded by the smoke, explosions, flames and light. The burning opium gave off a wonderfully intoxicating odor, but his legs were so badly burned that he could not budge. Gradually the opium oozed its way upwards along the length of his body, forming a huge bubble which enveloped him like a cocoon.

Little Cui couldn't move. Mr Zhang was too drunk to move; Mr Qiao was panicking; Mr Gou was panicking; the lieutenant was panicking; and the battalion commander was kneeling on his seat, screaming in pain. The train car itself was now on fire, and the smell of sulphur permeated the air. The paper and cloth stopped burning as the fireworks fizzled out. There were fewer explosions, and the smoke thickened; while the flames burned on, the smoke spread to every corner of the car; those who attempted to escape fell down; those who were kneeling down ceased screaming; the smoke thickened; the flames attacked the wooden seats; the train sped on; the wind rushed in through the windows; red tongues of flame darted out from the clouds of smoke, seeking an escape route. The flames burned brighter, white smoke and flames streamed out of the windows, illuminating the entire train in a gorgeous blazing spectacle. More flames trailed behind the train like a tail composed of a hundred torches.

The train came to a small station but did not stop. When the staff exchanger exchanged staffs with the engineer, he said to himself, "Fire!" When the signal man gave the green light he said to himself, "Fire!" When the switchman threw the switch, and when the railroad policeman stood at attention on the platform, they both said to themselves, "Fire!" The stationmaster was half drunk. By the time he made it to the platform, the train had already left the station. When he looked down the tracks, he thought he saw flames, but he told himself he was seeing things. The staff exchanger replaced the staff in its proper place; the signal man snuffed out his lamp; the switchman readjusted the switch; and the policeman shouldered his rifle and returned to the waiting room. They all remembered they had seen a fire on the train, but none of them felt it worthwhile mentioning. A few minutes later, all that remained of this particular fire turned to ashes in their minds, and they sat around chatting about how they were going to celebrate the New Year. They then set off firecrackers, drank wine and played mahjong — here, at least, all the world was at peace.

After leaving the station, the train increased speed. The wind fed the flames and sparks flashed in every direction. The night was as dense as black lacquer; the train burned like a giant lamp, spitting up and swallowing countless tongues of fire. All that remained now of the second class carriage was its shape, a charred skeleton engulfed in flames. Hungry flames licked at the air, but disappointed in finding no flammable objects, inched their way down the aisles in both directions and entered the third class cars. Smoke took up the vanguard — smoke scented with the putrid odor of raw meat and the sickening sweetness of charred flesh. First smoke, then flames, then the frenzied cries of "Fire! Fire! Fire!" as the third class passengers panicked. In the chaos which followed, some broke windows, but just stood before them too terrified to jump; some tried to make their way to the doors but collided with others who had the same intentions; some remained in their seats, rendered mute by their fear; some gathered up their bamboo baskets. . . . It was a scene of helplessness, chaos and terror. The flames burned before their very eyes, setting their torsos and heads on fire. People screamed, covered their heads with their hands, patted their clothing, rushed for the exits, leaped off the train. . . .

The blaze had discovered a new territory to colonize; with such an abundance of people and things, it went mad with joy. One flame shot out in a short leap while another flew off into the distance; one flame disguised itself in a cloud of smoke while another slipped out of the window; one flame wandered aimlessly about while another shunted back and forth through the car, leaving a trail of fire behind it. Assuming countless guises and forms, the flames came together in a fiery dance. Some merged to form balls of fire and flaming comets; others became burning walls of red and green flames; flashing on and off, they crept forward at the whim of the wind; suddenly they would break through a barrier of smoke and surge ahead like a giant wave of flame. With audible crackling, human flesh roasted and hair burned, the sounds growing more complex as boxes and baskets fell off the racks and passengers moaned and wailed; further fiery blasts were spurred on by the whistling wind. The entire train was on fire now; dense smoke and leaping flames turned it into a mass cremation of tragic proportions.

The train came to another station where it was scheduled to stop. The staff exchanger, signalman, ticket collector, policemen, porters, stationmaster, assistant stationmaster, clerks, secretaries, and factotums all stared at the train, but there wasn't a single fire extinguisher in the station. On the second class car and the two third class cars in front and behind, there were no sounds and no movement. All that remained were several slowly-rising columns of white smoke and a few steadily burning flames. It was a scene of perfect quietude.

The reports said that a total of fifty-two corpses were recovered on the train. Another eleven bodies were found along the line; these were the remains of passengers who had jumped from the train.

After the Lantern Festival, two weeks after New Year's Day, the investigation team arrived on the scene. There were dinner invitations from many quarters and a busy banquet schedule ensued. After three days of feasting and drinking, there was hardly any time left for a proper investigation. The members of the team had some personal business to attend to, and since this naturally came first, the investigation was postponed for another three days.

The chief conductor knew nothing about what happened, the chief ticket inspector knew nothing about what happened, the second ticket inspector knew nothing about what happened, and the man from Tianjin knew nothing about what happened. Also, the Shandong man knew nothing and Old Five knew nothing, so the cause of the fire was never discovered. The total number of tickets sold at all the stations along the line tallied with the number of tickets inspected on the train. Precisely sixty-three tickets were missing; it was assumed that all the tickets went up in smoke along with the train, since this was the exact number of corpses recovered. No stations reported selling any second class tickets. Since the second class car had been empty, it was eliminated as a possible source of the fire.

Old Five was questioned. Though he knew nothing about what happened, he was in the dining car when the fire started. His job was second class steward. Why had he left his post without proper authorization? Though the cause of the fire remained undetermined, this was a serious breach of railroad regulations and Old Five was dismissed from his job as a punishment.

The investigation team returned to their offices. Their detailed final report was written in an elegant literary style.

"I was supposed to get off on New Year's Eve. Then they insist I have to work that night. So who gives a damn if I keep that job or not." Old Five extended his long neck towards his wife. "Let 'em fire me. That's fine with me. If they don't want me, I can still take care of myself. Don't worry about it. You think getting kicked off the railroad means we're going to starve to death?"

"I'm not worried about that," Old Five's wife said, trying to console her husband, "but it still bugs me the way those fresh turnips you were bringing me got burned in the fire."

Translated by Don J. Cohn

Crescent Moon

YES, I've seen the crescent moon again — a chill sickle of pale gold. How many times have I seen crescent moons just like this one, how many times. . . . It stirred many different emotions, brought back many different scenes. As I sat and stared at it, I recalled each time I had seen it hanging in the blue firmament. It awakened my memories like an evening breeze blowing open the petals of a flower that is craving for sleep.

2

The first time, the chill crescent moon really brought a chill. My first recollection of it is a bitter one. I remember its feeble pale gold beams shining through my tears. I was only seven then — a little girl in a red padded jacket. I wore a blue cloth hat Mama had made for me. There were small flowers printed on it. I remember. I stood leaning against the doorway of our small room, gazing at the crescent moon. The room was filled with the smell of medicine and smoke, with Mama's tears, with Papa's illness. I stood alone on the steps looking at the moon. No one bothered about me, no one cooked my supper. I knew there was tragedy in that room, for everyone said Papa's illness was. . . . But I felt much more sorry for myself. I was cold, hungry, neglected.

I stood there until the moon had set. I had nothing; I couldn't restrain my tears. But the sound of Mama's weeping drowned out my own. Papa was silent; a white cloth covered his face. I wanted to raise the cloth and look at him, but I didn't dare. There was so little space in our room, and Papa occupied it all.

Mama put on white mourning clothes. A white robe without stitched hems was placed over my red jacket. I remember because I kept breaking off the loose white threads along the edges. There was a lot of noise and grief-stricken crying, everyone was very busy; but actually there wasn't much to be done. It hardly seemed worth so much fuss. Papa was placed in a coffin made of four thin boards; the coffin was full of cracks. Then five or six men carried him out. Mama and I followed behind, weeping. I remember Papa; I remember his wooden box. That box meant the end of him. I knew unless I could break it open I'd never see him again. But they buried it deep in the ground in a cemetery outside the city wall. Although I knew exactly where it was, I was afraid it would be hard to find that box again. The earth seemed to swallow it like a drop of rain.

3

Mama and I were both wearing white gowns again the next time I saw the crescent moon. It was a cold day, and Mama was taking me to visit Papa's grave. She had bought some gold and silver "ingots" made of paper to burn and send to Papa in the next world. Mama was especially good to me that day. When I was tired, she carried me piggy-back; at the city gate she bought me some roasted chestnuts. Everything was cold, only the chestnuts were hot. Instead of eating them, I used them to warm my hands.

I don't remember how far we walked, but it was very, very far. It hadn't seemed nearly so far the day we buried Papa, perhaps because a lot of people had gone with us. This time there was only Mama and me. She didn't speak. I didn't feel like saying anything either. It was very quiet out there. On that yellow dirt road there wasn't a breath of sound.

It was winter, and the days were short. I remember the grave — a small mound of earth. There were some brown hills in the distance, with the sunlight slanting on them. Mama seemed to have no time for me. She set me down on the side and embraced the head of the grave and wept. I sat holding the hot chestnuts. After crying a while, Mama burned the paper ingots. The ashes swirled before us in little spirals, then lazily settled back on the ground. There wasn't much wind, but it was very cold.

Mama began to cry again. I thought of Papa too, but I didn't cry for him. It was Mama's pitiful weeping that brought tears to my eyes. I pulled her by the hand and said, "Don't cry, Mama, don't cry." But she sobbed all the harder and hugged me to her bosom.

The sun was nearly set and there wasn't another person in sight. Only Mama and me. That seemed to scare Mama a little. With tears in her eyes she led me away. After we had walked a while, she turned and looked back. I did too. I couldn't tell Papa's grave from the others any more. There were nothing but graves on the hillside. Hundreds of small mounds, right to the foot of the hill. Mama sighed.

We walked and walked, sometimes fast, sometimes slow. We still hadn't reached the city gate when I saw the crescent moon again. All around us was darkness and silence. Only the crescent moon gave off a cold glow. I was worn out. Mama carried me. How we got back to the city I don't know. I only remember hazily that there was a crescent moon in the sky.

4

By the time I was eight, I had learned how to take things to the pawnshop. I knew that if I didn't come back with some money, Mama and I would have nothing to eat that night — Mama would never send me except as a last resort. Whenever she handed me a small package it meant there wasn't even thin gruel in the bottom of our pot. Our pot was often cleaner than a neat young widow.

One day I was sent to the pawnshop with a mirror. This seemed to be the only thing we could spare, though Mama used it every day. It was spring, and our padded clothes had just been placed in hock. I knew how to be careful. Carrying the mirror, I walked carefully but quickly to the pawnshop. It was already open.

I was afraid of that pawnshop's big red door, afraid of its high counter. Whenever I saw that door, my heart beat fast. But I'd go in just the same, even if I had to crawl over the high door-sill. Taking a grip on myself, I would hand up my package and say loudly, "I want to pawn this." After getting my money and the pawn ticket, I would hold them carefully and hurry home. I knew Mama would be worried.

But this time they didn't want the mirror. They said I should add another item to it. I knew what that meant. Putting the mirror in my shirt, I ran home as fast as my legs could carry me. Mama cried; she couldn't find anything else to pawn. I had always thought there were a lot of things in our little room. But now, helping Mama look for a piece of clothing to raise some money on, I saw that we didn't have much at all.

Mama decided not to send me to the pawnshop again, but when I asked her, "Mama, what are we going to eat?" she cried and gave me her silver hairpin. It was the last bit of silver she had left. She had taken it out of her hair several times before, but she had never been able to part with it. Grandma had given it to her when she got married. Now Mama gave it to me — her last bit of silver — to pawn together with the mirror.

I ran with all my might to the pawnshop, but the big door was already shut tight. Clutching the silver hairpin, I sat down on the steps and cried softly, not daring to make too much noise. I looked up at the sky. Ah, there was the crescent moon shining through my tears again.

I wept for a long time. Then Mama came out of the shadows and took me by the hand. Oh, what a nice warm hand. I forgot all my troubles, even my hunger. As long as Mama's warm hand was holding mine, everything was all right.

"Ma," I sobbed, "let's go home and sleep. I'll come again early tomorrow morning."

Mama didn't say anything. After we had walked a while I said, "Ma, you see that crescent moon? It hung crooked just like that the day Pa died. Why is it always so slant?"

Mama remained silent. But her hand trembled a little.

5

All day long, Mama washed clothes for people. I wanted to help her, but there wasn't any way I could do it. I would wait for her; I wouldn't go to sleep until she finished. Sometimes, even after the crescent moon had already risen, she would still be scrubbing away. Those smelly socks, hard as cowhide, were brought in by salesmen and clerks from the shops. By the time Mama finished washing the "cowhide" she never had any appetite.

I would sit beside her, looking at the moon, watching the bats flit through its rays, like big triangular water-chestnuts flashing across beams of silver then quickly dropping into the darkness again.

The more I pitied Mama, the more I loved the crescent moon. Gazing at it always eased my heart. I loved it in the summer most of all. It was always so cool, so icy. I loved the faint shadows it cast upon the ground, though they never lasted very long. Soft and grey, they soon vanished, leaving the earth especially dark and the stars especially bright and the flowers especially fragrant. Our neighbours had many flower bushes. Blossoms from a tall locust tree used to drift into our courtyard and cover the ground like a layer of snow.

6

Mama's hands became hard and scaly. They felt wonderful when she rubbed my back. But I hated to trouble her, because her hands were all swollen from the water. She was thin too; often she couldn't eat a thing after washing those stinking socks. I knew she was trying to think of a way out. I knew. She used to push the pile of dirty clothes to one side and become lost in thought. Sometimes she would talk to herself. What was she planning? I couldn't guess.

7

Mama told me to be good and call him "Pa" — she had found me another father. Mama didn't look at me when she told me this. There were tears in her eyes, and she said, "I can't let you starve!"

Oh, so it was to keep me from starving that she found me another Pa? I didn't understand much, and I was a little afraid. But I was kind of hopeful too — maybe we really wouldn't go hungry any more.

What a coincidence! As we were leaving our tiny flat, a crescent moon again hung in the sky. It was brighter and more frightening than I had ever seen it before. I was going to leave the small room I had grown so accustomed to. Ma sat in a red bridal sedan-chair. Ahead of her marched a few tootling musicians who played very badly. The man and I followed behind. He held me by the hand. The crescent moon gave off faint rays that seemed to tremble in the cool breeze.

The streets were deserted except for stray dogs that barked at the musicians. The sedan-chair moved very quickly. Where was it going? Was it taking Mama outside the city, to the cemetery? The man pulled me along so fast I could hardly catch my breath. I couldn't even cry. His sweating palm was cold, like a fish. I wanted to call "Ma!" but I didn't dare. The crescent moon looked like a large half-closed eye. In a little while, the sedan-chair entered a small lane.

8

During the next three or four years I somehow never saw the crescent moon.

My new Pa was very good to me. He had two rooms. He and Ma lived in the inner room; I slept on a pallet in the outside one. At first I still wanted to sleep with Mama, but after a few days I began to love "my" little room. It had clean whitewashed walls, a table and a chair. They all seemed to belong to me. My bedding was thicker and warmer, too.

Mama gradually put on some weight. Colour came back to her cheeks, and the scales left her hands. I hadn't been to the pawnshop in a long time. My new father let me go to school. Sometimes he even played with me. I don't know why I couldn't bring myself to call him "Pa" — I liked him a lot.

He seemed to understand. He used to just grin at me. His eyes looked very nice then. Mama would privately urge me to call him "Pa". I didn't really want to be stubborn. I knew it was because of him that Mama and I had food to eat and clothes to wear. I understood all that.

Yes, for three or four years I don't recall seeing the crescent moon; maybe I saw it and don't remember.

But I can never forget the crescent moon I saw when Pa died, or the one that rode before Ma's bridal sedan-chair. That pale chill light will always remain in my heart, shiny and cool as a piece of jade. Sometimes when I think of it, it seems as if I can almost reach out my hand and touch it.

9

I loved going to school. I had the feeling that the school-yard was full of flowers, though, actually, this wasn't so. Yet whenever I think of school I think of flowers. Just as whenever I think of Papa's grave I think of a crescent moon outside the city — hanging crooked in the wind blowing across the fields.

Mama loved flowers too. She couldn't afford them, but if anyone ever sent her one, she pinned it in her hair. Once I had the chance to pick a couple for her. With a fresh flower in her hair, she looked very young from the back. She was happy, and so was I.

Going to school also made me very glad. Perhaps this is the reason whenever I think of school I think of flowers.

10

The year I was to graduate from primary school, Mama sent me to the pawnshop again. I don't know why my new father suddenly left us. Mama didn't seem to know where he went either. She told me to continue going to school; she thought he'd probably come back soon.

Many days passed and there was still no sign of him. He didn't even write. I was afraid Mama would have to start washing dirty socks again, and I felt very badly about it.

But Mama had other plans. She still dressed prettily and wore flowers in her hair. How strange! She didn't cry; in fact she was always smiling. Why? I didn't understand. For several days whenever I came home from school, I'd find her standing in the doorway. Not long after, men began to hail me on the street:

"Hey, tell your Ma I'll be calling on her soon!"

"Young and tender, are you selling today?"

My face burning like fire, I hung my head till it couldn't go any lower. I knew now, but there wasn't anything I could do about it. I couldn't question Mama, no, I couldn't do that. She was so good to me, always urging, "Read your books, study hard."

But she was illiterate herself. Why was she so anxious for me to study? I grew suspicious. But then I would think — she's doing this because she has no way out. When I felt suspicious, I wanted to curse her. At other times, I would want to hug her and beg her not to do that kind of thing any more.

I hated myself for not being able to help Mama. I was worried. Even when I graduated from primary school, what use would I be? I heard from the girls in my class that several of the students who graduated last year became concubines; a few, they said, were working "in dark doorways". I didn't quite understand these things, but from the way my classmates spoke, I guessed it was something bad. The girls in my class seemed to know everything; they loved to whisper about things which they knew perfectly well were not nice. It made them blush, yet, at the same time, look quite self-satisfied.

My suspicion of Mama increased. Was she waiting for me to graduate, so that she could make me...?

When I thought like this, I didn't dare go home. I was afraid to face Mama. I used to save the pennies she gave me to buy afternoon snacks, and go to physical training class on an empty stomach. I was often faint. How I envied the other kids, munching their pastries. But I had to save money. With a little money I could run away if Mama insisted that I. . . .

At my richest, I never managed to save more than ten or fifteen cents. Even during the day, I used to gaze up at the sky, looking for my crescent moon. If the misery in my heart could be compared to anything physical, it should be that crescent moon — hanging helpless and unsupported in the grey-blue sky, its feeble rays soon swallowed up by the darkness.

II

What made me feel worst of all was that I was slowly learning to hate Mama. But whenever I hated her, I couldn't help remembering how she carried me piggyback to visit Papa's grave — and then I couldn't hate her any more. Yet I had to. My heart . . . my heart was like that crescent moon — only able to shine a little while, surrounded by a darkness that was black and limitless.

Men constantly came to Mama's room now; she no longer tried to hide it from me. They looked at me like dogs — drooling, their tongues hanging out. In their eyes I was an even tastier morsel than Mama. I could see it.

In a short time, I suddenly came to understand a lot. I knew I had to protect myself. I could feel that my body had something precious; I was aware of my own fragrance. I felt ashamed; I was torn by one emotion after another. There was a force within me that I could use to protect myself — or destroy myself. At times I was firm and strong. At times I was weak, defenceless, confused.

I wanted to love Mama. There were so many things I wanted to ask her. I needed her comforting. But it was just at that time that I had to shun her, hate her — or lose my own existence.

Lying sleepless on my bed and considering the matter calmly, I could see that Mama deserved to be pitied. She had to feed the two of us. But then I would think — how could I eat the food she earned that way?

That was how my mood kept changing. Like a winter wind — halting a moment, then blowing fiercer than ever. I would quietly watch my fury rising within me, and be powerless to stop it.

12

Before I could think of a solution, things became worse. Mama asked me, "What about it?" If I really loved her, she said, I ought to help her. Otherwise, she couldn't continue taking care of me. These didn't seem like words that Mama could speak, yet she said them. To make it even clearer, she added:

"I'm getting old. In another year or two, men won't want me even if I offer myself for nothing."

It was true. Lately you could see the wrinkles on Mama's face no matter how much powder she used. She no longer had the energy to entertain a lot of men; she was thinking of giving herself to only one. There was a man who ran a steamed bread shop who wanted her.

She could go to him right away. But I was a big girl now. I couldn't trail after her bridal sedan-chair like I did when I was a child. I would have to look after myself. If I would agree to "help" Mama, she wouldn't have to go to him. I could earn money for us both.

I was quite willing to earn money, but when I thought of the way she wanted me to do it, it made me shiver. I knew next to nothing; how could I peddle myself like some middle-aged woman? Mama's heart was hard, and the need for money was harder still. She didn't force me to take this road or that. She left the choice to me. Either help her, or we two would go our separate ways. Mama didn't cry. Her eyes had long since gone dry.

What was I to do?

13

I spoke to the principal of my school. She was a stout woman of about forty, not very bright, but a warm-hearted generous person. I was really at my wit's end, otherwise how could I have said anything about Mama. . . ? Actually, I didn't know the principal very well, and every word I spoke seared my throat like a ball of fire. I stammered and took a long time to get out what I had to say.

The principal said she was willing to help me. She couldn't give me any money, but she could give me two meals a day and a place to live — I could move in with an old woman servant who lived at the school. She said I could help the scribe with his writing — but not right away, because I still needed more practice with my handwriting.

Two meals a day and a place to live — that settled the biggest problem. I didn't have to be a burden to Mama any more.

Mama didn't ride in a bride's sedan-chair when she left this time. She simply took a rickshaw and went off into the night. She let me keep my bedding.

Mama tried not to cry as she was leaving, but the tears in her heart gushed out after all. She knew I couldn't come to see her — her own daughter. As for me, I had forgotten even how to weep properly — I sobbed open-mouthed, the tears smothering my face. I was her daughter, her friend, her solace. But I couldn't help her. Not unless I agreed to something I just couldn't do.

After she had gone, I sat and thought. We two, mother and daughter, were like a couple of stray dogs. For the sake of our mouths, we had to accept all kinds of suffering, as if no other parts of our bodies mattered. only our mouths. We had to sell all the rest of us to feed our mouths.

I didn't hate Mama. I understood. It wasn't her fault; it wasn't wrong of her to have a mouth. The fault lay with food. By what right were we deprived of food?

Recollections of past troubles flooded back on me. But the crescent moon that was most familiar with my tears didn't appear this time. It was pitch dark, without even the glow of fireflies. Mama had disappeared into the darkness like a ghost, silent, shadowless. If she were to die tomorrow, she probably couldn't be buried beside Papa. I wouldn't even be able to find her grave. She was my only Mama, my only friend. And now I was left alone in the world.

I could never see Mama again. Love died in my heart, like a spring flower nipped by frost. I practised hard with my writing so that I could help the scribe copy minor documents for the principal. I had to become useful — I was eating other people's food. I couldn't be like the other girls in my class, who did nothing but watch others all day long — observing what other people ate, what they wore, what they said. I concentrated on myself. My shadow was my only friend. "I" was always in my mind, because no one loved me. I loved myself, pitied, encouraged, scolded myself. I knew myself, as if I were another person.

My body changed in a way that frightened and pleased me, yet left me puzzled. When I touched them with my hand it was like brushing against delicate, tender flowers.

I was concerned only with the present. There was no future; I didn't dare to think too far ahead. Because I was eating other people's food, I had to know when it was noon and when it was evening. Otherwise I wouldn't have thought of time at all. Without hope there isn't any time. I seemed nailed down to a place that had no days or months. When I thought of my life with Mama, I knew I had existed for fifteen or sixteen years. My schoolmates were always looking forward to vacations, festivals, the New Year holiday. What had these things to do with me?

But my body was continuing to mature. I could feel it. It confused me. I couldn't trust myself. I knew I was growing prettier. Beauty raised my social stature. That was a consolation — until I remembered that

I never had any social stature to begin with; then the consolation turned sour. Still, in the end, I was proud of my good looks. Poor but pretty! Suddenly, a frightening thought came to me — Mama wasn't bad looking either.

15

I hadn't seen the crescent moon for a long time. Even though I wanted to see it, I didn't dare look. I had already graduated and was still living at the school. In the evenings I was alone with two old servants — a man and a woman. They didn't quite know how to treat me. I was no longer a student, yet I wasn't a teacher; nor was I a servant, though in some ways I resembled one.

At night I walked alone in the courtyard. Often I was driven into my room by the crescent moon. I hadn't the courage to face it. But in my room I would picture it, especially when there was a slight breeze. The breeze seemed able to blow those pale beams directly to my heart, making me recall the past, intensifying my forebodings of tragedy. My heart was like a bat in the moonlight — a dark thing in spite of the light; black — even though it could fly, still black. I had no hope. But I didn't cry. I only frowned.

16

I earned a little money, knitting for some of the girl students. The principal let me. But I couldn't make much because they knew how to knit too. The girls only came to me when they were too busy to do it themselves. Still, my heart felt lighter. I even thought — if Mama could come back, I could support her.

When I counted my money, I knew this was just an idle dream. But it made me feel better anyhow. I wished I could find her. If she would see me, she'd surely come away with me. We could get along, I thought. But I didn't altogether believe this myself. I was always thinking of Mama. Often, I saw her in my dreams.

One day I went with the students on an outing in the country. On the way back, because it was getting late, we took a shortcut through a small lane. There I saw Mama! Outside this steamed bread shop was a big basket with a large wooden object in it painted white to look like a steamed bread. Mama sat by the wall, pulling and pushing a lever that blew up the fire in the oven. While we were still quite a distance away I saw Mama and that white wooden steamed bread. I recognized her from the back. I wanted to rush over and embrace her. But I didn't dare. I was afraid the students would laugh at me. They wouldn't let me have such a Mama.

We came closer and closer. I lowered my head and looked at her through my tears. She didn't see me. The whole group of us brushed by her. Intent on pulling the bellows' lever, evidently she didn't see a thing.

When we were far beyond her, I turned around and looked back. She was still plying that lever. I couldn't see her features clearly; I had only the impression of a few stray locks hanging down over her forehead. I made a mental note of the name of the lane.

17

It was as if a little bug was gnawing at my heart. I had to see Mama or I'd have no peace.

Just at this time, a new principal was appointed to the school. The stout lady who was leaving told me I'd better start making other plans. As long as she remained she could give me food and lodgings, but she couldn't guarantee that the new principal would do the same.

I counted my money. Altogether I had two dollars and seventy some odd cents. This would keep me from starving for the next few days. But where was I to go?

There was no point in sitting around worrying. I had to think of something.

Go see Mama — that was my first diea. But could she let me stay with her? If she couldn't, it might provoke a quarrel between her and the steamed bread seller; at least it would make her feel very badly. I had to think of things from her viewpoint. She was my Mama, and yet she wasn't. We were separated by a wall of poverty.

After mulling it over, I decided not to go to her. I had to bear my own burdens. But how? I didn't know. The world seemed very small — there was no place for me and my little roll of bedding. Even a dog was better off. He could lie down anywhere and sleep. I wouldn't be permitted to sleep on the street. Yes, I was a person, but a person was less than a dog.

What if I should refuse to leave? Would the new principal drive me out? I couldn't wait for that. It was spring. I saw the flowers and the green leaves, but I felt no breath of warmth. The red of the flowers and the green of the leaves were only colours to me; they had no special significance. Spring, in my heart, was something cold and dead. I didn't want to cry, but the tears flowed from my eyes.

18

I went job-hunting. I wouldn't go to Mama. I wouldn't depend on anyone. I would earn my own food.

Hopefully, I searched for two whole days. But I brought back a harvest of only dust and tears. There was no work for me to do. It was then that I truly understood Mama, really forgave her. At least she had washed smelly socks. I wasn't even able to do that. Mama took the only road that was left. The learning and morality the school had given me were just jokes, playthings for people with full stomachs and time to spare. The students wouldn't permit me to have a Mama like mine; they sneered at women who sold themselves. That was all right for them; they got their meals regularly.

I practically made up my mind — I would do anything. If only some one would feed me. Mama was admirable. I wouldn't kill myself — although I had thought of it. No, I wanted to live. I was young, pretty, I wanted to live. Any shame would be none of my doing.

19

Thinking like that, it was as if I had already found a job. I dared to walk in the courtyard in the moonlight. A spring crescent moon hung in the sky. I saw it and it was beautiful. The sky was dark blue, without a speck of cloud. Bright and warm, the crescent moon bathed the willow branches with its soft beams. A breeze, laden with the fragrance of flowers, blew the shadow of the willow branches back and forth from the bright corner of the courtyard wall to the darkened section. The light was not strong; the shadows were not deep. The breeze blew tenderly. Everything was warm, drowsy, yet gently in motion. Below the moon and above the willows a pair of stars like the smiling eyes of a fairy maiden winked mischievously at that slanting crescent moon and those trailing branches. A tree by the wall was a galaxy of white blossoms. In the moonlight, half the tree was snowy white, half was dappled with soft grey shadows. A picture of incredible purity.

That crescent moon is the beginning of my hope, I said to myself.

20

I went to see the stout lady principal again, but she wasn't home. A young man let me in. He was very handsome, and very friendly. Usually, I'm afraid of men, but this young man didn't frighten me a bit. I couldn't very well refuse to answer his questions — he had such a winning smile. I told him why I wanted to see the principal. He was very concerned. He promised to help me.

That same night, he came and gave me two dollars. When I tried to refuse, he said the money was from his aunt — the stout principal. She had already found me a place to live, he added. I could move in the next day. I was a little suspicious at first, but his smiles went right to my heart. I felt it was wrong to doubt a person who was so considerate, so charming.

21

His smiling lips were on my cheek, and I could see the crescent moon, smiling too, upon his hair. The intoxicated spring breeze had blown open the spring clouds to reveal the crescent moon and a pair of spring stars. Trailing willow branches stirred along the river bank, frogs throbbed their love songs, the fragrance of young rushes filled the spring night. I could hear water flowing, bringing nourishment to the tender rushes so that they might quickly grow tall and strong. Young shoots were growing on the moist warm earth; every living thing was absorbing spring's vitality and giving off a lovely perfume.

I forgot myself; I had no self. I seemed to dissolve into that gentle spring breeze, those faint moon beams. Suddenly, a cloud covered the moon. I had lost the crescent moon, and myself as well. I was the same as Mama!

22

I was regretful, yet eased. I wanted to cry, but was very happy I didn't know how I felt. I wanted to go away and never see him again. But he was always on my mind, and I was lonesome without him.

I lived alone in a small room. He came to me every night — always handsome, always tender. He provided me with food, he bought me clothing. When I put on a new gown, I could see that I was beautiful. I hated the clothes, but I couldn't bear to part with them.

I didn't dare to think; I was too indolent to think. I drifted about in a daze, rouge on my cheeks. I didn't feel like dressing up, yet I had to. There was no other way to kill time. While putting my finery on, I adored my image in the mirror; then, when I finished, I hated myself.

Tears came easily to my eyes now, though I managed not to weep. My eyes — always moist and glistening — looked lovely.

Sometimes I would kiss him madly, then push him away, even curse him. He never stopped smiling.

23

I knew there was no hope from the start. Any wisp of cloud could cover a crescent moon. My future was dark.

Sure enough, not long after, as spring was changing to summer, my spring dream ended.

One day, just about noon, a young woman came to see me. She was very pretty, in a vapid, doll-like way. The moment she entered the room she began to weep. There was no need for her to say anything; I knew already.

She hadn't come to raise a row, nor did I want to quarrel with her. She was a simple, honest sort. Crying, she took my hand. "He deceived us both!" she said.

I had thought she was also a "sweetheart". But no, she was his wife. She didn't berate me. She just kept repeating, "Please let him go!"

I didn't know what to do. I felt very sorry for the

young woman. Finally, I consented and, at once, she was all smiles. She appeared to be completely guileless, and quite naive. All she knew was that she wanted her husband.

24

I walked the streets for hours. It had been easy enough to agree to what that young woman had asked, but what was I to do now? I didn't want the things he had given me. Since we were parting, I ought to make the break complete. But they were all I had to my name. Where was I to go? Would I be able to eat that day? His gifts at least were worth a little money. Very well, I'd keep them. I had no choice.

Quietly, I moved away. Though I had no regrets, there was an emptiness in my heart. I was like a lone and drifting cloud.

I rented a small room. Then I went to bed and slept right around the clock.

25

I was good at economizing. Since childhood I had known how precious money was. I still had a couple of dollars, but I decided to go out and look for a job immediately. Though I had no great hopes, it seemed like the safest course.

But job-hunting hadn't become any easier just because I was a year or two older than last time. I kept trying, not that I thought it would do any good, but because I felt it was the proper thing to do.

Why was it so hard for a woman to earn a living? Mama was right. She took the only road open to a woman. Though I knew it was waiting for me, not far off, I didn't want to take that road yet.

The more I struggled, the more frightened I became. My hope was like the light of a new moon; in a little while it would be gone.

Two weeks later, just as I was about to give up, I stood in a line of girls in a cheap restaurant. The restaurant was very small; the boss, who was looking us over, was very big. We were a rather attractive bunch — all primary school graduates, but we waited for that great broken-down tub of a boss to pick one of us as if he were an emperor.

He chose me. Though I wasn't the least grateful, at the moment I couldn't help feeling good. The girls all seemed to envy me. As they left, some had tears in their eyes. A few cursed under their breath — "How can women be worth so little!"

26

I became the small restaurant's Second Hostess. I didn't know anything about waiting on tables and I was rather scared. The First Hostess told me not to worry — she didn't either. She said the waiter took care of that. All the hostess had to do was serve tea, hand out damp face cloths and present the bill at the end of the meal.

Strange. First Hostess wore her sleeves rolled up to her elbow, but the white linings were quite spotless. Tied to her wrist was a fancy handkerchief embroidered with the words "Little Sister, I love you." She was always powdering her face, and the lipstick on her big mouth made it look like bloody ladle. When lighting a cigarette for a customer, she would press her knee against his leg. She also poured the drinks: sometimes she took a sip herself. To some customers she was very attentive; others she would completely ignore. She had a way of batting her eyes and pretending she didn't see them. It was up to me to look after the ones she neglected.

I was afraid of men. I had learned from that little experience of mine — love or no love, men were monsters. The customers at our restaurant were particularly repulsive. They put on a great show of grabbing for the bill. They played noisy drinking games and ate like pigs. They picked fault over the smallest trifles, and cursed and raged.

While serving them tea or handing out face cloths, I kept my head down and blushed. They talked to me and tried to make me laugh. But I wanted nothing to do with them. At nine o'clock when my first day's work was over, I was worn out. I went to my little room and lay down; without even taking my clothes off, I slept until the next day. When I awoke, I felt better. I was self-supporting, earning my own keep. I reported for work very early.

27

When First Hostess showed up, after nine, I had already been on the job two hours. Contemptuously, but not altogether unkindly, she explained, "You don't have to come so early. Who eats here at eight o'clock in the morning? And another thing, droopy puss, don't always be pulling such a long face. You're supposed to be a hostess, not a pallbearer. Keep your head down like that all the time and nobody'll order any extra drinks. What do you think you're here for? You're dressed all wrong, too. Your gown should have a high collar — and where's your chiffon handkerchief? You don't even look like a hostess!"

I knew she meant well. If I didn't smile at the customers, I'd lose out and so would she, for we all split the tips equally. I didn't look down on her; in one sense, I even admired her — she knew how to earn money. Playing up to men — that was the only way a woman could get along.

But I didn't want to imitate her, though I could see clearly enough that the day might be coming when I would have to be even more free and easy than she to earn my food. But that would be only when all other means failed. The "last resort" was always lying in wait for us women. I was just trying to make it wait a little longer.

Angrily, I gritted my teeth and struggled on. But a woman's fate is never in her own hands. Three days later the boss warned me — he'd give me two more days; if I wanted to keep the job, I'd have to act like First Hostess. Half in jest, First Hostess also dropped me a hint:

"One of the customers has been asking about you. Why don't you quit holding back and playing so dumb? We all know the score. Hostesses have married bank managers — there've been cases. We're not so cheap. If we're not too prissy, we can ride around in a goddam limousine with the best of 'em!"

That burned me up. "When did you ever ride in a limousine?" I queried.

Her big red mouth opened so wide with surprise, I thought her jaw was going to drop off. Then she snapped, "None of your nasty lip. You're no lily-arsed lady. You wouldn't be here if you were!"

I quit. I took my pay — a dollar and five cents — and went home.

28

The final shadow had taken another big step towards me. To avoid it, I first had to come closer to it. I didn't care about losing the job, but I was really afraid of that shadow. I knew how to sell myself. Ever since that affair, I understood quite a bit about relations between men and women. A girl had only to relax her hold on herself a little, and the men would sense it and come running. What they wanted was flesh; when they had satisfied their lust, they would feed you and clothe you for a time. Afterwards, they might curse and beat you, and cut off your income.

That's the way it is when a girl sells herself. At times she's very content. I've known that feeling myself. It's all sweet love talk for a while; later you become depressed and ache all over. When you sell yourself to one man, at least you get words of love and bliss. But when you're on sale to the general public, you don't even get that. Then you hear lots of words Mama never used.

The degree of fear was different too. Though I just couldn't accept the advice of First Hostess, I wasn't quite as afraid of a private affair with one man. Not that I was thinking of selling myself. I had no need of a man — I was less than twenty. I only thought that it might be fun to go around with one. How was I to know that as soon as I went out a few times with a new friend he would demand what I feared the most!

It was true I had once abandoned myself to the spring breeze, and let a young man have his will. But later I knew he had taken advantage of my innocence, hypnotized me with his honeyed words. When I awoke, I realized it was all an empty dream, with nothing to show for it but a few meals and some new clothes. I didn't want to earn my food that way again. Food was a proper practical object that should be earned in a proper practical way. But if that proved impossible, a woman had to admit she was a woman, and sell her flesh.

More than a month passed. I still was unable to find a new job.

29

I ran into some of my old classmates. A few had gone on to middle school; some were just living at home. I wasn't much interested in them. Talking with them, I could see that I was cleverer than they. In school, they used to be the smart ones. Now the tables were reversed. They seemed to be living in a world of dreams. All very smartly turned out, they were like merchandise in a store. Their eyes shone when they met a young man and their hearts seemed to melt in a poetic reverie.

Those girls made me laugh, but I had to forgive them. Food was no problem to them; it's easy to think of love when your belly is full. Men and women weave nets to

ensnare one another. The ones with the most money
have the biggest nets. After bagging a few prospects,
they leisurely take their pick. I had no money. I couldn't
even find a quiet corner to weave my net. But I had to
catch someone, or be caught myself. I was clearer on
such matters than my ex-classmates, more practical.

30

One day I ran into the doll-faced young wife again. She
greeted me as if I were one of her dearest friends, but
there was some confusion in her manner.

"You're a good person," she stammered, very
earnest. "I was sorry later I asked you to let him go.
I would have been better off if he stayed with you. Now
he's found himself another. He's gone away with her
and I haven't seen him since!"

Questioning her, I discovered that she and he had
married for love. Apparently she still loved him, but he
had run off again. I was sorry for the little wife. She
was still dreaming; she still believed that love was
sacred.

I asked her what she was going to do now. She said
she had to find him, that they were mated for life. But
suppose you can't find him? I asked. She bit her lips.
She had parents and in-laws; she was under their control. She envied me my freedom.

So someone actually envied me. I wanted to laugh.
My freedom — what a joke! She had food, I had
freedom. She had no freedom, I had nothing to eat.
We both were women, both were frustrated.

31

After meeting the little doll-face, I gave up the idea of selling myself to one man. I decided to play around; in other words, I was going to use "romance" to earn my meals. I couldn't be bothered about moral responsibility any more when I was hungry.

Romance would cure hunger, just as a full stomach was necessary before you could concentrate on romance. It was a perfect circle, no matter where you started from.

There wasn't much difference between me and my classmates and the little doll-face. They had a few more illusions; I was a bit more straightforward. There is no truth more vital than the empty stomach.

I sold my meagre possessions and bought myself a complete new outfit. I didn't look bad at all. Then I entered upon the market.

32

I had imagined I could play at romance, but I was wrong. I didn't know as much about the world as I had thought. Men weren't trapped quite that easily. I was after the more cultured types, men I could satisfy with a kiss or two. Ha-ha, they didn't go for that line, not one bit. They wanted to take advantage the very first time we met. What's more, they only invited me to see a movie, or go out for a walk, or have some ice-cream. I still went home hungry.

The so-called cultured men never failed to ask what school I graduated from, what business my family was in. It was plain enough — they didn't want you unless you had something to offer. If you couldn't bring them any real gain, the best they were willing to give was ten cents worth of ice-cream in exchange for a kiss.

It was strictly a cash on delivery proposition. The doll-faces didn't understand this, but I did. Mama and I both understood. I thought of Mama a lot.

33

They say some girls can earn a living playing at romance. But I just didn't have the capital; I had to drop the idea. For me it had to be straight business. My landlord ordered me to get out. He was a respectable man, he said. I didn't even give him a second glance. I moved back to the small flat where Mama and my first new Papa used to live. This landlord didn't say anything about being respectable. He was much nicer and more honest.

Business was very good. The cultured types came too. As soon as they found out I was for sale, they were willing to buy. With this kind of arrangement they got their money's worth, with no reflection on their social status.

When I first started I was very scared. I wasn't yet twenty. But after a couple of days I wasn't afraid any more. I could turn them limp as sacks of wet sand. They were pleased and satisfied; they advertised me to their friends.

By the end of several months, I knew a lot. I learned to size a man up the first time we met. The rich customer would always inquire about my background, and make it plain that he could afford me. Very jealous, he would always want me all to himself. Even in brothels he wanted to monopolize — because he had money.

To that type of man I wasn't very courteous. If he raged I didn't care. I could quiet him down by threatening to go to his wife. Those years at school weren't spent in vain. I didn't scare easily. Education has its advantages. I was convinced of that.

Some men would show up with only a dollar in their hands, terrified of being cheated. To this sort, I would explain the terms of our transaction in careful detail. They would then meekly go home and get some more money. It was really a scream.

The worst of the lot were the small-time punks. Not only didn't they want to spend any money, but they were always trying to make something on the deal — stealing half a pack of cigarettes, or a small jar of cold cream. It was bad policy to offend these boys — they had connections. Get tough with them, and they put the cops on you.

I didn't offend them. I played them along until I got to know an official on the police force, then I finished them off one by one. It's a dog-eat-dog world; the worse you are the better you make out.

Most pitiful of all were the young student types, with only a dollar and a handful of small change clinking in their pockets, nervous perspiration standing out on their noses. I pitied them, but I took their money just the same. What else could I do?

Then there were the elderly men — all quite respectable, some of them grandfathers. I didn't really know how to treat them. But I knew they had money; they wanted to buy a little happiness before they died. So I gave them what they were after.

These experiences taught me to recognize the true nature of money and man. Money is the more powerful of the two. If man is an animal, then money is his gall.

I discovered I had caught a disease. It made me so miserable I wanted to die. I rested, I strolled about the streets. I longed for Mama. She could give me some comfort. I thought of myself as someone who hadn't long to live.

I went to the little lane where I had last seen her plying the bellows' lever. But the steamed bread shop had closed down. No one knew where they had moved to. But I persisted. I simply had to find her. For days I roved the streets like a ghost. It was no use. I wondered whether she was dead, or whether the shop had moved to somewhere outside the city, maybe hundreds of miles away.

In this gloomy frame of mind, I broke down and cried. I put on my best clothes, made up my face, and lay down on my bed and waited for death. I was sure I wouldn't last long.

But I didn't die. There was a knock at the door. Someone had come looking for me. All right, show him in. With all my strength, I gave him a full charge of my infection. I didn't think I was wrong. The fault wasn't mine to begin with.

I began to feel a little better. I smoked, I drank, I

behaved like an old hand of thirty or forty. There were dark circles under my eyes, my hands were feverish. I didn't care. Money was everything. The idea was to eat your fill first; then you could talk about other things.

And I ate not badly at all. Why not have the best! I had to have good food and nice clothing. That was the only way I could do a little justice to myself.

35

One morning as I sat draped in a long gown — it must have been about ten o'clock — I heard some footsteps out in the courtyard. I had just got out of bed. Sometimes I didn't get dressed until noon. I had become very lazy lately. I could sit around like this for an hour, sometimes two, thinking of nothing, not wanting to think of anything either.

The footsteps approached my door, softly, slowly. I saw a pair of eyes peering in through the door's small glass panel. After a moment, they vanished. I sat listless, too lazy to move. A few minutes later, the eyes came back again. This time I recognized them. I got up and quietly opened the door. "Ma!"

36

What happened next I can't exactly say. Nor do I remember how long we cried together. Mama had aged terribly. Her husband had gone back to his native village, sneaking away without a word. He didn't leave her a cent. She sold the shop's few implements, gave the store back to the landlord and moved into a cheap room.

She had already been searching for me over half a month. Finally, she thought of coming to her old flat, just on the off chance that she might run into me. Sure enough, there I was. She hadn't dared speak to me. If I hadn't called her, perhaps she would have gone away again.

When we stopped crying at last, I began to laugh hysterically. What a farce! Mother finds daughter, but daughter is a whore. In order to bring me up, Mama had been forced to become one. Now it was my turn to look after her, so I would have to remain one.

This oldest profession is hereditary — a woman's speciality!

37

Though I knew that words of comfort were just empty talk, I was hoping to hear them from Mama's mouth. Mama was always good at fooling people, and I used to take her cajolery as consolation.

But now she had forgotten how to do even that. She was scared stiff by hunger, and I didn't blame her.

She began checking through my things, questioning me about income and expenses, apparently not the least troubled by the nature of my work. I told her I was sick, hoping she would urge me to rest a few days. Nothing of the sort. She said she'd buy me some medicine.

"Are we always going to remain in this business?" I asked her. She didn't answer.

Yet, in a way, she really loved me and wanted to protect me. She fed me, looked after my health. She was always stealing glances at me, the way a mother watches a sleeping child.

The only thing she wouldn't do for me was tell me to quit my profession.

I knew well enough — though I wasn't too pleased about it — that aside from this, there was nothing else I could do. Mama and I had to have food and clothing — that decided everything. Mother and daughter or no, respectable or no, the need for money was merciless.

38

Mama wanted to look after me, but she had to stand by and watch me be ruined. Though I wanted to be good to her, sometimes she was very annoying. She tried to run the whole show — especially where money was concerned. Her eyes had lost their youthful shine, but the sight of money could make them gleam again. She acted like a servant when there were customers around, yet if any man should pay less than the agreed price, she'd curse him and call him every name under the sun.

It made things awkward for me. Of course, I was in business for money, but that didn't mean we had to curse people. I knew how to be rude to a customer, but I had my own methods. I brought him around easy. Mama's way was too crude; she offended people. From the point of view of money, that was something we shouldn't do.

Maybe I was young and naive. Mama only cared about money, but she had to be that way; she was so much older. Probably in another couple of years I'd be the same. A person's heart ages with the years. Gradually, you get to be hard and stiff — like silver dollars.

No, Mama didn't stand on ceremony. If a customer didn't pay in full, she'd keep his brief-case, or his hat, or anything worth a little money like a pair of gloves or a cane. I hated rows, but Mama was right. "We have to make every dollar we can," she said. "In this racket, you age ten years in one. Do you think anybody will want you when you look seventy or eighty?"

Sometimes, when a customer got drunk, she'd drag him out to a lonely spot and strip him of everything, right down to his shoes. The funny thing was the man never made a fuss about it afterwards. Maybe he didn't know how it happened, or maybe he caught pneumonia from the exposure. Or maybe, remembering how he got into that state, he was too embarrassed to complain. We didn't care, but some people had a sense of shame.

39

Mama said we age ten years in one, and she was right. After two or three years I could feel that I had changed a lot. My skin grew coarse, my lips were always chapped, my eyes bloodshot. I would get up very late, but I always felt tired.

I was aware of these things, and my customers were even less blind to them. Old customers gradually stopped coming around. As to new customers, though I worked still harder to please them, they got on my nerves. Sometimes I couldn't control my temper; I'd rant and rave so, I didn't recognize myself. Talking nonsense became a habit with me.

My more cultured customers lost interest because my "charming little love-bird" quality — their favourite poetic phrase — was gone. I had to learn to behave like a street-walker. Only by painting my face like a clown could I attract the uneducated customers. I spread my lipstick on thick, I bit them — then they were happy.

I could almost see myself dying. With every dollar I took in, I seemed to come closer to death. Money is supposed to preserve life, but the way I earned it, it had the opposite effect. I could see myself dying; I waited for death.

In this state of mind, I didn't want to think of anything. There was no need. I only wanted to live from day to day — that was enough.

Mama was the mirror of my coming self. After peddling her flesh for years, all that was left of her was a mass of white hair and a dark wrinkled skin. Such is life.

40

I forced myself to laugh, to act wild. Weeping a few tears would never have washed away my bitterness anyhow. My way of living had no attraction, but it was life after all, and I didn't want to part with it. Besides, what I was doing was not my fault. If death seemed frightening, it was only because I loved life so dearly. I wasn't afraid of the pain of dying — my life was more painful than any death. I loved life, but not the way I was living it.

I used to picture an ideal life, and it would be like a dream. But then, as cruel reality again closed in on me, the dream would quickly pass, and I would feel worse than ever. This world is no dream — it's a living hell.

Mama could see that I was feeling low, and she would urge me to get married. A husband would give me food, and she could get a cash payment for her old age. I was her only hope. But who would marry me?

41

Because I had known so many men, I forgot completely the meaning of love. I loved myself — no, I didn't even love myself any longer. Why should I love anyone else? Still, if I were to marry, I would have to pretend, to say that I loved him, that I was willing to spend the rest of my life with him.

And that is what I did say — to several men. I swore it, but none of them wanted to marry me. The rule of money makes men sharp. They were quite willing to have an affair with me. That was much cheaper than going to a brothel.

If it didn't cost anything, I guarantee all the men would say they loved me.

42

Just about this time, I was arrested. Our city's new chief of police is a stickler on morals; he wants to clean out all the unregistered brothels. The licensed women can go on doing business, because they pay tax.

After my arrest, I was sent to a reformatory where I was taught to work — washing clothes, cooking, knitting. But I already knew how to do all that. If I could have earned a living by any of those methods, I would have quit my own bitter profession long ago.

I told that to the people at the reformatory, but they didn't believe me. They said I was a loafer, immoral. They said that if I not only learned to work, but also loved to work, I could become self-supporting, or find a husband.

They were very optimistic. I didn't share their confidence. They were very proud of the fact that they had "reformed" about a dozen women and found them husbands. For a two-dollar licence fee and a guarantee from a responsible shopkeeper, any man could come to the reformatory and pick a wife. It was a real bargain — for the man.

To me it was a joke. I flatly refused to be "reformed". When some big official came down to investigate us, I spat in his face. But they wouldn't let me go. I was a dangerous character. Since they couldn't reform me, they sent me to another place. I went to jail.

43

Jail is a fine place. It convinces you that there's no hope for mankind. Never in my dreams did I imagine any hole could be so disgusting.

But once I got here, I gave up any idea of ever leaving

again. From my own experience, I know that the outside world isn't much of an improvement.

I wouldn't want to die here, if I had any better place to go. But I know what it's like outside. Wherever you die, it's all the same.

Here, in here, I saw my old friend again — the crescent moon. I hadn't seen it for a long time.

I wonder what Mama is doing.

That crescent moon brings everything back.

Translated by Sidney Shapiro

This Life of Mine

I studied a bit when I was a boy. Not much, mind you, but enough to read *Seven Knights and Five Heroes, The Three Kingdoms,* and things like that. I know quite a lot of the stories in *Liao Zhai,* by heart — I could tell you them with all the details if you liked. They make good listening. Not that I can read the originals — that classical language is too hard for me. The bits I know I learned from those "*Liao Zhai* Stories Retold" columns in the papers. They're terrific. They turn the classical stuff into ordinary Chinese, and put jokes in too!

My handwriting's not bad either. It's as good as anything in the official documents they used to write in government offices in the old days. I'd have made a first-rate clerk. My writing has a good balance to it, I lay the ink on thick and glossy, and my lines are very neat. Of course, I know my limits. I wouldn't say I'd have been good enough to write memorials to the emperor, but I could guarantee to do a good job of copying out any of the ordinary official documents you see these days.

Considering how good I am at reading and writing I ought to have got a job in a government office. It wouldn't have brought much glory on my family, but it'd have been a sight more respectable than any other job. Besides, however low you start you're bound to get some promotion. I've seen more than one top official whose writing's not up to mine, and who can't even string a sentence together when he's talking. If men like that can get to the top as officials, there's no reason why I shouldn't have done.

But when I was fifteen the family made me start an apprenticeship. There's many a trade, and every trade has its masters. There's nothing degrading about learning a trade — it's just that it's a bit less satisfying than having a government job. Learn a trade and you're stuck with it for the rest of your days. Even if you make a pile you're nothing compared with a high official. But I didn't make a fuss about it with my parents. I just went off and served my apprenticeship. I was only fifteen, and you don't make your own choices at that age. Besides, my parents told me that they'd find me a wife when I'd finished my apprenticeship and started earning. In those days I thought getting married would be fun. Stick it out for two or three years, I thought, then earn my living at my trade and have a nice young bride too. I reckoned that would be really living.

I was apprenticed to learn papier-mâché work. In the good old days you never had to worry about where your next meal was going to come from if you were in that line of business. When someone died they didn't cut their corners the way they do now. Don't get me wrong. I don't mean that there'd be endless ups and downs before they finally died, instead of simply pegging out and being done with it. What I'm getting at is that when someone died back then the bereaved spent their money like nobody's business. No effort, no expense was spared to put on a good show. Take the shops that sell things for the dead, for instance. They used to spend tidy little sums in those places.

The moment somebody passed away, a paper carriage had to be made. These days a lot of people wouldn't even know what one of those was. Then three days later there was another ceremony when a lot of papier-mâché goods had to be burned: carriages, sedan chairs, mules, horses, trucks, servants, soul banners, wreaths and all the rest. If someone had died of childbirth fever you had to paste up an ox and a chicken coop as well. For when they recited sutras on the seventh day you had to paste up storehouses, gold and silver mountains, giant coins, clothes and flowers for every season of the year, antiques, and every kind of furniture you could imagine. Then when the coffin was brought out of the house there were all sorts of papier-mâché goods apart from paper pavilions and archways. However poor you were you had to run to a couple of boys to carry the stuff. On the thirty-fifth day they burnt canopies, and for the sixtieth day we used to make paper boats and bridges. So it took a dead man sixty days to get away from us paper-pasters. As long as a dozen or so rich men died in a year we didn't go hungry.

It's not just the dead that the paper-pasters look after. They take care of the gods too. In the old days the gods weren't the pathetic creatures they are today. Take Lord Guan Yu, for instance. In the old days people always had yellow paper flags and canopies made for him on his festival on the 24th of the sixth month, as well as horses, grooms, seven-star banners and all the rest of it. But nowadays almost everyone seems to have forgotten about him.

Whenever smallpox broke out in the old days the plague goddesses kept us busy. For the Nine Goddesses we had to make nine sedan chairs, a red horse and a yellow one, as well as phoenix crowns and cloaks of many colours. On top of that there were the robes, sashes, shoes and hats for the Smallpox Brothers and Sisters and all their attendants. But now that hospitals give vaccinations and the goddesses are left idle, the paper-pasters are too. Apart from that there were lots of papier-mâché things people needed to fulfil vows they'd made, but now that superstition's out, that's all gone by the board too. The world really has changed.

Apart from what we did for gods and spirits we did jobs for the living too — "white work" we called it, papering ceilings. Back in those days, before all these foreign buildings, people had their ceilings and walls repapered right down to the floor when they moved or had a wedding or any other celebration. That made the whole place spick and span. Really rich families even got us to put the gauze on their windows in spring and the paper in autumn. But since then everyone's got poorer and poorer; sometimes they don't even have the ceilings done when they move in. The rich have all had their houses foreignized. They have their ceilings plastered, and that saves them a lifetime of trouble. And now that people have glass in their windows there's no call for pasting gauze or paper on them any more. When everyone started wanting foreign things that didn't leave much of a living for us old-fashioned craftsmen. Not that we didn't try. When rickshaws came in we made rickshaws. When cars came in we made cars. We could change with the times. But how many bereaved families wanted a papier-mâché rickshaw or car? With so many big changes afoot our little changes were all for nothing. It doesn't matter how deep the water is, it'll never drown the duck.   There was nothing we could do about it.

2

As I've told you already, if I'd stuck to that trade I'd have starved to death years ago.   That skill wasn't much use for very long, and my three-year apprenticeship wasn't good for anything else, but there was one thing about it that stood me in good stead for the rest of my life.   That benefit stayed with me long after I laid down my tools and changed my trade.   Even when they talk about what sort of man I was after I'm dead they'll remember that I served a three-year apprenticeship when I was a lad.

As an apprentice you don't just learn your craft, you learn to behave yourself as well.   When I first went to the shop I was scared stiff of everybody, and the rules were terribly strict.   Apprentices didn't get to bed till late but had to be up early. You had to take orders from everyone and humble yourself to wait on them hand and foot.   You had to put up with being hungry, cold, overworked and miserable, and be cheerful about it too.   Your tears you kept to yourself.   The shop I lived in as an apprentice was my boss's home.   So on top of my master's bad temper, I had to put up with his wife's bad temper too.   I was caught between them. Three years of that would soften the most pig-headed character, and toughen up an easy-going lightweight.   I can tell you straight: apprentices aren't born with character — it's beaten into them.   Character's like wrought iron: it has to be beaten into shape.

All that bullying and beating was quite simply unbearable. I really wanted to do myself in. But when I look back on it now all the rules and the strict teaching were pure gold. By the time I'd been through that training I could face anything else that life was going to throw at me. For instance, if I'd had to enlist I'd have made a good soldier. In the army they only drill some of the time, but the only time an apprentice had off was when he was in bed. I'd find the time to go off for a shit so that I could have a bit of a shut-eye as I squatted there, because when we were working nights I'd sometimes only get three or four hours' sleep a day. I learnt how to wolf down a whole meal at once, because no sooner would I have my bowl in my hand than the master or the mistress would be yelling for me. If it wasn't that then I'd have to be dealing with a customer who'd come to place an order. I'd have to treat him ever so respectfully, and be very careful to remember what my master had told me about our prices. So of course I had to bolt my meals. After a training like that I was tough enough to take anything, and to do it with a smile too. I may be a bit rough, but I reckon that's something educated people can't do. At those athletics meetings they have in the foreign schools these days the students seem to think they've really done something when they've run round in a circle a couple of times. Hunh! They hold each other up and hug each other and slap surgical spirit on their thighs. They even lose their temper and go around in buses. What do young gents like them know about discipline and training? As I was saying just now, what I had to suffer taught me how to take being overworked and treated unfairly. I'm never ever idle, and when I work I never lose my temper or cut up awkward.

I can take hardship as well as any soldier, but soldiers can't be as polite and pleasant about it as I can.

Here's something else to prove my point. When I'd served my apprenticeship I wanted to let people know I could earn my living with my own skill, so like all the other craftsmen the first thing I did was to buy myself a pipe. Whenever I had a moment to myself I'd put in a pinch of tobacco and puff away at it, nice and slow, as if I really was somebody. I started drinking too. I often bought a couple of jars of cat's piss. I used to smack my lips and purse my mouth as I drank the stuff. That was the beginning: once you've started one habit it's easy to start a second. Anyhow, it was all good fun. But it led to trouble. I like a smoke and a drink, and there was nothing very remarkable about that — more or less everybody does. But as time went on I started on opium. There was nothing illegal about it in those days and it was very cheap. At first I only smoked it for fun, but then I got hooked on the stuff. It wasn't long before I started feeling the pinch, and I wasn't working with anything like the same energy. So without waiting for anyone else to tell me what to do I chucked them all: opium, drink and tobacco too. I never touched any of them ever again. I joined a temperance sect. When you join that you're not allowed to touch opium, tobacco or booze: break the rule and you'll have very bad luck. That was why I didn't just kick the habits but joined the sect too. With very bad luck in store for me if I did, I wasn't going to break the rule, was I? When I look back on it today I can see that I got that determination and toughness from being an apprentice. I can take any hardship, however great. Mind you, when I first gave up smoking and drinking it was agony to see other people doing it. It was like having thousands of insects crawling all over you. But I couldn't break the rule because I didn't want the bad luck. Of course, the bad luck or whatever lay in the future: What I had to go through at the time was terrible. I had to stick it out. Sticking it out was the only way to succeed. Worrying about bad luck mattered less to me than that. The reason why I could stick it out was because of the training I'd had as an apprentice.

Talking of my craft, I reckon that from that point of view too my three years as an apprentice weren't wasted. Any craft has to change with the times. The techniques are fixed, but you can be flexible in how you use them. Thirty years ago bricklayers used to pay a lot of attention to grinding bricks into shape so that the joins were exactly in line. They did very skilful work. Now they can work in concrete, set artificial stone and all the rest of it. Thirty years ago joiners specialized in carving patterns on wooden furniture and now they make foreign-style furniture. It was the same with my trade. The only difference is that we could adapt even faster than any other craft. What we prided ourselves on was being able to copy anything we see. For instance, if there was a funeral and you told us to make a papier-mâché banquet we'd make you chicken, duck, fish and pork out of papier-mâché. If a family lost an unmarried daughter and you told us to make up a complete trousseau, whether for forty-eight or for thirty-two porters, we could make the lot for you — everything from flour-jars and bottles of cooking oil to cupboards and mirrors. Our skill was to be able to make anything we'd see. We didn't have a lot of skills, but we have to be quite clever. An idiot could never be a good paper-paster.

Our trade was a mixture of work and conjuring. Success or failure depended completely on the right combination of different coloured papers. That was something you had to give a lot of thought to. As for me, well, I was a bit crafty. Not many of the beatings I got as an apprentice were because I couldn't master the skills. Most were because I was too clever by half, naughty and disobedient. I suppose that none of my cleverness would have come out if I'd been apprenticed to a blacksmith or a sawyer; you always beat the iron and saw the timber the same old way. It was a piece of luck that I was apprenticed as a paper-paster. Once I'd learned the basic techniques I started making up my own styles. I made things as skilfully as I could. I wanted them to be as lifelike as possible. Sometimes I'd waste masses of time and material and still not be able to make what I could see in my mind's eye. But that just made me think even harder and keep on adjusting it. I never gave up till I'd got it right. That really was a good habit. It's those three years of my apprenticeship I have to thank for being clever and knowing how to put that cleverness to some use. Those three years gave me the habit of using my own head. I'd be the first to admit that what I've achieved in my life has been no great shakes, but I can get the rough idea of anything that ordinary people can do the moment I see it done. I can build a wall, plant a tree, mend a watch or a clock, tell whether a fur is real or fake and choose the right day for a wedding. I know all the tricks of all the trades. I wasn't taught any of them. I just used my eyes, then had a go at it myself. Hard work, endurance, keeping my eyes open and learning as I go along are a way of life with me. And those habits all came from my three years as an apprentice in the funeral outfitter's. It's taken me till now, when I'm practically dying of starvation, to realize that if I'd stayed at school for a few more years and buried my nose in books like the old-style scholars or the graduates of modern schools I'd have probably stayed stupid for the rest of my life. I'd have been completely ignorant. Pasting paper didn't bring me a good job or make me rich, but it made my life very interesting — poor, but interesting. In a way, I've lived.

By the time I reached my early twenties I was a big man among my friends and relations. Not just because I had some money and a position in society, but also because I did things carefully and never spared myself. Once I'd served my apprenticeship I used to go and sit in the street teahouse waiting for other people in the trade to come and hire me. I became quite somebody in the street — I was young, quick and I knew how to behave in public. If anyone came to hire me, I'd go off to work; but even if there was no work I wouldn't be idle. My friends and relations were always asking me to fix up all sorts of things for them. I was scarcely married myself before I was acting as a matchmaker for other people.

Helping people is a kind of relaxation and I needed some sort of relaxation. Why was that? Well, as I told you a little while back, we had two kinds of work in our trade, burning jobs, papier-mâché, and white jobs. Doing burning jobs was interesting and clean, but not white jobs. When you're repapering walls and ceilings the first thing you have to do is to strip all the old paper off. That's a mucky business. If you've never done it you couldn't possibly imagine how much dirt there is in the walls and ceilings. It piles up there for ages and ages, and it's the driest and finest dust there is. It really gets up your nose. By the time we'd stripped the paper from three rooms we'd all be covered in dust, looking like devils. When we'd made good the straw lining on the wall and put the new paper up the stinking powder on the new silver-patterned paper got up your nose too. The dust and the powder on the paper could give you consumption — that's what they used to call T.B. those days. I hated that kind of work. But if someone came and offered you some when you were waiting for a job on the street you couldn't refuse. You had to take whatever work you could get. On that sort of job I usually stayed down below, cutting the paper out, passing it up and pasting it. That was so I wouldn't have to go up top. It meant I could keep my head down as I worked and swallow a bit less dust. So even if the rest of me got filthy all over, my nose could be a kind of chimney. When I'd done that sort of job for a few days I was ready to do something else for a bit of a change. That was why I was always glad to help out friends or relations who wanted anything done.

Whether I was doing burning jobs or white jobs the work always had something to do with weddings and funerals. My friends used to look me up to place their orders, and while they were about it they'd ask me to fix other things up for them too, like the marquees, porters, cooks and carriages for weddings and funerals. As time went by I found that sort of thing more and more interesting. I learnt the clever ways of doing things, so that my friends and relations could put on a good show on the cheap, instead of being taken for a ride like idiots. I learnt a lot of lessons fixing up that kind of thing and found out how to get on with people. As time went by

I became a very clever man, even though I was still in my twenties.

3

From what I've told you already you'll have guessed that I couldn't go on earning a living pasting paper. That's obvious. Once the times started changing it was like a downpour at a temple fair — everyone scattered. I seem to have been going downhill all my life. I just couldn't help myself. The more I wanted the world to be peaceful and prosperous, the faster I hurtled downhill. These changes took your breath away: everything changed all at once. It wasn't just change, it was a hurricane, blowing us all goodness knew where. We didn't have a clue about what was happening. My trade and most of the other jobs that paid well when I was young were suddenly swept away. They disappeared, just as if they'd been thrown into the sea. Although the paper-pasting trade is still carrying on in a way, it's more dead than alive. It'll never recover. I could see that long, long ago. In the good old days I could certainly have opened a little shop and taken a couple of apprentices of my own if I'd wanted to. It would have been a safe way of earning a living. It's lucky I didn't. I'd never have been able to make ends meet if there were no big orders from one year's end to the next. Making a paper carriage or papering a couple of ceilings a year would never have kept me fed. Just look! Did I get a single really good order in those dozen years and more? I reckon I was right to change my trade.

But that wasn't the only reason for making a sudden

switch. When the times are changing you can't do anything about it. You can't stand out against them. A battle to the death with the times is just asking for trouble. But the things that happen to you and you alone are sometimes even worse. They can drive you crazy, just like that. They can easily force you to drown yourself in a river or a well, to say nothing of chucking in your trade and trying your hand at something else. Personal things may be little enough, but they can be too much for you to bear alone. A grain of rice is nothing, but it takes a hell of an effort for an ant to carry one away. Same with personal things. You've only got so much breath in you, and if you've got too much to cope with you suffocate, you're left gasping for breath. What little things we people are.

It was my cleverness and affability that brought me disaster. When you hear me saying that you're probably thinking I'm talking nonsense, but it's absolutely, one hundred per cent true, every word of it. If it hadn't hit me myself I'd probably never have believed that such things could happen. It came and looked for me and found me. I practically went round the bend at the time. When I think about it now, over twenty years later, I can smile about it, like remembering a story. What I understand now is that what may look like a good thing for you isn't necessarily so. A thing's only really good if it's good for everyone else, not just for you. Then you're like a fish in the water. What's good for you but bad for everyone else is only good for you at their expense. What use is cleverness and affability then? That's a truth I've cottoned on to now, so I just nod and smile when I remember what happened. But at the time it was almost more than I could take. In those days I was still young.

Was there ever a youngster who didn't like being well turned-out? You'd never have known I was only a craftsman from the way I dressed and carried myself as a young man when I was helping people out and fixing things up for them. In the old days furs were very expensive and you weren't allowed to wear them. Nowadays you can win on the horses or in a lottery one day and buy a fox-fur overcoat the next. Doesn't matter if you're a child of fifteen, or a twenty-year-old who still hasn't had his first shave. It was never like that in the old days. The way you dressed was settled by your age and what you were. If you had a squirrel collar to your jacket or your waistcoat in those days you looked good and were rich. I always used to stroke that collar. My jacket and waistcoat were made of blue satin, and the satin wasn't half tough in those days — a jacket would last you a good dozen years. When I was papering walls and ceilings I was a filthy monkey. But once I got home, had a good wash and got dressed up I became a really well turned out young man. I hated being a filthy monkey, which made me all the fonder of being that well-dressed youngster. With my long, black plait, the front of my head shaved smooth and shiny, and my satin waistcoat with its squirrel collar I really was someone.

I suppose the thing a handsome young man most dreads is marrying an ugly wife. For some time I'd dropped some casual hints to my parents: I was quite willing not to marry at all, but if I did she'd have to be up to scratch. Of course, there wasn't free marriage in those days, but the boy and the girl were allowed to have a look at each other beforehand. If I was going to marry anyone I was going to take a look at her first. I wasn't going to be conned by all the matchmaker's blarney.

I got married when I was twenty. My wife was a year younger than me. Say what you like, she was a neat, trim young wife. I saw her with my own eyes before we got engaged. I couldn't say that she was a great beauty, but pretty and able she was, because that was what I wanted in a wife. If she hadn't been I'd never have agreed. Those two words "pretty" and "able" give you a very good idea of the sort of man I was. In those days I was young, handsome, and a very good worker. The last thing I wanted to marry was some stupid cow.

There's no denying it: our marriage was made in heaven. We were both young and able. Neither of us was tall. To our friends and relations we looked just like a pair of neat little tops, spinning all over the place and making the older folk smile. We two used to exchange quick answers and clever remarks with each other in front of everyone. We were always showing off. It was just to get people to say what a fine young couple we were. When other people praised us it increased our love and respect for each other. I suppose there was something about it of one hero admiring another, the tough guy liking the tough guy.

I was very happy. To be frank with you, my parents never made much money, but they did have a house, so I could live rent-free. There were plenty of trees and bushes in the yard, and a couple of canaries hanging in cages under the eaves. I had my craft, I had friends, and I had an adorable young wife. If I hadn't been happy with that I'd have been just asking for trouble.

I couldn't find a single fault in my wife. Well, sometimes I thought she was a bit wild. But then any clever young wife is a bit high-spirited. She liked talking because she was a good talker. She didn't do much to avoid men because that's a married woman's right, especially a capable new wife like her. Of course she wanted to stop being bashful the way she'd had to be as a girl. She wanted everyone to know that she was a married woman, and no bones about it. You couldn't say there was anything wrong with that. Besides, she was so friendly and considerate to her parents-in-law and looked after them so well. It was only natural for her to be a bit free and easy with younger people. She was very cheerful and open, and wanted to be warm and friendly to everyone, young and old alike. I never blamed her for being so lively.

When she was in the family way and after she became a mother she was prettier than ever, and even more open — I really can't bring myself to say she was free and easy. A young woman who's expecting and a young mother are the loveliest things in the world. The sight of her sitting in the doorway showing her breast as she fed the baby only made me love her more than ever. I couldn't even think of blaming her for not behaving herself.

By the time I was twenty-four I had a son and a daughter. Not that raising kids is anything to the credit of the husband. When he feels like it he can cuddle the baby and play with it, but it's the mother who does all the hard work. I'm no fool. I don't need anybody to tell me that. Honestly, when it comes to having babies and bringing them up a man's no use even if he wants to lend a hand from time to time. But anyone with a lick of sense will keep his wife happy and give her a bit of freedom. Only a real bastard would mistreat a

pregnant woman or a young mother.   Once my missus
had the kids I let her have her own way more.   I reckoned it was only fair.

Well, as they say, the husband and wife are the tree
and the children are the blossom.   You can only tell
that a tree's well-rooted when it comes into blossom.
By then you ought to have a lot fewer suspicions and
worries, if any at all.   Kids tie their mother down hand
and foot.   So even if I did think she was a bit wild — I
really don't like using a nasty word like that — I had
to stop worrying.   She was a mother, wasn't she?

4

To this very day I can't make head nor tail of it.

This thing I can't make out is what drove me well-
nigh crazy at the time.   My wife ran off with another
man.

I say it again, to this day I can't make head nor tail of
it.   I'm not pig-headed, I've been on the streets a long
time and I know what makes people tick.   I can see my
own faults just as well as my strong points.   But as
for that business, well, I've looked at all my faults, and
I can't find any reason why I should have been humili-
ated and punished like that.   That's why I said that it
was my own cleverness and good nature that caused the
disaster.   I really can't find any other explanation.

There was an older apprentice, he's the man I hate.
Everyone in the street called him Blacky, and I'll use
that name too.   Even though I hate him I won't tell
you his real name.   His nickname was Blacky because
his face was dark — not just dark, but really black.   His

face was like one of those iron balls people used to roll between their fingers. Black, but very shiny. Black, but smooth. Black, but with a beautiful shine to it. When he'd got a few drinks inside him or was hot his face would start going red. It looked like black clouds in the sunset with a bit of red showing through them. There was nothing special about his features — I was a lot more handsome than him any day. He was very tall, but gangling, not sturdy. The only reason people didn't detest him was because of that shiny black face of his.

We used to be good pals. We were apprenticed to the same master, and he looked so stupid, black and rough that I'd have had no cause to be suspicious of him even if I hadn't liked him. My cleverness hadn't taught me to be cautious about people. Quite the opposite. I knew that nobody was going to pull the wool over my eyes. I trusted other people because I had confidence in myself. I was sure that none of my friends were going to pull any fast ones on me. Once I decide to have anything to do with someone I treat him as a real friend. Even if there's been anything fishy about that other apprentice I had to treat him with respect and look after him properly. After all, he was senior to me, and we were under the same master. We'd learnt our trade in the same shop and were trying to make a living in the same street. Whether we were in work or not we were bound to meet several times a day. If there was a job we'd be on it together, and if there wasn't he'd come to my place for a meal and some tea. Sometimes we'd play a few hands of cards, the old-fashioned sorts. That was before mahjong came in in a big way. I was very friendly, and he didn't stand on ceremony either. He'd eat and drink whatever was put in front of him. I never laid on anything special for him, and he never fussed. He could eat a lot, but he wasn't choosy about it. It was a real pleasure to see him holding a bowl in his hand and eating hot soup noodles with us. He ate till the sweat came pouring down his neck, slurping noisily away and getting redder and redder in the face. He'd end up looking like an enormous coal briquette turned half red. Who'd ever have thought a man like that could have got such nasty ideas?

As time went on I could see from other people's faces that everything wasn't as it should be. But I didn't let it bother me. If I'd been a simple-minded idiot I'd probably have put two and two together and kicked up an almighty row straight away. I might have got to the bottom of it, but I might just have gone grasping at shadows and ended up with mud on my face. But I was too clever to kick up some kind of stupid row. Instead I thought it all over calmly and quietly.

First of all I thought about myself. But I couldn't find anything I'd done wrong. Even if I did have my faults, at the very least I was better looking and cleverer than him. I was a much better proposition.

Then I thought about him. There was nothing about his looks, or the way he carried himself, or his money to give him those sort of nasty ideas. He wasn't the type to bowl a woman over at first sight.

To end with I had a very careful think about my young wife. She'd been with me for four or five years by then, and you couldn't say we two hadn't been happy together. Even if she was only pretending to be happy and wanted to go off with someone she really loved —

and in the old days that would have been well-nigh impossible — surely that Blacky couldn't be the man for her. He was a craftsman, same as me, and he wasn't a cut above me or anything. He was no richer than me, no better looking, and no younger. So what was she after? I just couldn't see it. Even if you said she'd lost her head because he'd led her astray, what did he have to lead her astray with? His dark face? His skill? The way he dressed? The money in his pocket? It made no sense. Hunh! I could have led a few women astray if I'd wanted to. I may not have had much money, but I was a good looker. What did Blacky have going for him? Besides, even if she had lost her head and forgotten herself, she'd never be able to bring herself to leave the two kids.

I refused to believe what everyone was saying. I couldn't send Blacky packing or start questioning her like some great idiot. I'd thought it all over. There was nothing wrong. All I had to do was to wait patiently till everyone realized they'd been making a fuss over nothing. And if there was something behind the rumours I'd find out soon enough. I couldn't humiliate myself, my friend and my wife unless there were very good reasons. Clever people don't cut up rough.

But soon after that Blacky and my wife both disappeared. To this day I've never seen either of them again. How could she have done a thing like that? I wished I could see her and hear the truth from her own mouth. I never have understood it. It'll never make sense to my way of thinking.

I really longed to see her again, just so that I understand why it had happened. I'm still completely in the dark.

No need to go into the details of how I suffered. Nobody could imagine what I went through at home, a handsome lad with a couple of motherless children to rear. Nor could you imagine how terrible it was in the street for a clever, respectable bloke whose darling wife had run off with a man who'd been his fellow apprentice. The people who sympathized with me couldn't tell me what they felt. And when strangers heard about it they didn't blame Blacky but kept saying I'd been made a monkey of. We talk a lot about family duty and loyalty in this society, but people always like to have someone who's been made a monkey of to point their fingers at. I kept my mouth shut and gritted my teeth. What I kept seeing in my mind's eye was those two in a pool of blood. I reckoned I'd better not set eyes on them, because if I did it would be the knife — no need to say any more.

All I wanted at the time was to have it out with them. That's the only thing that would have made me feel human again. It all happened a long time ago, and I've had plenty of time to think very carefully about what it did to my life.

I didn't keep quiet. I asked everywhere about Blacky, but it was no use. The pair of them had disappeared as surely as a couple of stones dropped into the sea. When I couldn't get any hard news my temper gradually cooled down. The funny thing is that once I'd stopped being angry I started to feel sorry for her. Blacky was only a craftsman, and he could only make a living at that trade in big cities round Beijing and Tianjin. There was no call for fancy papier-mâché models for burning in the countryside. So if they'd gone a long way away how was he going to keep her? Hunh! A man who'd steal his best friend's wife would like as not be willing to sell her later. I couldn't get that worry out of my mind. I really hoped that she'd leave him and suddenly turn up again to tell me how she'd been taken in and what a terrible time she'd had. If she'd been willing to go on her knees in front of me I'm sure I wouldn't have sent her away. When you love a woman you love her for ever, no matter how she's wronged you. But she didn't come back, and there was no news of her. Sometimes I hated her, and sometimes I felt sorry for her. Sometimes my head was in such a whirl that I didn't sleep a wink all night.

After a year or so I was a lot less worked up about it all. It's true, I couldn't forget about her for the rest of my life, but I stopped worrying about her. I accepted that it really and truly had happened, and there was no need to waste any more time worrying about her.

So how did it affect me, when all's said and done? It's something I want to talk about: it was one of the most important things that happened in my life, and I've never been able to make head nor tail of it. It was like losing the person dearest to me in all the world in a nightmare: she disappeared in the wink of an eye. It was a nightmare, but it was so true I just couldn't take it. A nightmare like that will change you completely, even if it doesn't drive you crazy. It leaves you half dead.

5

I didn't even dare stick my head out of doors at first. I couldn't face the warm, bright sunshine.

What was worst was the first day back on the street. If I'd walked boldly along with my head held high there'd sure as anything have been people to say I was born shameless. If I'd slunk along with my head down then I'd have been admitting that I was spineless and weak. Whatever I'd done would have been wrong. But I had nothing to be ashamed of. I hadn't wronged anyone.

I gave up my self-imposed ban and started smoking and drinking again. No need to worry about bad luck now: what could have been worse than losing a wife. I didn't want anybody's pity and didn't deliberately provoke anyone. I smoked my pipe, drank my booze, and buried my sorrows in my heart. There's nothing like a disaster hitting you out of the blue to cure you of superstition. Before that I'd never have dared to offend a single one of the gods, but now I believed in nothing, not even in the Buddhas. From what I've been able to make out, superstition is all about hoping for something good that you don't expect, so when you're hit by troubles you never allowed for you stop hoping for anything. I burnt the money god and the kitchen god's shrine, though I'd made them myself. A lot of my friends and relations said I'd turned into an imitation foreigner. Imitation foreigner or not, I wasn't going down on my knees to anyone. If you couldn't depend on people then gods were even more unreliable.

I didn't turn into a misery. The distress of a thing like that can drive some people to their graves, but I didn't let death get anywhere near me. I'd always been sparky, and if I was going to go on living I was going to stay sparky. Smoking, drinking and stopping believing in the gods were all just ways of keeping myself sparky. Whether I really felt like it or not, I stayed cheerful. I'd always been able to manage it as an apprentice, and after all those ups and downs I needed it more than ever. Even now, when I'm near enough starving to death, I'm still smiling. I couldn't even tell you myself whether the smiles are real ones or not, but keep on smiling I surely do, and the nearer I get to dying the more I force myself to do it.

From the time that business happened right up until today I've been a useful, friendly sort of bloke, but under it all my heart's been empty. That emptiness was what my troubles left behind them, a little hole that's always there, like a bullet-hole in a wall. I'm useful, I'm friendly, and I like to give people a hand, but if I'm unlucky and things turn out badly, or I get my fingers burnt when I least expect it, I don't get worked up or blow my top. That's because of the emptiness inside. That emptiness keeps me cool when I'm at my warmest. However happy I am there's always that touch of grief, and when I'm laughing I'm usually crying too, so I can't tell which it really is.

So that's how my heart changed. If I hadn't told you about it and I can't even explain the whole of it myself — I don't suppose anyone would ever have guessed. There were some other changes in my life that were obvious to anyone. I changed my trade. I couldn't go on as a paster. I couldn't face going back to the street to wait for work. All the other men in the trade who knew me were bound to know Blacky too. If they'd started giving me funny looks I'd have been too choked to eat. Back in those days, when there weren't many papers about, the looks in people's eyes were even more terrible than being reported in the papers. If you want a divorce these days all you have to do is go to a government office and tell them why, but things like that weren't so free and easy in the old days. I had to drop all my old friends. I couldn't even go to see my old master and his wife. It was just like wanting to jump straight from one world into another. It was the only way I could lock that business away in my heart. The changes over the years have meant less and less work for pasters, but if it hadn't been for that business I'd never have made so quick and clear a break with my old trade. Giving up my trade was nothing to regret, but I'm not grateful to that business for the way I had to do it. Anyhow, change my trade I did, and that was a change anyone could see.

Deciding to give up my trade didn't mean that I knew what to do next. I just had to drift like an empty boat at the whim of the waves. As I've told you already, I could read and write well enough to be a government clerk. Besides, that's a very respectable job, and if I could get a job as a government clerk that would of course have done something to give me back the good name I'd lost when my wife ran away. It's a ridiculous idea when I think about it now, but at the time I sincerely believed that it would be a brilliant solution. So although I was still a man who'd been made a monkey of I felt a lot more cheerful. It was as if I had it all wrapped up: I was going to be a government clerk and get my good name back. I started to hold my head high again. Oh well! You can learn a trade in three years, but it'll take you thirty to get a job with the government. You just keep coming up against one brick wall after another. As I've told you, I could read, but I dare say that a lot of people who knew whole books off by heart would still have starved. And I told you that I could write too, but I suppose I wasn't such a great calligrapher after all. I'd overestimated myself. But with my own eyes I've seen big officials spending all their days living off the fat of the land who can hardly write their own names. I even wondered whether I was too well educated to be an official. I was too clever to make myself look thick.

Slowly it dawned on me. Jobs in government weren't given on ability; you had to know the right people. I didn't stand a hope, no matter how capable I was. I was a tradesman, and so were all the people I knew. My dad was a nobody, very able and decent, but a nobody just the same. I ask you, who could I have turned to for a job like that?

When life forces you to take a certain route, that's the route you have to take. You're like a train. The rails are there, and they're the way you have to go. Try showing off and you'll crash. That's how it was for me. I'd decided to chuck in my trade, I couldn't get a job in a government office, and I couldn't go on kicking my heels for ever. So there it was. The rails were there in front of me, and along them I had to go. There was no turning back.

I joined the police.

In the big cities joining the force and pulling a rickshaw are the poor man's two sets of railway tracks. If you can't read a word and haven't got a trade, all you can do is to pull your rickshaw. You don't need any capital, and as long as you don't mind sweating for it you can get your corn bread. If you can read a bit, want something more respectable, and can't support yourself in your trade then all you can do is become a policeman. Never mind about anything else for the moment, but you don't need good connections to be recruited into the force, and once you're in you've got a uniform to wear and six dollars in your pocket. It's a government job when all's said and done. I had no other choice. I wasn't in such a bad way that I had to pull a rickshaw, and I didn't have an uncle or a brother-in-law who was a big official. Being a policeman was not too high and not too low for me. If I wanted to I could wear a uniform with brass buttons on it. Joining the army would have looked better, and even if I hadn't got a commission at the very least I'd have had the chance of a bit of looting. But I couldn't have gone for a soldier: I still had a couple of motherless kids. Soldiers have to be rough, and coppers have to be civilized. To put it another way, if you're a soldier you can make a lot of money the rough way, but as a copper you're poor and civilized all your life: poor as hell, but barely civilized.

If there's one thing I can tell you that these fifty or sixty years have taught me it's this: if you know what you're doing you keep your mouth shut till it's time to talk, but if you just like pleasing people you have to say something even if you haven't really got anything to say. My tongue just won't keep quiet. I've got a whole lot to say about everything, and I like giving people nicknames that fit. I got my comeuppance on two counts. On the first I lost my wife, and had to keep my mouth shut for a year or two. On the second I joined the police. Before joining the force I used to call policemen "tramps", "gentlemen of leisure" and "stinkyfeet". All I'd meant was that coppers hung around the streets, made a lot of fuss about nothing, and got stinky-

feet from walking about so much. But now I was a
stinky-foot too.

It's quite true: life's always making us play jokes on
ourselves. I'd slapped myself in the face, but not because I'd done anything wrong — at worst I'd just cracked a few jokes too many.

It was only now that I realized what a serious business
life is. Never ever crack a joke. It was just as well
I had that empty hole in my heart. I'd called other
people stinky-feet before, and now I had to call myself
one. In the old days we'd have said that was retribu-
tion. I've never been able to find out what new-fangled
term they use for it nowadays.

I had no option — I had to join the police — but I
really did feel a bit hard done by. It's true, I didn't
have any very special skills. But I can tell you that
nobody knew more than I did about what went on in
the street. Isn't that what coppers are meant to be in
charge of? But take a look at the officers we had over
us. Some of them couldn't even talk the local language,
and they'd have needed a good long time to work out
whether two and two made four or five. Hunh! They
were officers, and I was only a recruit. A pair of their
leather boots would have cost me six months' pay. No
experience and no ability, but they were officers. There
were a damn sight too many of them. And there was
nobody you could turn to.

I remember one instructor. The first day he was
drilling us he forgot to shout "Halt!" and shouted
"Brake!" instead. No need to ask: that fine gentleman
had been a rickshaw coolie. All you have to do is know
the right people. One day you're pulling your rickshaw
and the next day your aunt's husband lands himself

a top job and you can fix yourself up as an instructor. So what if you do shout "Brake!"? Nobody's going to dare laugh at the instructor. Of course, there weren't many of his sort, but you can imagine what a shambles the police drill was from the fact that we had even one instructor like that. Of course, the indoor classes couldn't be taught by instructors like him: you had to have some smattering of education to be able to muddle through them. I suppose you could divide the indoor instructors into two types. There were the old men who were mostly opium addicts, and if they'd been able to teach you anything then with their connections they'd have got top jobs ages ago: it was only the ones who were beyond explaining anything who stayed as mere instructors. The other kind were the young boys who kept going on about foreign rubbish — about the Japanese police, about French police law, and all that. Anyone would have thought we were a bunch of bloody foreigners. The only good thing about those classes was that the instructors got carried away by the sound of their own voices, so we could take a quiet snooze during them. None of us knew the first thing about Japan or France — we just let the instructors waffle on. I could give a fine class on America, but I'm not an instructor, more's the pity. Whether those kids wet behind the ears really knew anything about abroad I've no way of saying, but I can tell you for sure that they didn't know the first thing about China. Those two kinds of instructors were of different ages and knew different things, but they had one thing in common: they were only fit to be instructors. They couldn't climb any higher and wouldn't sink any lower. They had good connections and were thoroughly useless — just the right men to instruct a bunch of coppers who because of their six silver dollars didn't dare raise a squeak.

That was what the instructors were like, and the other officers weren't much different. Think it over: Would anyone who could be a county magistrate or the head of a government bureau want a commission in the police? I told you before, you only join the force as a constable because you have to: you can't get anything better and you won't sink any lower. The same goes for the officers. From top to bottom they're as much use as performing bears just fooling around for a living. The ordinary coppers are on the streets all day. However hopeless they are they've got to be able to talk their way out of trouble, act on their own initiative, turn big problems into little ones and make little ones disappear. They mustn't give their officers any bother, and they've got to live and let live. Whether it's done honestly or by trickery, they have to have that skill. But those officers! They don't even need those little skills. They say it's much easier to be the King of Hell than one of his demons, and they're right.

6

I hope nobody will accuse me of being arrogant and ignorant if I go on a bit more about this. When I told you I felt hard done by it was the truth. Just think: my six dollars a month was the same as a servant's pay, but I didn't get any of the servant's extras, just the six dollars flat. And that was for a fine, strong young man who stood straight, looked good, could use his tongue and could read and write too. Six dollars: that was all that my whole heap of qualifications was worth.

Out of the six dollars three and a half were docked for food, and on top of that a bit more went in presents, so all I was left with was about two dollars. Of course, I was issued with a free uniform, but nobody wants to go home in his uniform when he's off duty. So even if you didn't really want to, you still had to get yourself a jacket made, and if you spent your money on that then you'd worked for a whole month for nothing. Besides, everyone's got a family, a mother and a father — well, let's not bring them into it now, let's say just a wife. You had to have the rent for a room, and you had to feed and clothe her. And all on a couple of dollars. Neither of you could afford to be ill, you couldn't afford a kid, you couldn't smoke, and you couldn't eat any little extras. And even then it wasn't enough to keep you fed every month.

I can't understand why anyone would let his daughter marry a policeman, even though I often used to be a go-between for my colleagues. The moment I told the girl's family about him being a policeman they'd curl up their lips, and even though they didn't say anything directly it was quite obvious what they meant: "Hunh! A cop!" But I didn't let those curled lips put me off, because nine times out of ten the next thing would be that they'd nod in agreement. Is that because there are too many girls in the world? I don't know.

However you look at it, a copper really has to put on a good show, even if he's broke. I don't know whether to laugh or to cry about it. When you're in uniform you're neat, clean, respectable and someone to be looked up to. You have to control traffic, pedestrians, arguments and fights. You're a government servant, but all you get for your pains is your food and two dollars a month. You know yourself that you're not getting enough, but you have to hold your back straight, and when you come to marrying and raising a family you've still got to get by on your two dollars. When I went to propose marriage for my friends the first thing I always said was, "The lad's got a government job." But was there anyone lower than us in the government service? That was something people didn't want to go into too deeply: if they had it would have ruined everything.

It's true. All coppers know how badly they're treated, but you've still got to do your night patrols, even in the wind and rain. There's no slacking, because you can be fired for that. You're treated badly, but you can't complain. You're dead tired, but you can't take it easy. You know you're never going to get anything out of the force, but you daren't risk chucking the job in. You can't bear to lose it, but you don't put your back into it. Coppers just have to get by from one day to the next, putting on as good a show as they can. Although they're not putting their back into it they make it look as though they are. It's like *taijiquan* boxing.

I just can't think why there should be a job like that, or why so many men are prepared to do it. If I'm a human being in my next life, and if I don't drink the forgetfulness soup before I'm reborn and can still remember what happened in this one, I'll yell at the top of my voice, "This business is a complete disgrace, it's a con, it's disguised murder!" I'm too old now, and I'll soon starve to death, so I can't even bother to shout that. I'm kept busy enough working for my next meal of corn bread.

Mind you, when I first joined the force I didn't see all this straight away. None of us were clever enough for that. Quite the opposite. When I first joined I was rather pleased with myself. I had a smart uniform, boots and a cap, and I looked really good in them. Very well then, I told myself, I've got a government job, and a bright and capable lad like me is bound to get some promotion before long. I was fascinated by the brass stars and gold braid of the sergeants and the officers, and I could just see myself looking like that. It never occurred to me then that stars and braid weren't given out for cleverness and ability.

The novelty soon wore off and I got fed up with that uniform. It didn't make anyone respect you — it just told people that the stinky-feet had arrived. The uniform itself was horrible too. In summer it felt like cowhide, and made you so hot you were soaked in sweat. But in winter it felt more like paper than leather. You weren't allowed to wear anything else underneath, so you just had to let the gales blow right in through your chest and out through your back. And those leather boots kept your feet cold in winter and hot in summer: they were never comfortable. If you wore thin socks with them they were like a couple of big baskets. Your toes and heels rattled around inside them, but you could never find the boots. But when you were wearing padded socks they turned very tight. You couldn't get the padded socks into your boots at the same time as your feet. How many people made their fortunes from contracting for uniforms and leather boots I don't know. All I know is that my feet were always in a terrible state. In summer it was foot rot and in winter it was chilblains. And, of course, even if your feet were in a terrible state you still had to patrol your beat and stand at your post, or that was the end of your six dollars. It made no difference how hot or cold it was. Everyone else could go off somewhere for a bit of shelter. Even the rickshaw men could take a half day off. But we coppers had to walk our beat or stand at our posts, and if you were being roasted or frozen to death so much the worse for you. You'd sold your soul for those six dollars.

I can't remember where, but somewhere I read that if you don't get enough to eat it makes you weak. Whatever it meant, it's near enough to the truth as far as cops on the beat go. The saddest and most ridiculous thing was that although we always had empty bellies we had to hold ourselves straight and look the part on the street. Beggars sometimes bend themselves double and pretend that they've had nothing to eat for three days when they've really got full stomachs, but a copper always has to stick his belly out as if it's got three big bowls of chicken noodles inside even when it's empty. There's some sense in a beggar pretending to be hungry, but I can't see any good reason why a copper should have to pretend he's had a good meal. It's downright ridiculous if you ask me.

Nobody likes the way coppers deal with problems and try to fudge things. Well, there are reasons why. But before I explain it all in detail I want to tell you a terrible story. It'll be much easier to tell you this terrible story first then go back to explain all the reasons, and more interesting too. So we'll do it this way.

7

There should have been a moon that night, but it was hidden by black clouds. It was pitch-black everywhere, and I was on a night patrol in a quiet, out-of-the-way district. I had iron-heeled boots, and in those days we coppers all had to carry a Japanese sword. There was not a sound to be heard apart from my iron heels and sword. I felt lonely, bored and almost scared. Whenever a cat scampered in front of me or I heard a cock crow it got at me. I made myself throw out my chest, but I felt very worried inside, as if something bad was going to happen to me. It wasn't quite fear, and it certainly wasn't blind courage. I just felt very uncomfortable, and my hands were sweating a bit. Usually I was brave enough: guarding a dead body or a storeroom by myself didn't bother me at all. I don't know why I was feeling so jittery that night. The more I tried to laugh myself out of it the more I felt danger lurking. I didn't walk any faster, but I couldn't get back to where there was light and friends a moment too soon.

Suddenly there was firing. I stood where I was, feeling a bit braver. There's nothing like real danger to stop you feeling scared. Fear comes from alarms and uncertainty. I pricked up my ears like a horse at night. Then there was another burst, and a third. It was quiet again. I waited and listened. The silence was unbearable. It was like waiting for thunder after you've seen the lightning. My heart was racing. Then the shots started up again, from everywhere this time.

I wasn't feeling so brave any longer. The first volley had bucked me up, but too much shooting was really dangerous. I was only human, and I wanted to live. I started running, but before I'd gone more than a few paces I slammed to a halt. I listened again. The firing was getting heavier. It was pitch-black and I couldn't see anything. There was just the shooting. I didn't know why or where. There I was, all by myself in the dark, listening to the firing in the distance. Which way should I run? What was it all about? I needed to think it over carefully, but I hadn't got time. There wasn't any point in being brave, and if you don't know what you're doing you can't be brave anyway. Best to run, run anywhere — couldn't be worse than standing there shaking in my boots. So I ran, ran like crazy, clutching my sword. I was like a frightened cat or dog — I could find my home without even having to think. I'd forgotten I was a cop. The first thing I had to do was to run back and see those motherless kids of mine. At least we could all die together.

I had to cross a lot of main roads to get home. As soon as I got to the first one I realized that it was going to be hard to get any further. I could half make out lots of dark shadows in the road: men running fast and shooting. Soldiers! They were the plait soldiers.* I'd cut my plait off a few days earlier. I was really sorry I hadn't coiled my hair up on the top of my head like some other people, but cut the whole plait clean off. The soldiers hated cops, but if I'd been able to let my plait down there and then it might have been enough to stop them shooting me. As far as they were concerned if you had no plait you were a fake foreigner and

---

* Soldiers of the Qing armies who had kept their long plaits as a mark of loyalty to the throne at a time when some people were cutting their plaits off.

deserved to be shot. But I'd lost that little darling. I froze. All I could do was hide in the dark and watch before making my next move. Groups of soldiers were running down the road, one after another, firing all the time. I didn't know what they were doing. After a while they all seemed to have gone away, so I peered out. There was no sign of movement, so I rushed across the road as fast as a night bird and got to the other side. In the instant I was crossing I caught a glimpse of a red glow. There was a fire at the crossroads. As I stayed there, lurking in the shadows, the fire soon lit up a whole area in the distance. When I stuck my head out for another look I could more or less make out the crossroads. The shops on the corners were all ablaze, and by the light of the fire I could see the soldiers rushing about shooting. I understood now. It was a mutiny. Soon the fire got brighter as it spread, and I could tell from the distance of the light that everything by the crossroads and the other junction was ablaze. It's a terrible thing to say so, but the fire was really beautiful. You'd see a sudden flash of white against the black sky in the distance, then it would go black again. Then there'd be another flash of white, and all of a sudden a great ball of red would burst out. There was a girder so red-hot it was terrifying. Amid all the red glow were clouds of black smoke rising up with the tongues of flame. Sometimes the smoke hid the flames, and sometimes the flames burst through the smoke. The black smoke was pouring out and changing shape all the time as it rose into the sky. It made a pall that covered the flames, just like heavy clouds blotting out the setting sun. A little later the glow grew brighter and the smoke turned a whitish grey, all clean and bright. There

weren't many flames, just a bright glow stretching half-
way across the sky. From close to, you could hear all
the noise of the fire and the smoke rising high into the
sky and the flames leaping everywhere. The smoke was
like a horrible black dragon, and the flames were like
red-hot iron bamboo shoots pushing up all over the
place. The flames were wrapped in smoke and the
smoke was wrapped in flames, and they all coiled up
and up together till suddenly they separated out and
sparks came raining down from the black smoke. There
were even a few huge balls of fire. Once the sparks
and the fireballs had fallen the smoke seemed a lot
happier and lighter and went on rolling up into the sky.
As the fireballs came down and met the flames underneath in mid air they started doing a mad, happy dance
again till they exploded into millions of sparks. If the
fireballs landed further away where there was anything
inflammable a new fire started. The new smoke masked
the old fire and turned it black in an instant. Then the
new fire burst through the black smoke and joined up
with the old fire. There'd be tongues of fire and pillars
of fire everywhere, spitting, swaying and roaring about
like crazy. Crash! A house came falling down, sending
up sparks, cinders, ash and white smoke. The flames
were crushed under the ruins, and they all slithered out
sideways like thousands of fire-snakes with their tongues darting out. Without a sound, without any sound
at all, the fire-snakes slowly and patiently crept back
up. Once they were back on top they joined with the
fire already up there. It was all bright, pure and roaring away.   It kind of lit up your heart.

So I watched it. No, I didn't just watch it, I was
smelling it too. I was savouring all the different smells

to tell them apart. That must be the silk dealer's with black letters on a gold sign, and that must be the Shanxi oil and liquor shop. It was by the smells that I could tell the different balls of fire apart. The light ones that rose up high must have been from the tea dealer's, and the heavy black one from the cloth merchant's. They weren't my shops, but I knew them all, and I can't tell you how miserable it was to smell them being cremated and watch them go up in a ball of fire then come down again.

I was so miserable watching and smelling it all that I forgot all about my own danger. I was like a child, completely absorbed in watching the excitement. My teeth were chattering so loud I could hear them, not because I was scared but because I was so carried away by the beauty of this terrible disaster.

There was no hope of getting back home. I had no idea how many soldiers were out on the streets, but from the fires everywhere I reckoned that they were in all the busy shopping areas. What they were really interested in was looting, but goodness knows how many shops they'd sent up in flames while they were about it. There was no way of telling that they weren't bumping people off just for the hell of it while they were about it. To them a cop with his plait cut off was no better than a bedbug. It'd have been no trouble for one of them to give his trigger a squeeze and finish me off.

When I thought about that I decided to get back to the police station. It wasn't far away: just across one road. But it was too late now. The moment the shooting started everyone, rich and poor alike, had fastened their doors. Apart from the soldiers on the rampage the streets were completely deserted. Once the fires began the shopkeepers started rushing around in the glare. The bolder ones among them stood in the street watching their own or other people's shops going up in flames. None of them dared try to put the fires out, but they couldn't bear to go. They just stood there, not saying a thing and watching the flames licking about the place. The timid ones were scrambling with each other to find somewhere to hide down an alley, skulking in little groups, peering out into the street from time to time. They didn't make a squeak. They just shook with fear.

As the fires got fiercer and the shooting started to die out the people who lived down the alleys probably realized what was going on. First some of them opened their doors and peered out. Then some of them cautiously made their way to the street, where there were flames and people but no police. The doors of the pawnshops and the jewellers that the soldiers had looted were still wide open. . . . A shopping street is scary when it's like that, but it makes you bold too. A street without cops is like a classroom without a teacher: even the well-behaved children go wild. First one door opened, then all the doors opened, and the streets were full of people. The shops had already been looted, so why not join in? You'd never have imagined decent, law-abiding people looting in normal times, would you? Hunh! Give them a chance and they'll soon show you what they're really like. Once the word "loot" had been spoken the strong young lads went first for the pawnbrokers, the jewellers and the clock and watch dealers. When the men went home they came out again with their women and children. The shops that the soldiers had looted already were no trouble, of course:

you could just go in and take what you pleased. And the doors of the shops that hadn't been looted didn't keep people out for long. Grain chandlers, tea merchants, general stores and everything else — all the doors were smashed in.

It's a scene I've only ever seen once in my whole life. Everyone shouting, yelling, rushing about like lunatics, crowding together, quarrelling, smashing doors in, yelling and shouting. Men and women, old folk and children. Crikey! Once a door was down they'd rush in like a swarm of bees, pushing and grabbing all over the place. There'd be some who got pushed over and were lying on the ground howling. The nimble ones were up on the counter looking greedily about, fighting, rushing forward in a solid mass, then all falling over and scattering all over the street. People were carrying stuff on their backs, in their arms, or on their shoulders, or dragging it along. They were scurrying along with their heads held high just like an army of conquering ants. They kept coming back over and over again, bringing their wives and children, who gladly came with them.

Of course the poor came out. But the middle classes didn't hang back either.

The valuables went first. Then it was the things like coal, rice, firewood and charcoal. Some people took whole vats of sesame oil. Some people managed two sacks of flour on their shoulders. The street was covered in broken bottles and jars, with rice and flour all over the pavement. Loot! Loot! Loot! They all wished they had extra hands and could run faster. One man was moving a huge jar of white sugar by rolling along the ground with it in his arms, like a dung beetle pushing a turd.

However tough you are there's always somebody tougher. Some people know how to use their heads. One man fetched a vegetable chopper, stood at the entrance to an alley and just waited. "Put it down!" One wave of the chopper and the sack or the clothes would be on the ground. Then quietly and with no trouble at all he'd take it home. "Put it down!" If you weren't quick about it, down came the chopper, the sack of flour was ripped open, and the two of them would be rolling about fighting in a snowstorm. Other people hurrying past, threw them a piece of advice, "What are you fighting for? There's plenty more." Then the two wrestlers came to their senses and ran back to the street. Loot! Loot! There was plenty more.

I squeezed into a crowd of shopkeepers and hid there. I didn't say anything, and they seemed to understand my problem: they kept quiet and squeezed around me. It wasn't just me, a policeman, who didn't dare show my face: they didn't either. They couldn't protect their wealth and property. Anyone who'd tried to interfere would have been throwing his life away. The soldiers had their rifles and the people had their vegetable choppers. So they kept their heads bowed as if they were ashamed of something. What they were most afraid of was of looking the looters in the eye. What with the shame and the anger the looters would have thought nothing of killing a few shopkeepers at a time like that when law and order had broken down. So they protected me. Just think. The people round there must have been able to recognize me. I used to walk that beat nearly every day. If I caught one of them pissing against a wall I'd usually give him a bad time. Of course they hated me. If they'd met me just then, when they were

having such a marvellous time stealing, one of them
would have done for me with a brick. Even if they
didn't recognize me, I was still wearing my uniform
and carrying my Japanese sword. It was no time for a
cop to go sticking his neck out. All the apologies in the
world for being so rude wouldn't have been enough to
make them spare me.

All of a sudden the street emptied and the people on
the pavement all rushed into the alleys. A mob of soldiers were sauntering ever so slowly down the road. I
took off my cap and peered over an apprentice's
shoulder. I could see a private carrying a string of things
that looked like crabs. I could tell they were gold and
silver bracelets. He was carrying a lot of other stuff too.
I wasn't sure, but I reckoned he must be carrying a lot
more valuables on him from the slow way he was walking. He looked so natural you really wanted to admire
him. Sauntering casually along the middle of the road,
so nice and easy, holding his string of bracelets. The
blazing shops were like enormous torches lighting up the
whole city for them.

Once the soldiers had gone the people all came out of
the alleys again. Just about everything had been taken
by now, so they started carrying off the shop doors and
even the shop signs over the entrances. I've often seen
the word "thorough" in the papers, and our worthy
citizens did some really thorough looting that night.

It was only then that the shopkeepers dared to show
their faces and shout, "Help! Fire! Don't let everything
get burned!" It sounded so sad it brought tears to your
eyes. At last the people with me started to move. What
was I to do? They were going to fight the fires, leaving
me all by myself, a cop. Where was I going to run to?

I grabbed hold of a butcher who took off his tunic that was soaked in pork dripping. I hid my cap under my arm and ran back to the station, keeping close to the wall. I clutched my sword in one hand and held the lapels of the tunic together with the other.

8

I didn't do any looting, and none of what other people looted had belonged to me, so you could say that the whole business was nothing to do with me at all. But I'd seen it and I'd understood. Understood what, you ask. I can't put it in a nutshell, but what I understood came close to changing my character. My wife leaving me had been one thing I was never to forget, and now there was another to keep it company: I was never to forget that mutiny either. Losing a wife had only been my own business and all I had to do was remember it. There was no need to drag national politics and world problems into a family matter. But this mutiny had affected thousands and thousands of people, so whenever I thought of it I thought of everyone, of the whole city. To put it bluntly, that business helped me to make my mind up about a whole lot of big issues, like all the problems that the papers are always going on about. Yes, I've just thought of a good way of putting it. That business gave me a bit of insight, and that insight has helped me to understand a lot more problems. I don't know whether anyone can see what I'm getting at when I put it that way, but I think it gets it nicely.

As I told you before, there was an empty place in my heart after my wife disappeared, and after the mutiny it was even bigger. There was plenty of room in there for a whole lot of things. But let's get back to the mutiny. When I've told you the whole story you'll be able to see why it was so big.

When I got back to my room at the station I found all the rest of them still awake. That was understandable enough, but none of them seemed at all anxious or bothered. They were smoking and drinking tea just as if they were staying up all night for a wedding or a funeral. They weren't at all sympathetic when I came in looking such a sorry sight — they actually laughed. I'd been longing to pour my woes out to them but I could see at a glance that I'd have been wasting my breath. I wanted to turn in, but the officer stopped me. "Don't go to bed. It'll soon be light, and we'll all have to go out and calm things down." It was my turn to laugh then. When all that arson and looting was going on there hadn't been a copper to be seen. Waiting till daylight before going out to calm things down was absolute nonsense. But orders were orders, and we had to wait till dawn.

Even before then I found out that the top police commanders had all known about the mutiny in advance but hadn't wanted to tell the junior officers and the men. In other words, the mutiny was beyond the control of the police, and if the troops wanted to mutiny they could. They didn't care whether the junior officers and the men got killed as they patrolled their beat or stood at their posts as usual that night without a clue about what was going to happen. It was a very clever idea, and a vicious one too.

When all the other cops heard the firing they'd done the same as me and run straight back. We weren't fools.

We were just the right men for officers like them. From top to bottom the whole force was a bunch of clowns on the job. That's the absolute truth.

Although I was dead tired I was longing to get back on the streets and have a good look round. The scenes of the previous night were imprinted on my mind and I wanted another look at them by daylight for comparison so I could get the whole picture. The time really dragged till dawn: I suppose it was because I was feeling too impatient. In the end the sky did slowly get brighter and we fell in. I really wanted to laugh: some of the lads had let the plaits down from on top of their heads and combed them out. The officers pretended not to notice. Some of them gave their uniform a good brush down and shined up their boots. With all the losses in the city some men could still care about shining their boots. I couldn't help smiling.

Going out on the streets wiped the smile clean off my face. This was the first time I'd ever understood what was meant by the word "catastrophe". There were still a few big stars in the sky that had not yet set, and in the grey morning light the clouds were bluish, looking fresh and pale. There was the smell of burning everywhere, and white smoke was drifting across the sky. All the shops had their doors wide open, and every single window was broken. The adults and the young apprentices were all standing or sitting in the doorways. None of them was saying a word, and they couldn't bring themselves to start clearing up the mess either. They were like a flock of sheep without a shepherd. The fires weren't spreading any longer, but white smoke was still rising quietly from the wreckage they'd left, and bright little flames were still burning. Whenever there was a breath of wind the charred timbers of the houses started glowing again, and the flames fluttered in the breeze like little flags. The first shops to have gone up in flames were now just huge piles of cinders. The end walls were still standing, but all there was inside them were smoking grave mounds. The last places to catch fire were all still standing with their walls and roofs complete. The only thing was that their doors and windows had all been burned out and left as blackened, gaping holes. There was a cat sitting in one of those doorways. The smoke was making it sneeze, but it wasn't going to budge.

What were normally the busiest shopping streets were now just stretches of charred wood and broken tiles. Masses of charred wooden uprights just stood there in silence. It was the same whichever way you looked — there they were, looking lazy, bored and as if they couldn't stop the smoke pouring out even though they wanted to. I've no way knowing what hell's like, but I expect it's something like that. When I looked down I could remember what the street used to be like with all its lovely, grand shops, but when I looked up again all that was left was ashes. The contrast between what I could remember and what I could see brought tears to my eyes. Was this what they meant by a catastrophe? Crowds of shopkeepers and apprentices were standing dumbstruck beside the wreckage, their hands in their sleeves, staring numbly at what was left of the fire. When they saw us they just gave us a look of total indifference. They showed no emotion. It was as if they didn't need to feel anything now that their hopes had been completely wiped out.

As we went through the area where the fires had been

all the shops had their doors and windows open but there
was no sign of movement. The pavements and the roads
were covered with debris, which was an even more de-
pressing sight than the fire damage. One look at the
ruins was enough to tell you there'd been a fire, but the
sight of the smashed-up, deserted shops and things baf-
fled me. I just couldn't understand why a prosperous
shopping area had suddenly been turned into an enormous rubbish dump. Anyhow, I was sent there to stand
guard. I hadn't a clue about what I was supposed
to do. I just stood there very correctly, not moving at
all. There was something cold about the ruined streets
that had me fascinated. Some women and children were
picking up broken things outside the shops. As the shopkeepers weren't saying anything I didn't interfere.
Standing there seemed completely pointless.

When the sun came up the streets looked more of a
mess than ever. They were as ugly as beggars in the
sunlight, which brought out the shape and the colours of
every single little thing on the ground. The strange,
clashing styles and chaos of it all was oppressive. There
was nobody selling vegetables, hurrying to the market
early, or selling breakfast snacks. There wasn't a rickshaw or a horse. The whole street was a cold, deserted
shambles. Even the sun that had just come up seemed
to be hanging its head in dejection as it just hung there
pointlessly. A postman walked past me, his head hanging low and a long shadow behind him. I shivered.

A bit later one of the officers came, followed by a
constable. The two of them walked along the middle of
the road in very high spirits, as if something marvellous
had just happened. The officer told me to keep good
order on the streets: martial law had been ordered. I

saluted, wondering what on earth he was talking about. The officer seemed to notice that I was looking stupefied, so he added under his breath that I was to make the scavengers clear off as martial law had been ordered. I didn't want to do as he'd told me, but I couldn't openly disobey an order, so I went out of the shop and waved my hands at the women and children. I couldn't bring myself to say anything.

As I maintained public order like this I walked towards the pork butcher's shop to tell him I'd bring his tunic back when I'd had it washed. The bucther was sitting in the doorway of his little shop. I'd never have imagined that even a little shop like his would have been looted, but it had been cleaned right out. The butcher did not even look up when I spoke to him. I took a glance inside and saw that the chopping blocks, the meat hooks, the cash box, the fat tray and everything else that was portable had been stolen. All he had left was his counter and the earth base for the meat shelves.

I went back to my post. My head was splitting. If I'd had to look at that street much longer I'd have gone round the bend.

Martial law had indeed been brought in. A squad of a dozen soldiers and an officer came along with fixed bayonets and a sign authorizing them to enforce the law with summary executions. Hunh! It was the plait soldiers again. After they'd finished their own looting and burning they were coming out again to do some summary executions. What kind of joke was that? I even had to salute their sign.

After saluting I had a quick look around to see if there were any more scavengers around and give them a warning. People who'd even steal a butcher's block didn't deserve any sympathy, but being executed by the plait soldiers of all people was taking injustice too far.

It happened faster than I can tell you. A boy of fourteen or fifteen didn't get away. He was surrounded by bayonets while he still had a plank and an old shoe in his hands. They pulled him to the ground, the sword came flashing out, and the boy shouted, "Mum!" His blood spurted ever such a long way. His body was still twitching when they hung his head from a telegraph pole.

It left me too weak even to spit. Everything was spinning round in front of my eyes. I'd seen people killed before and wasn't scared of that. It was because I realized it was so unjust! So unjust! When I told you before that this business had given me a bit of insight that was what I meant. Just think: you take a whole string of gold and silver bracelets back to the barracks then come out again to execute a boy who's stolen an old pair of shoes and call it enforcing the "law" with summary punishments. If that's the kind of law there is in the world then f- - - its mother and its grandmother. Forgive me for putting it so crudely, but things like that aren't very civilized.

Later on I heard it said that the mutiny had some political significance, which was why the very soldiers who did the looting had come out to restore order afterwards. The whole thing had been worked out in advance from beginning to end. Political significance? Search me. All I wanted to do was to swear at everyone. But what would have been the point in a stinky-foot like me swearing at everyone?

9

I don't really want to say another word about that business, but to round the story off I've got to back to it. I'll bring it up and leave it at that. There are plenty of people who are cleverer than me, and they can work out what it all meant.

How could a mutiny have "political significance"?

If they were deliberately training the troops in looting, why did they send us cops out on our beats beforehand?

What were we police for? Were we meant just to stop people pissing in the street but to ignore people looting shops?

If peaceful, law-abiding citizens were looters, why did we police only arrest petty thieves?

Did the people want police or didn't they? If they didn't, then why did they call for us whenever a fight was going to start, and pay their police tax every month? If they did want us, why were they pleased when we didn't do our job? We let the looters loot, and the victims didn't utter a word of protest.

Very well then. I've just given you a few examples. There are many, many other problems beside these. I can't solve them, so there's no point in going on about them. Those examples left me completely at sea. No matter how I thought about them it didn't seem right. I couldn't make out what was what. Even what made sense at one minute was all nonsense the next. My little bit of brain just wasn't up to sorting out problems that big.

I can only say it in a very old-fashioned way. The whole people — officials, soldiers, police, and decent citizens — aren't good enough. That was why the empty hole in my heart got bigger. Living among all these people who weren't good enough all I wanted to do was to muddle through. I didn't want to do anything properly. I understood now.

There's another good way of putting it that's worth remembering: a mess. For anyone like me who can't think of how to cope it's just the word, ready made, handy, and it doesn't muddle you either. A mess, and that's all. If you think that's a bit too short, call it a f- - - ing mess and you'll have it perfectly.

10

No need for any more arguments to convince you. Anyone can see what our people are like. To get back to us coppers, it was quite right that we were slack and incompetent. Nothing surprising about that. Take arresting gamblers, for example. In the old days the gambling joints had very big shots as their backstage bosses. It wasn't just that the officials couldn't raid them. Even murders there weren't taken seriously. People were always getting bumped off in those places. After the police force was set up they still stayed open. We didn't raid them: the reason's so obvious you won't need me to tell you why. But if we didn't make any raids at all that didn't look too good. What were we to do? Someone had an idea. Clean up a few small, simple cases, arrest a few old men and women, seize a few packs of cards, and slap on a few fines. That way we police had done our job and had done something to keep up our reputation. That's one example, and I could give you a dozen more. From the very beginning the force was just faking it. The whole police force was full of useless people doing useless things. Society didn't need real cops, and the coppers weren't going to work themselves to death for six dollars a month. That was very obvious.

Things got a lot worse for us after the munity. The young lads in the city had done a lot of looting and made their dirty pile. Some of them were going round wearing two jackets, one on top of the other, or a ring on every finger. They'd go swaggering down the road, sneering at us police and snorting at us with contempt. We could only walk past with our heads hanging. Well, you could hardly blame people for looking down at us after we'd made not a squeak in the face of as big a challenge as that. They were gambling everywhere: it was all stolen money, so even if every penny of it went it was no real loss. We didn't dare make any raids, and even if we had we'd never have got all the places — there were just too many of them.

We could hear gamblers shouting "a pair", "long and short" and so on from the other side of their walls, but we pretended not to hear and just slunk past. After all, they were only fooling about inside their own courtyards, not coming out on the streets. People wouldn't even allow us that bit of self-respect. The lads who were wearing two coats wanted to show that they weren't at all scared of us cops. Their granddads and fathers hadn't even seen the police, let alone be scared of them, so why should their generation take any nonsense from the police? So they came out to gamble on the streets. If you had dice you could begin the game, squat down and start rolling them. If you had a couple of stone bowls you could have a game of kicking bowls for any number of players from two to five. "Ten cents a kick. What about it? O.K. Roll back, roll back!" Clink, the bowls meet, and it's ten cents. That wasn't chicken feed. You could make several dollars in an hour. All this was happening under our very noses. Was I going to do anything about it or not? Say I'd tried to. All I had was a sword that couldn't even slice beancurd properly and I was on my own. The gamblers were a bunch of young lads. There was no point in asking for trouble. The only thing a cop could do was take a longer way round and leave them to it. But with my lousy luck I'd have to run into an inspector. "Are you blind? Couldn't you see them gambling?" When I got back the least I could expect would be a reprimand. And there was nowhere I could complain to about getting rough justice.

There were so many things like that. As far as I'm concerned, if I'd had a pistol instead of the useless sword I'd have been willing to take anyone on. Of course, it's not worth throwing your life away for six dollars a month. Still, everyone's got a temper, especially when you're thoroughly fed up. But I couldn't get my hands on a pistol. All the guns were for bandits and soldiers.

When I saw soldiers riding rickshas without paying and hitting the rickshamen with their belts I had to smile and wave them past. They had guns and were prepared to use them. Killing a cop was nothing to them. One year soldiers murdered three of our lads in a third-class brothel. We didn't even ask for the ringleader to be handed over. Three of our lads killed for nothing, and not one of the soldiers had to pay with his life. None of them even got a flogging. They could shoot whenever they felt like it, but we were bare-handed. We did things the civilized way!

To put it in a nutshell, there's no place for a police force in a society that honours barbarism and thinks it's glorious to destroy the peace. Anyone who can understand that and what I was telling you before about how badly we were fed can get more or less the whole picture. What else could we do except fake it? As a policeman I'm not asking anyone to forgive us for it. I just want to tell it and bring it all out into the open. Then everyone can understand the way things are.

While I'm about it, let me tell you about the thing that got me down worst of all.

After one or two years in the force I was really someone among the lads. Whenever there was a case our officers always sent me in first to deal with it. The other lads weren't jealous, because I never hung back when it came to helping any of them out. Whenever there was a vacancy for a platoon commander they'd all whisper, "You're bound to be the one who gets promotion this time." Anyone would have thought they really wanted someone like me as a sergeant. Although I never did make it to platoon commander everyone knew how good I was.

You'll have been able to guess my secret of coping from all the stuff I've told you already. For example, if someone came in to report a burglary the sergeant and I would go along to investigate. After a very sketchy look round the doors, windows and yard I'd give them some very glib patter about where our posts were in that part of town and how many patrols we made each night. I'd put in plenty of detail and make it all sound really good, as if we were the most careful and conscientious people in the world, all flogging our guts out. After that we'd find a door or a window that wasn't fastened very

well and start our counter-attack. I'd talk in a very
gentle voice but I'd let them hear the steel behind it:
"This door's not very secure. You ought to fit a lock.
I tell you, when you fit your lock, fit it nice and low.
The best place is right near the doorstep, so that it's hard
for thieves to find it. It's a good idea to keep a little
dog in the house too. If you've got a dog indoors, however small it is, it'll start barking at the slightest movement. It's better than keeping three big ones in the yard.
Look, sir, we'll keep a special eye on things, and you
be a bit more careful. If we work together I can guarantee that you won't lose anything else. Right then, we'd
better be going back. We'll send a few more lads out
on night patrol. You can go to bed now, sir."

That little speech got us right off the hook. He'd have
to fit his locks and get his little dog. If the householder
was a friendly sort he'd even make us a cup of tea. That
was what I was good at. I'd do what was necessary so
that we didn't accept any responsibility, but nobody
could see that we were just faking it. I'd make ever such
a nice speech and with my blarney I'd get rid of all our
responsibility. And I could guarantee that there
wouldn't be any trouble in store. All the lads knew how
to do it, but they couldn't talk and act the part anywhere
near as well as I did. There are a lot of ways you can
say the same sentence, and if you get your manner right
you can take back what you're saying even as you say
it, like a spring. I was better than they were at that,
and they couldn't pick it up. It was a natural gift.

How do you think I handled it if I came across burglars when I was on night patrol by myself? I'd take
a good grip on my sword to stop it clanking, and let
them get on with climbing their walls while I got on with

my patrol. We left each other alone. Well, if I'd given one of them a grudge against me he could have hidden in the shadows and got me with a brick. I couldn't have taken that. What's his name, that idiot Wang the Ninth, lost an eye that way. And he wasn't even trying to catch burglars. One day he and Dong Zhihe had been cutting people's plaits off in the street whether they wanted it done or not. Each of them had a pair of scissors in one hand, and whenever they saw a plait they'd grab it and cut it off. Someone remembered. When that idiot Wang the Ninth was on the beat by himself they got him in the eye with a handful of lime. "That'll teach you to cut my plait off, you f --- er." From then on he was blind in that eye. Do you think I'd still be alive today if I hadn't done my job the way I did? Whenever the police think they ought to do something people always think we're sticking our noses in where we're not wanted. So what else could we do?

I wasn't going to lose the sight of an eye for nothing, like that idiot Wang the Ninth. I kept my eyes to watch the world with. While I was tiptoeing quietly out of the way of burglars my mind wasn't asleep. I was thinking of my two motherless children and working out what we were going to eat for the rest of the month. I suppose some people do their accounts in the big foreign-style coins, counting in fives and tens. I had to work things out in copper cash, one by one. If I had a few cash in hand I felt easy, and if I was a bit short I was worried. If I'd tried nabbing burglars we'd have all been broke. When you're dead broke and there's no other way out anyone can take to thieving. Bellies don't care about being respectable.

II

After the mutiny there was another big upheaval: the Great Qing Empire became the Republic of China. A change of dynasty isn't something that happens often, but it didn't mean much to me. To be frank, this great change that only comes once in several hundred years was less exciting than the mutiny. They said that once the Republic started, the people would be in charge of everything. If they were, I never noticed. I was still a cop, my pay didn't go up, and it was the same old routine every day. I'd been pushed around before and I was still being pushed around. The coachmen and servants of the old officials always used to push us around, and the underlings of the new officials weren't any more polite to us either. The mess was still a mess. The change of dynasty didn't make any real difference. One difference was that you saw more men with their plaits cut off: I suppose that was progress of a sort. The old sorts of cards and dice gradually became less popular as rich and poor alike all started playing mahjong. As before, we didn't dare raid the gambling joints, but you had to admit that the gear they used had been reformed and was more civilized.

The citizens of the Republic were nobodies, but the Republic's officials and soldiers really were something. Goodness knows where all those officials and soldiers sprang from like mushrooms after rain. You shouldn't talk about officials and soldiers in the same breath, but they really did have quite a lot in common. Someone who'd been up to his knees in mud as a peasant one day and become an official or a soldier the next didn't need any lessons in how to glare. The more stupid they were, the fiercer the glare. They were so stupid that they shone with it. Those stupid fools couldn't tell whether you were talking to them politely or not: whatever you said to them they treated you like dirt. They were so stupid you almost felt sorry for them, but they loved it. Sometimes they made me think that the reason I'd never become either a civil official or an army officer was because I wasn't stupid enough.

Almost any official could demand a few policemen to guard his home. We became kind of bodyguards doing their private business at the public expense. I got detached to guard an official's residence. In principle, looking after an official's private home should have been no part of our duties. Once I was detached I was promoted to be a constable, third grade. As a recruit I hadn't been qualified for detachment. That was when I first got into the grades. On top of that, duties were very light at the residence. There was nothing to do apart from standing at the gateway and keeping guard at night. At the very least you could save a pair of leather boots a year. It was less work and no danger. Even if the master and the mistress had a fight it was none of our business to break it up, so there was no risk of getting knocked to the ground and injured by mistake. All the night patrols involved was taking a couple of turns round the compound without the slightest chance of running into a burglar. The walls were too high and the dogs too fierce for petty thieves, and the top burglars didn't bother. They probably burgled retired officials' houses: there was plenty of loot there, and the authorities wouldn't try so hard to catch them. They never tangled with powerful men still in office. Instead of being supposed to raid gambling dens, we were now protecting the ladies and gentlemen while they played mahjong.

When they had visitors for mahjong we'd have a very easy time. There'd be a whole line of horses and carriages outside, and it'd be as bright as day inside with servants coming and going between the two or three mahjong tables and the four or five opium lamps all the time. There'd be such a commotion all night that there wasn't the slightest risk of burglars, so we could get a good night's sleep. Next morning, when the game broke up, we'd come out again to stand at the gate and salute. It gave the gentlemen a bit of class. Weddings and funerals in the home were even better for us. At weddings there were operas we could watch for free. They always had top singers, and gave much fuller versions of the operas than you'd ever see at the theatre. Although there weren't operas at funerals, the deceased couldn't be taken out after only a few hours. The coffin had to stay there for thirty or forty days while there were lots of scripture recitations. That was fine, because we got the free meals too. One of them died, and we were rewarded with feasts. The worst thing was when a kid died. There'd be no funeral ceremony, and we'd have to listen to them all crying for real. The next worst was when one of the daughters of the family eloped, or one of the concubines was thrown out for doing something terrible. We got nothing to eat or drink, and no operas either. And we had to feel pretty bad for the masters and mistresses then.

What I particularly liked about this kind of duty was that I could come and go a lot more freely, so that I would often get back home to see my kids. When I was in the main police station or the local station it was well-nigh impossible to get a bit of extra leave. That was because your duties in the station or on the beat were all set: it wasn't easy to get them changed. But when I was guarding a residence there was nothing else for me to do after my spell of sentry duty on the gate. I just needed to have a word with the other lads and I could disappear for hours on end. This was the perk that really had me worried about being transferred back to the station. My kids had no mother, so I really wanted them to see as much of their dad as possible.

The fact that I didn't have to go out had its advantages too. I never got exhausted, and I didn't have much to worry about. What did I do with all that spare time? There were plenty of newspapers in the residence, and when I was at a loose end read them from the front page to the back page. Posh papers, trashy rags, news stories, editorials, I read them all, whether I understood them or not. It was a big help to me. I found out about a whole load of things, and learnt how to read a whole lot more words. There are a lot of words that I couldn't pronounce to this very day, but I got to recognize them so well that I could guess what they meant. It's like the way you give a friendly smile to some people you always meet in the street even though you don't know their names. Apart from newspapers I used to go all over the place borrowing light fiction. Mind you, you get much more out of reading the papers. There's a lot more in them, and they use harder words, so that they broaden your mind. The only thing is that as there's so much in them and they use so many difficult words they take a lot of effort. When I get to the bits I can't understand I go back to light fiction. But light fiction's always the same old stories. When you've read one chapter you can guess what's going to happen in the next. That's why it's so easy to read. You just do it for fun. In my experience papers cheer you up and light fiction relaxes you.

There were some snags about being in the residences. The first problem was food. In the main station or the local station our mess fees were docked from our wages whether we liked it or not, but we got our meals every day. When we were detached to guard a residence there'd only be four or five of us, so we couldn't possibly afford to hire a cook to take care of our meals. No cook would ever have looked twice at a silly little proposition like that. We weren't allowed to use the kitchen in the house either. The reason why those gentlemen wanted us coppers was so they would have men in uniform working for them for nothing. They didn't give a damn about our bellies. So what were we to do? We couldn't build our own stove, and we couldn't buy a whole lot of bowls and pots and pans because we didn't know when we'd be transferred. Besides, the reason they wanted us police on the gate was to give the place a bit of class. It wouldn't have done at all if we'd had our bowls and dishes all over the place and rattled our knives and pans. So we had no option. We had to buy our meals.

That was very awkward. If we'd had the money I'd have been free to buy whatever I wanted. Goes without saying. Plenty to drink, a couple of good dishes, and I'd have been in clover. But don't forget that I only had those six dollars a month. I didn't mind eating badly, but I hated having to decide what to do for every meal. Just thinking about it had me almost in tears. I wanted to save money, and I wanted some variety. I couldn't always be gnawing away at dry corn bread and hot pepper pancakes, force-feeding myself like a Beijing duck. I could never find anything that was both cheap and tasty. But when I thought about the money I just had to accept my fate. I just had to make do with a few dry buns and a bit of old pickled turnip. It didn't seem very healthy. The more I thought about it the worse I felt and the harder it was to make up my mind to do it. I'd starve myself till evening before eating my lunch.

I had those kids to feed at home. The less I ate, the more there was for them. Everybody loves their children. When I had to eat the food provided in the station I had no way of saving any money on it, but now I was free to eat as I pleased I could cut down a bit so as to give the children more. So if eight dry buns were what I really needed I'd make do with six and drink a couple of extra bowls of hot water to make me feel full. It was enough to bring tears to my eyes.

When I looked at the officials' homes they made no end of money. You could easily find out how much salary they earned, but what they actually got was much more than that fixed sum. What I mean is that someone earning eight hundred dollars a month would never have been able to live in that sort of style on eight hundred alone. Of course there was more to it than that. This is how it worked. If your pay was six dollars a month that was all you got, and if you had an extra dollar in your pocket people would give you dirty looks and start spreading stories about you. But if you earned five hundred dollars you wouldn't be held to that. The more you got, the more you'd be looked up to. That may look a bit unfair, but that's the way it was, whether you want to believe it or not.

The papers and propaganda places were always going

on about freedom. Anything that has to be argued for like that can't have existed before: stands to reason. I'd never had any freedom, and even after it had been talked about for a time I still didn't get any. But I did see it in the officials' homes. So there was something to be said for the Republic after all. Even if you didn't get any freedom yourself you could at least broaden your horizons by seeing someone else's.

Look, back in the days of the Great Qing there were rules about everything. If you were meant to wear a blue cotton jacket you wore a blue cotton jacket, and it was the same even if you were rich. I suppose you could call that dictatorship. But once the Republic came in there was bags of freedom in the officials' residences. As long as you had the money you could eat or wear whatever you liked. Nobody was going to interfere. So if you want freedom you have to grab money as if your life depends on it, and as there are no censors* under the Republic you're free to do so. If you've never spent any time in an official's residence you probably won't believe me. So take a look for yourself. Even a petty official does a lot better for himself now than one of the highest ministers in the old days. Take food. With communications so much better now you can have game or seafood whenever you like — as long as you've got the money. When you get fed up with them you can switch to Western food and foreign liquor for a change. I don't suppose any Chinese emperor in history ever had a Western meal. The same goes for clothes, jewellery, entertainment, and all the other things you

---

* Censors in the Qing state were officials whose duties included ensuring that other officials were uncorrupt.

need: you can sit at home and enjoy all the best things in the world. The people who live in luxury these days really do live in luxury, and, of course, they have a lot more freedom to grab money than they used to. I wouldn't like to comment on anything else, but I do know that the concubine in one residence used perfumed powder that cost fifty dollars for a tiny box. It was from Paris or somewhere. Where's Paris? Search me. Anyhow, powder from there costs the earth. My neighbour Li the Fourth had to sell a fine fat baby boy, and all he got for him was forty dollars. That shows how dear the powder was. It must have been very fine and smelt lovely, it really must.

Anyhow, that's enough about that. If I keep on saying nasty things about it anyone might think I was against freedom. As if I'd dare!

Let me try approaching it another way. Even though I've got to wrap my meaning up a bit, there were some changes that won't bore you at all. I was telling you a moment ago about how free and rich they were in their official residences, but don't get the wrong impression that all those fine gentlemen do is to throw their money away in handfuls. There're not such fools. It's true that the concubine's powder cost more than a baby, but a concubine is a concubine, and she has her own winning ways and the good fortune that comes with them. The reason why the master would buy her such expensive powder was because he could get the money elsewhere. Look, if you were an official I could tell you a whole lot of the secrets of the rules of the official residence. Your electricity, water, coal, phone, lavatory paper, carriages, awnings, furniture, stationery and flowers all come for free. On top of that you can have the services of a few policemen for nothing. That's all in the rules and regulations. If you don't understand that you're not fit to be a top official.

I'll tell you something that's absolutely true. Officials come empty-handed and leave stuffed to the gills. They're like bedbugs when they've woken up from hibernation: they come as just skin, and a moment later they've got big round bellies full of blood. Crude the comparison may be, but it's spot on. You grab money freely and you save it like a dictator. Put the two together and your lady concubine can use powder that's come all the way from Paris. If that's a bit hard to follow, too bad. You can work it out if you want to.

I suppose I ought to say something more about myself. You'd have thought that after they'd had our services for free for a year or more they'd have had the common decency to give us at least a meal at festivals and the New Year. It would have been a kind gesture. Hunh! Forget it! The master kept all his money to spend on his lady concubine. We police were nothing. We had to be very grateful if we could get the master to put in a good word for us at the station when we were transferred.

Just imagine! The order came down and I was transferred somewhere else. I packed up my bedroll then went to see the master of the house, as polite as could be. He didn't make a fuss. He hardly condescended to notice me. Anyone would have thought I'd been nicking his things. I said something to ask him to put in a good word for me at the station. I wanted him to say I'd done a decent job at his house. He barely lifted an eyelid: he couldn't even be bothered to fart in reply. All I could do was leave. He didn't even give me the money to hire a cart to move my bedroll: I had to carry it myself. What a f --- ing job, and what f --- ing kindness.

12

More and more of us were needed in government offices and officials' residences. A special guard unit of five hundred men was set up, just to be unpaid bodyguards. To show that we really could protect our lords and masters we were each issued with a rifle and several clips of ammunition. I wasn't in the least interested in the rifles — in those rifles, that is. They were old, heavy, and clapped out. Goodness only knows where they'd been found. All they were was a weight on your shoulder: apart from that they were completely useless. We always kept our ammunition on our belts. We were never allowed to load our rifles. In a crisis all they ever let us do was to fix our bayonets after the officials had fled.

But that didn't mean that we could ignore those wrecks. We had to work on them. They had to be cleaned, inside and out, every day, including the bayonet. Even though we could never make them shine, our hands were never allowed to be idle.

On top of that, once we had rifles we had to carry a lot of other stuff about with us too: leather belts, bayonet scabbards, ammunition pouches. The whole lot had to be spick and span. We couldn't be sloppy, the way Pig wears his sword in *Journey to the West*. We even had to wear puttees.

For all this extra trouble, and nine or ten more pounds

of equipment to carry, I got an extra dollar. I now earned seven dollars a month, thank Heavens.

I carried my rifle, wore my puttees, stood sentry duty
and got my seven dollars a month for over three years,
going from one residence or government office to the
next. When my lords and masters went out I saluted
them; and I saluted them when they came back in. That
was my duty. It really wore me out. Compared with
being idle, I was busy; compared with being busy, I had
nothing to do. It was worse than standing at your post
in the street. There you'd always have something to keep
an eye on and give your mind to. You never had to use
your head at all at the entrance to an office or a residence. If the office had nothing to do or the residence
was a mess you could do what you liked even on sentry
duty. You could stand there leaning on your rifle, or
even put your arms round it and take a snooze. You
didn't have to make any effort on a job like that, but
it wore you right out. The servants always had something to hope for, like the chance of getting duties with
some nice pickings. But we knew we hadn't got a hope
of things getting better. We just wasted every single day,
and lost all our self-respect in the process.

You might think that with nothing to do like that I'd
have fattened myself up and at least had that to make
myself presentable. Hunh! We never put on any fat.
We spent all our days thinking about our seven dollars,
we were so worried about being hard up. When you're
worrying you can't possibly put on weight. As for me,
my kids were of school age by then, and of course I
wanted them to go. But schooling cost money. Nothing
odd about that: that's the way it's always been. But
how was I going to find the money? Officials got all

sorts of free perks, but we cops didn't even have a free school to send our children to. If I'd sent them to a private school there'd have been the fees, presents for the teachers at festivals, books and stationery. It'd all have cost money. It'd have cost even more to send them to a state school, what with the uniform, the handicraft materials, and all the exercise books. On top of that, when the children got hungry at home they could break off a piece of corn bread, but you had to give them snack money for school. If I'd tried to make them take a hunk of corn bread with them they'd never have agreed. It doesn't take much to make a kid feel embarrassed.

I didn't know what to do. There I was, a grown man, having to watch my children running wild at home. Just because there was no hope for me in this life did that mean things had to be even worse for my children? I could see the young ladies and gentlemen in the officials' residences going to school. They had rickshas to take them there and bring them home, and when they got back there'd be nurses and maids to take their satchels and carry them inside. They had tangerines and apples and brand-new toys. It was one way for their children and another way for mine. But weren't all children the citizens of tomorrow? I really wished I could resign and chuck the job in. I thought of becoming a servant and making a few extra bucks to pay for my children's education.

But everyone gets into their own rut in life, and once in your rut you never get out of it. After several years in a government job — even as lousy a one as that — I was completely in a rut. I had friends I could talk and joke with, and I knew the ropes. It didn't really interest me, but somehow I hadn't the heart to leave. Besides, vanity is often more powerful than money. Becoming a servant after you've got used to working for the government is going down in the world, even if the money's better. It's silly, it's very silly, but that's what people are like. When I discussed it with my friends they all shook their heads. Some of them asked me what I wanted to change for when we all got along fine. Some of them said that the grass always looks greener on the other side of the hill. It didn't matter what we poor blighters did, we'd never get rich, so I might just as well stick it out. Other people told me that even some high school graduates were now police recruits, so that a job like ours wasn't so bad. Why go to all that trouble? Even the officers advised me to stick it out as best I could. It was a government job, and with my abilities I was bound to get a promotion one day. As everyone was saying this I perked up a bit. I began to feel that if I was pig-headed I'd be letting my pals down. Very well then. I'd stick it out. What about the kids' schooling? It had to go by the board.

I had a piece of luck soon after that. There was a very high official called His Excellency Feng who was such a big shot that he wanted a dozen bodyguards: four on the gates, four to carry messages, and four to go round with him as escorts. The four escorts had to be able to ride. That was before cars, when top officials were particular about their carriages. Under the Qing, top officials always had horsemen in front of and behind their sedan chairs and carriages, didn't they? Well, this Feng wanted to bring back some of the prestige officials had before, so he wanted an escort of four armed horsemen riding behind his carriage. I suppose it was hard to get men who could ride: they only found three in the whole guard battalion. Just three would have looked ridiculous. Even our officers were racking their brains. I saw that I could be on to a good thing: there were bound to be fodder allowances for a horseman. For the sake of my children's education I decided to take the risk. If I could make a bit on the side from the fodder allowances I'd at least be able to afford to send them to private school. You might say that I shouldn't have been thinking along those lines, but I was risking my neck for it — I couldn't ride. I told the officer I was willing to volunteer. When he asked me whether I could ride I didn't say I could and didn't say I couldn't, and as he couldn't get anyone else he didn't press the point.

You can do anything in the world if you've got the nerve. I had it all worked out the first time I met the horse. If he threw me and killed me the kids would probably be no worse off in the orphanage than at home. And if I wasn't killed they'd go to private school. So I wasn't scared of the horse; and because I wasn't scared of him, he was scared of me. It's like that with everything. Beside that, I was nimble and quick-witted, so after I'd chewed the fat for a few minutes with the three men who really could ride I knew quite a few of the tricks of it. I got hold of a docile animal and had a try. My hands were sweating, but I insisted that I knew what I was doing. For the first few days I took a lot of punishment. I felt shattered all over, and my backside was raw and bloody. I gritted my teeth. By the time the injuries had healed I felt a lot braver and was starting to enjoy it. I rode and rode, as fast as the carriage. I'd got the animal under control.

I'd got the horse under control, but I hadn't got my

hands on any fodder allowance. I'd taken all that risk for nothing. His Excellency had a dozen or so horses in his stables with rooms to look after them. The fodder was nothing to do with me. It made me almost sick with anger, but after a while I cheered up again. As His Excellency was such a big shot with so many top jobs he simply didn't have the time to go home for his meals. When we went out with him we were out all day. He of course got meals wherever he went. But what about us escorts? We four talked it over and decided to put it to him that wherever he ate we ought to eat too. His Excellency wasn't a bad bloke. He cared about his horses, he cared about his dignity, and he cared about his subordinates. The moment we mentioned it to him he agreed. That was a real boon, as I don't need to spend very long explaining to you. If we could get half of our meals out each month for free I'd save half of the money I was spending on food. I was delighted.

As I told you, His Excellency Feng cared about his dignity. When we went to see him to negotiate about the meals he took a very close, long look at us then shook his head. "That'll never do," he said to himself. We four wondered if he was talking about us, but obviously he wasn't. He asked for brush and ink and wrote a note there and then. "Take this to your colonel, and tell him to have it done within three days." We took the note, and when we looked at it we saw that it was an order to the colonel to get us new uniforms. Our ordinary uniforms were made of cotton drill, and His Excellency wanted them changed to woollen cloth, with gold braid on our pockets, down our trouser seams and round our cap bands. Our boots were to be changed to riding boots. Instead of rifles we were to carry carbines, and be issued with a pistol each as well. When we read the note even we thought it was going too far. Only senior officers wore woollen cloth and gold braid. We were just four constables: we had no good reason to be wearing that sort of thing. We could hardly ask His Excellency to take his note back, but we felt very awkward when we went to see our colonel. He might not have dared offend His Excellency, but there was nothing to stop him taking it out on us.

But what do you think happened? When the colonel read the note he didn't so much as sigh. He did exactly as instructed. That'll show you how powerful His Excellency was. We four were cock-a-hoop. Black worsted uniforms with shining gold braid, black leather knee-length boots, gleaming spurs at our heels, carbines slung over our backs, and pistols at our sides with long yellow tassels outside the holsters. To put it very simply, we four looked finer than the rest of the city police put together. When we walked along the street all the other coppers standing on duty saluted us. They must have taken us for senior officers.

When I was a paster I always used to make a piebald horse as part of my better jobs. Now I was in this splendid uniform I went to the stables and chose myself a piebald horse. The horse was a vicious brute that bit and kicked, but I chose him because I used to make paper horses like that and wanted to ride a real one. He had piebald markings like a chrysanthemum and looked terrific. Vicious he was, but he had style when he galloped with his head down, frothing at the mouth, his mane like a row of wheat blowing in the wind and his ears pricked like a couple of little gourd ladles. Just a touch on the stirrup and he'd fly. Nothing else in my whole life ever went really right for me; but I must admit that when I was riding that piebald horse I felt proud and very pleased with myself.

Perhaps you'll say that this job was a good one. Shouldn't I have been able to get by very happily with that fine uniform and that horse? Hunh! I hadn't been wearing the uniform for three months before His Excellency fell from power and the guard battalion was disbanded. I went back to being a constable, third class.

13

Why was the guard battalion disbanded? I don't know. I was transferred to Police Headquarters and given a bronze medal. Anyone would have thought I'd done something heroic by standing at the gateways of official residences. At Headquarters I did all sorts of things: dealing with population registers, working on the shop tax ledgers, doing gate duty and looking after the quartermaster's stores. During those two or three years I got a good general idea of how everything worked at HQ. With all this on top of my experience on the street and on the gates of government offices and official residences I reckon I was an all-round expert. I knew all about everything that happened inside and outside the force. In police matters I was an old hand. But it was only then, after ten years' service, that I finally made it to constable, first class, on nine dollars a month.

Most people probably think all cops are youngsters on street duty who like meddling in things that are none of their business. In fact there were another whole crowd of us hidden away in HQ. If there were ever a general police inspection you'd see all sorts of rare and peculiar cops. Hunchbacked, short-sighted, toothless, lame — you name it, we had it. These freaks were the salt of the force. They had the qualifications and the experience. They could write well and handle every kind of official document and case. They knew all the tricks of the trade. Without them the men on the beat would have messed everything up. But they never got promotion. They were always doing things for other people, but they got none of the credit for it. Usually they weren't even given the chance to put in a dignified appearance. They worked away, putting up with the exhaustion and the unfairness of it all, till they were too old to move the bedclothes; but they'd only ever be constables, first class on nine dollars a month.

You must have seen men in the street wearing clean grey cotton civilian jackets, but with their police boots still on their feet, dragging their heels so slowly that you'd think they can barely move their feet. They're bound to be old cops. Sometimes they go up to the liquor vat, shout for a bowl of liquor and down their fire-water very correctly with a dozen peanuts and deep sigh. Their hair may be going grey, but they still keep themselves so clean-shaven you could take them for palace eunuchs. They're very correct, affable, and capable — and they can't even take their damned boots off in their free time.

I learned a lot from working with them. But it scared me a bit too. Was that how I was going to end up? They were so nice, and so pathetic too. The sight of them sometimes gave me quite a scare. I couldn't say anything for a long time after that. It was true, I was younger than them, but not necessarily any

cleverer.   Did I have any hope?   Was I young myself?
I was thirty-six already.

There was another good thing about the years I spent
at HQ: no danger.   That was the time when there were
wars every spring and autumn.   I won't go into how
other people suffered because of them: you'll get a good
enough idea from what happened to the police.   Once
a war started the soldiers became real fiends, and we
cops had to grovel to them.   Whenever they wanted
grain, carts, horses, men or women they always made
the police collect them and hand them over on time.
If they demanded five tons of griddle cakes we'd have
to go round all the houses, noodle shops and everywhere
griddle cakes were made to tell people to make them;
and when they'd been made we had to escort the street-
sweepers as they carried them to the barracks.   As likely
as not we'd get slapped in the face for our pains.

If we'd just had to wait on our military lords and
masters that wouldn't have been so bad; but they deliberately made things hard for us.   Wherever we cops
were they always made trouble.   We couldn't control
them, but it was wrong to do nothing.   It was humil-
iating.   There are plenty of fools in the world, I know,
but I just can't understand the stupidity of soldiers. Just
because they're wearing army insignia they go completely
insane.   Even if they've got to be like that, at least
you'd expect them to look after their own interests. But,
no, they can't see beyond the ends of their noses.   You
won't find fools like them anywhere else in the world.
Take my cousin.   He'd been a soldier for over ten years,
and for the last few of them he was a platoon commander, so he ought have some sense. During one of
those wars he was escorting a dozen or so prisoners back

to barracks, walking in front of them, ever so pleased
with himself. You'd have thought he was an emperor
or something. The lads under him all noticed that he
hadn't disarmed his prisoners and wondered why. But
he refused to. He patted himself on the chest and said
it was no mistake. They were half-way back to the
barracks when a shot was fired and he was killed in
the street. He was my own cousin, and I didn't want
to see him dead, but I could hardly blame the man
who shot him. That example will give you some idea
of how impossible soldiers are. Tell a soldier not to
drive a truck into a wall and he'll deliberately crash it
and kill himself sooner than take your advice.

Apart from any other advantages, one good thing
about working in HQ was that I was spared the dangers
and humiliations of war. Of course, once fighting started
the price of coal, rice, firewood, charcoal and everything
went up, and we police suffered the same as everyone
else, but at least I could stay in the office and didn't
have to go out and cope with the troops. That was
something to be grateful for.

But I was worried about being stuck there for the
rest of my life, and never ever getting anywhere. You
can get ahead if you know the right people; and even
if you don't another way ahead is to clear up some rob-
beries. But I didn't know the right people and wasn't
on the street. How was I going to get a leg up? The
more I thought about it the more worried I felt.

14

The year I was forty I finally hit it lucky and they made
me a sergeant. I didn't mind any more about all the

years I'd spent in the force and all that hard work. I didn't even care what I'd earn as a sergeant. All I felt was that my luck had turned.

A child can play cheerfully for hours with some broken bit of rubbish he's picked up. That's why kids can be so happy. If grown-ups were like that too we might be better at coping with life. If I'd thought it over more carefully I'd have realized the whole business was a disaster. It was true I'd been made a sergeant, but, to be frank, how much more did a sergeant earn than a constable? Not much. But the responsibilities were far heavier. You had to cope with your superiors and keep them in the picture all the time. With the lads under you you had to keep your wits about you and be friendly and straight at the same time. You had to carry out the duties assigned you, and when dealing with the public you had to avoid being either too hard or too soft. It was a harder job than being in charge of a whole county. The county magistrate is a local emperor, but a police sergeant is nothing like that. He has to be able to do some things properly and just go through the motions with others. He has to think of everything, whether it's real or faked up, because if you forget about something it'll go wrong. And when things go wrong you're in real trouble. Getting promoted is very hard, but falling is easy. A demoted sergeant has a hard time wherever he's sent. The lads get their teeth into him. There's an awful lot of "you ex-sergeant. . ." and the like. To your superiors you're an awkward customer and they deliberately give you a hard time, and try as you can you just can't take it. So what can you do? If you're demoted from sergeant to constable the best thing is to pack your bags and leave. Chuck it all in.

But what else could I have done if I'd packed my bags when I'd just made sergeant at forty?

If I'd really thought about it at the time my hair would have turned white on the spot. It was just as well I didn't. I was simply happy, and I ignored all the snags. What I thought then was that as I'd made sergeant at forty I might be an inspector at fifty, or even before. My career wouldn't have been for nothing. We hadn't graduated from school and we didn't know the right people, so for one of us to make inspector would have been something. When I thought like that I was ready to work my guts out. I felt a hundred times keener about my work. Anyone would have thought it was really something special.

After two years as a sergeant my hair started turning grey. It wasn't that I was giving everything a lot of careful thought, but I was worried every day about getting into trouble for doing something wrong. By day I worked with a smile and put my back into it, but I didn't sleep properly at night. Something would suddenly come into my mind and give me a terrible fright, so I'd be tossing and turning. Sometimes I could think of a solution and sometimes I couldn't, but either way I'd not get back to sleep.

Apart from the work I was worried about my children. The boy was twenty and the girl eighteen. Fuhai, my son, had spent a few days at private school, a few at charity school and a few at the state primary school. When it came to reading, if you'd put all the words he knew together he could probably have managed book two of the primary school Chinese textbook. But when it came to getting up to no good he really learned a lot from private school, charity school and state school. If the schools had exams in getting up to no good he'd have scored a hundred per cent. He'd lost his mother as a young child and I'd been out all the time trying to make some sort of a living. He wasn't a natural trouble-maker. I wasn't angry with him for failing to make something more of himself and I didn't blame anyone else either. I just resented my lousy luck which stopped me from making enough money to get him properly educated. I don't think I did them wrong. I never inflicted a stepmother on them who'd have given them a bad time. It was none of my fault that my luck was so lousy I could only be a cop. We're all the victims of our fate.

Fuhai was a big lad, and could he eat! He could get through three big bowls of noodles with sesame sauce, and still complain he was hungry sometimes. Two dads like me couldn't have earned enough to keep him. I couldn't afford to pay for him to go to middle school, and he wasn't clever enough to pass the exam for a free place. I had to find him a job. But what could he do?

One thing that had been in my mind for a very long time was that I'd rather my boy pulled a rickshaw than joined the force. I'd had enough of it in my lifetime: There was no need to make it a hereditary job. When he was twelve or thirteen I tried to get Fuhai an apprenticeship, but he cried and yelled and refused to go. That was that. I decided to wait till he was a couple of years older before deciding. You can't help having a specially soft spot for a motherless child. When he was fifteen I fixed him up with another apprenticeship. He didn't refuse to go this time, but whenever my back was turned he came running home. Every time I took him back there he came sneaking home again. So all I could do was to wait for him to get a bit older and come round to the idea. Oh dear! He wasted the years from fifteen to twenty. He could eat and he could drink, but work he wouldn't. In the end I got desperate. "What on earth do you want to do? Tell me!" He hung his head and told me he wanted to join the force. He thought that by walking round the streets in uniform he'd be able to earn his living and keep himself amused at the same time, instead of being cooped up indoors all day as an apprentice. I didn't say anything, but I tell you it hurt. I put in a word for him and he was taken on as a constable. Never mind whether it hurt me. At least he had a job, which was better than me having to support him. Like father, like son. If I was a copper my son had to be a copper, even though he couldn't possibly have been as good a one as I was. It'd taken me till I was forty to make sergeant, but where'd he be when he was forty? He'd be lucky if he hadn't been kicked out by then. He hadn't a hope. I hadn't married again because I'd been able to grit my teeth and stick it out. But before long, I supposed, I'd have to be fixing him up with a wife. How was I going to keep them?

Yes, having my boy in the force was another big weight on my mind.

And what about the girl? She was eighteen or so by then, and being shut up at home all day was no kind of life for her. Of course, the best thing would have been to get her married off as soon as possible. But who to? A policeman? Another damned policeman? Join the force and all your descendants join it too, just like falling into a trap. But it had to be a copper. She was no looker, and as for education, a motherless child like her could only read a few simple words. The most I'd be able to provide by way of a dowry was a couple of cotton dresses. And her only skill was that she could take hardship. Coppers' daughters are born to marry coppers. It's in their stars, and there's nothing you can do about it.

Oh well! If she had to be married off, so be it. At least I'd have a bit less to worry about once she was off my hands. It wasn't that I was being cruel. Just think: if I'd left it till she was in her twenties she might have stayed on the shelf for the rest of her life. I've always tried to do right by everyone, but who did right by me? But I don't want to go on moaning and whining away. I just want to set the facts out straight. Anyone can see who was in the right and who was in the wrong.

The day she left home to be married I really wanted to sit there and weep. But I didn't. If I'd started I'd never have stopped. My eyes watered, but not a tear fell.

15

With my boy in a job and my girl married I thought that the time had come for me to spread my wings. If any good opportunity turned up elsewhere I'd chuck in my police job and go away to see something of the world. I didn't care about whether I'd get rich or not, but I wasn't going to be a failure all my life.

Yes, I really did have my chance. Do you remember His Excellency Feng I told you about? He was given a post in the provinces. As I told you, I like reading the papers, and as soon as I saw the news I went off to see him and ask if he'd take me with him. He remembered me and agreed. He told me to find three other good men to make up four of us to go with him to his new post. I had enough sense to ask him to contact Police Headquarters for four men on secondment. What I had in mind was that if things turned out badly later on my pals wouldn't hold it against me as they could report back here again. That left us a line of retreat. So, you see, my plan wasn't at all bad: to ask HQ for the transfer of four specified men.

This really was something to celebrate. My experience told me that I'd definitely be made police chief there. I'm not bragging. Every dog has his day, so why shouldn't a man? I deserved my moment of glory. I was over forty and I'd yet to make my mark.

The order did indeed come and I was made commander of the guard. I could have jumped for joy.

Well I don't know whether it was my rotten fate or His Excellency's lousy luck. He was fired before he even took up the post. I'd been happy over nothing. All my hopes burst like a bubble. It was a good thing the four of us were only on secondment and hadn't given in our notice: His Excellency could send us back to Police Headquarters. I was upset about the whole business and worried about whether I'd still be a sergeant. My face got a lot thinner.

Luckily I was sent to guard a quarantine station. There were six of us altogether and I was in charge. It wasn't a bad posting. There wasn't much to do, and the quarantine station paid for our meals. I can't be sure, but I reckon His Excellency must have put in a good word for me.

Now that I didn't have to pay for my own food I could start saving a bit of money for Fuhai's wedding. It was the only thing I still had to do, and the sooner I got it out of the way the better.

I finally got him married when I was forty-five. His wife's father and brother were both coppers. Marvellous, wasn't it: my whole family and my in-laws too were all in the force. If we'd all been put together we could have staffed a small police station.

Sometimes there's no accounting for the things people do. I don't know quite why, but after getting a wife for my son I felt I ought to start growing my moustache to make me look more like a grandad. I didn't give any thought to what I was doing but just started to let it grow, as bold as you please. With that little black moustache on my upper lip and a bag of Guandong tobacco for my pipe I felt really good. Why shouldn't I have? The girl had been married off, the boy had a wife, and everything was going smoothly for me. So what was there to stop me feeling really good?

It was the moustache that ruined everything. There was a sudden change of police chief, and one of the first things the new man did after he arrived was to have an inspection of all the city police. He was an old soldier, and all he understood was standing to attention and falling in by markers. He didn't understand about anything else. As I've told you already, there were a lot of old-timers in the police stations and at HQ. They weren't much to look at, but they'd all been on the job for so many years that they had a lot of experience. I was paraded with all the old men at HQ as our quarantine station didn't come under any of the local police districts. That's why we had to stand with the old men from HQ.

We'd fallen in and were waiting to be inspected. The old timers and I were all talking and laughing and feeling fine. We reckoned that as we had to do all the important jobs and knew how to cope with anything we'd been hard enough treated by not being promoted. Nobody was going to kick any of us out. Sure, we were getting on a bit, but we worked as hard as ever. Even if anyone said we were worn out and useless we'd all put in at least fifteen or sixteen years' service and poured out our blood and sweat for the force when we were young. That alone ought to have been enough to earn us a bit of consideration. Nobody just kicks a dog out when it gets old. That's what we all thought, and that's why we didn't take the inspection seriously. We thought the new police chief would just glance at us from a distance and that would be that.

When the new chief arrived he had an enormous chest covered in medals. He shouted and jumped around as if he were some kind of machine. My heart started pounding. He wasn't looking at the men in the right order. The moment he saw our squad he fell on us like a tiger. He stood there with his legs apart and his hands behind his back, nodding at us. Then suddenly he shot at us like an arrow, grabbed an old clerk by the belt and jerked him forward. It was like a wrestling match. He nearly pulled the old clerk over, shook him to and fro by his belt, then suddenly let him go. The old man landed on his backside. The chief spat in his face twice and shouted, "Are you a policeman? You can't even fasten your belt. Take him out and shoot him."

We all knew that nobody, not even him, could have a man shot for that. It wasn't fear that made our faces all go pale but fury. The old clerk was left there sitting on the ground in a quivering lump.

The police chief looked at us then swung his finger right across. "Get out, the whole lot of you! Never let me set eyes on any of you again! You're not fit to be policemen, you scum!" That little speech didn't seem to be enough for him, because he charged up to us again and yelled at the top of his voice, "All of you with whiskers take your uniforms off and go, right now."

I wasn't the only one with a moustache: all the others were sergeants and officers. If they hadn't grown them I'd never have dared sport those damned whiskers. When you're young and strong you flog your guts out for six or seven dollars a month. Because you're a copper your son can't go to school and get an education. Because you're a copper your daughter has to marry a pauper too and eat corn bread all her life. But once you grow a moustache you're finished. They didn't give me a brass farthing by way of compensation or pension. After twenty years' service they just kicked me out like an old brick that was in their way. If you can get your three meals a day before you're fifty you're doing all right, even if you don't make any money. After fifty you've got a choice: jump in the river or hang yourself. That's what coppers come to in the end.

In twenty years' service I never did anything wrong, but I had to pack my traps and go, just like that.

The lads saw me off with tears in their eyes, but I was still smiling. There was too much injustice in the world: I was keeping my tears to shed another day.

16

Despite what those charitable people who dish out gruel think you can't save a poor man's life with a few bowls of gruel. Gruel just keeps you going for a few days' more misery, but sooner or later you're bound to die. My experience has been much like that gruel: it's kept me going for a few more days' misery by finding me a few odd jobs. I had to go back to being a policeman. What else could I call myself? It goes around with me everywhere, like a horrible mole or tumour. I didn't want to say I'd been a policeman, and I didn't want to go back to being one, but how else was I going to eat? It was disgusting.

Before I'd been out of work for long I got a job that His Excellency Feng found for me in charge of the clinic at a coal mine. Later I was put in charge of the police sub-station in the mining village. That was quite a piece of luck. I could put my skills and knowledge to some use. After my twenty years' service I took the workers in that village really well in hand. When there was any gambling, fighting, strikes, trouble-making or drunkenness I only had to open my mouth and explain things in a clear, straightforward sort of way and they'd accept everything I said. I trained the lads under me myself. Some of them had been transferred from elsewhere, and some I'd taken on myself. They'd all been coppers before, which made it harder to train them as they thought they knew a thing or two about the police themselves and wanted to see how good I was. It didn't bother me. I'd been every kind of copper, and knew it all, from headquarters to the beat. With that experience behind me I reckoned they couldn't hurt me. I could cope with anything, inside the force or outside it. That's no boast, I tell you.

If I'd been able to carry on there for a few years more I'm certain that at the very least I'd have saved up enough to buy myself a decent coffin. I was being paid more or less the same as an officer, and there were bonuses at the end of the year too. But when I'd only been there for about six months and had just got things more or less sorted out I was given the boot. My crimes were being too old and doing the job too conscientiously. The lads would have been able to make a lot on the side if I'd been prepared to turn a blind eye. By keeping both my eyes wide open I laid up trouble for myself. I had the same problem dealing with civilians. Because I knew all about police work my conscience made me want to do a thorough job there and do things properly. But there's another thing. If people aren't genuine there's no point in policing them: the better you do it, the more they'll hate you. Of course, if I'd had a few years on the job everyone would probably have seen the benefits of it. But they didn't give me the time to do it properly. They kicked me out first.

It's only now that I've come to understand that whatever you try to do in this society is like policemen's boots. If they're too big it serves you right. And if they pinch because they're too small that serves you right too. If you want to make a go of anything you've got to make sure that everyone's going to like it. Otherwise they'll kick you in the face. I failed that time because I forgot the magic words: muddle through. That's why I had to pack my traps.

This time I was out of work for over six months. Ever since my apprentice days I'd always kept myself busy, whether there was really anything to do or not. I've never been a slacker. Although I was pushing fifty by then I wasn't much less energetic than any youngster. I couldn't bear being idle. With no proper work to do from when I got up in the morning till when the sun set at night I felt hopeless. I just moved about, like the sun. But while the sun lit up the world my heart was always pitch black. I got desperate with boredom, bad-tempered, and thoroughly fed up with myself; but I couldn't find a job. Reminding myself of my ability to work and my experience was no consolation. Work and experience hadn't brought me enough savings to support me in my old age; I was on the brink of starvation. I didn't want to live on charity. I had spirit and ability and I wanted to earn my own living. So I kept my eyes and ears open as carefully as if I'd been a thief. Whenever there was any news of a possible job I'd go there, but I'd always come back empty-handed, my head hanging between my shoulders. I wished I could fall over and break my neck. It'd have made me feel a lot better. But till it's time for you to die society buries you alive. I could feel myself slowly sinking into the ground in broad daylight. I'd done nothing wrong, but I was being punished like this. I sucked that pipe of mine from morning till night, just sucked it as there was no tobacco in it, for a bit of interest. That was all the interest that life offered me. I was just a joke.

It wasn't easy, but in the end I found another job: as a private in the Henan Salt Authority's Smuggling Prevention Force. If I had to be a private, so be it. As long as I had something to eat I'd be fine. So I borrowed some money, got some things together, shaved off my moustache and went to take up the new job.

Within six months I'd cleared my debts and been promoted to platoon commander. I only spent half of what anyone else did so as to pay back my debts. And I did twice as much as the others, which was why I was made platoon commander. Although I felt hard done by it didn't stop me working: I was scared of losing my job. Lose your job and you age three years. Even if you don't starve to death you feel so low it could kill you. But goodness only knows whether hard work can stop you losing your job.

I started longing — yes, I started longing again — that as I'd become a platoon commander I could get to company commander. Hoping again, wasn't I? This time I played it very carefully. I did what everyone else did. If the others demanded bribes, so did I. I wasn't going to ruin everything again for the sake of my conscience. Conscience is worth nothing these days. If I could make it to company commander and hold the job for a few years then my pay and the bribes ought to be enough for a decent coffin. I really didn't have any great ambitions. I wanted to go on working as long as my legs would carry me, and have a coffin to be buried in once I couldn't get out of bed. That way I wouldn't be eaten up by wild dogs. I kept one eye on heaven and one eye on the ground. If I did right by heaven I hoped I'd be allowed to lie in peace under the ground. It wasn't that I was trying to make the most of being an old man. I was only fifty, but all my efforts up till then had been for nothing. So I had to keep my head down and think about my grave. What I thought was that if my ambition was so small surely heaven would look on it with a kindly eye.

A letter came from home to tell me I had a grandson.

If I told you I wasn't happy, that would be inhuman.
But I must also admit that after my excitement wore off
my heart turned cold and I found myself grumbling to
myself, "Hunh! Another little copper!" A grandfather
shouldn't say anything as discouraging as that about his
grandson, but if you've read all I've said already you'll
probably be able to forgive me. To the rich, children
are hope. To the poor they're a burden. When your own
belly's empty you can't worry about your children and
grandchildren. With us it's not a matter of

> Noble ideals passed on in the family;
> Learning continuing down through the ages.

I had some tobacco in my pipe again when I sucked
it and thought about the future. Now I had a grandson
my responsibilities didn't end with my coffin. My son
couldn't possibly support his family as only a constable,
third class. Even if I didn't bother about him and his
wife I couldn't ignore my grandson. My head was in a
terrible whirl. I was getting older every year, but there
were more and more mouths in the family to be filled
with corn bread. I gave a few deep belches: It was as
if there was a belt of air across my chest. To hell with
it. I'd better stop worrying. It got you nowhere, and
there was no end of it. Your days on earth are numbered, but troubles are handed down from generation to
generation. My descendants were going to have to eat
corn bread for ever.

If the wind and the rain always happened the way the
weather predictions say there'd never be any gales or
downpours. If troubles came slowly, the way we think
about them beforehand, nobody would ever be driven

crazy by worry. Just as I was working out what to do about my grandson my son died on me.

He didn't even die at home. I had to go and fetch his body.

Ever since his marriage Fuhai always wanted to do well. Although he wasn't very able he did his level best. When I went to join the Salt Authority's Smuggling Prevention Force he wanted to come with me. He believed he could do a lot better for himself in the provinces. I stopped him coming because I was worried that our jobs wouldn't be safe. If both of us had been thrown out of work at the same time it'd have been a disaster. But no sooner had I set my foot outside the house than he went off to Weihaiwei. He earned an extra couple of dollars a month there. When you're by yourself away from home a couple of dollars extra doesn't really leave you with any more than your old ways at home, but when a poor man wants to do well all he can see is the extra money: he doesn't usually bother to do his sums. As soon as he got there Fuhai fell ill, but he couldn't bring himself to spend money on medicine. By the time he was flat on his back medicine couldn't help him.

Bringing his coffin back left me completely broke. My daughter-in-law was a young widow still nursing a baby. What was I to do? I couldn't go off and work in the provinces again, and back here I couldn't even find work as a constable, third class. I was only fifty, but I was finished. I envied Fuhai for dying young. He could shut his eyes and forget about it all. If he'd lived to my age the best he could have hoped for would have been to do as well as me. He probably wouldn't even have been able to manage that. My daughter howled till she was more dead than alive herself, but I didn't shed a tear or make a sound. All I could do was to prowl around the room giving a bitter laugh from time to time.

All my previous efforts had been for nothing. Now I've got to use all my skills to get a bit of gruel for the kid. I've been a watchman in empty houses; I've sold vegetables; I've worked as a plasterer's mate. I've done everything short of pulling a rickshaw. Whatever I do I put my back into it and I'm very careful. Although I'm over fifty I work as hard as a lad in his twenties, even though there's only gruel and corn bread in my stomach. I haven't got a decent thick padded jacket to wear in winter. But I don't ask for anyone's charity. I earn my dinner through my own skill and effort. I've held my head high all my life, and I'm not going to lose my pride before I die. I often go hungry all day; I often haven't got the coal to light the stove; I often can't even find a few leaves of tobacco. But I never complain. When I was working in the public service I treated everyone right. I was completely straight. What else do I need to say?

What I've got to look forward to now is dying of starvation. I won't possibly be buried in a coffin, and my daughter-in-law and grandson will have to die soon after me. It's just as well. Whoever made me become a copper? I often get blackouts — it's like a touch of death. But I'm still laughing. Laughing at the cleverness and ability I've shown all my life. Laughing at this amazing and unjust world. I hope that after I've laughed my last this world will change.

Translated by W. J. F. Jenner

老舍短篇小说选

熊猫丛书

*

《中国文学》杂志社出版

（中国北京百万庄路24号）

中国国际图书贸易总公司发行

（中国国际书店）

外文印刷厂印刷

1985年第1版

00320

编号：（英）2—016—32

10—1　1990 P